BE NEAR ME

BOOKS BY ANDREW O'HAGAN

The Missing
Our Fathers
Personality
Be Near Me

ANDREW O'HAGAN

BE NEAR ME

McCLELLAND & STEWART

Library and Archives Canada Cataloguing in Publication

O'Hagan, Andrew, 1968-
Be near me / Andrew O'Hagan.

ISBN 13: 978-0-7710-6834-8
ISBN 10: 0-7710-6834-4

I. Title.

PR6065.H33B4 2007   823'.914   C2006-904042-7

Typeset by Faber and Faber Ltd.
Printed and bound in Canada

This book is printed on acid-free paper that is 100% recycled, ancient-forest friendly (100% post-consumer recycled).

McClelland & Stewart Ltd.
75 Sherbourne Street
Toronto, Ontario
M5A 2P9
www.mcclelland.com

1   2   3   4   5   10   09   08   07   06

for
Mary-Kay Wilmers

Be near me when my light is low,
  When the blood creeps, and the nerves prick
  And tingle; and the heart is sick,
And all the wheels of Being slow.

Be near me when the sensuous frame
  Is rack'd with pangs that conquer trust;
  And Time, a maniac scattering dust,
And Life, a Fury slinging flame.

Be near me when my faith is dry,
  And when the flies of latter spring,
  That lay their eggs, and sting and sing
And weave their petty cells and die.

Be near me when I fade away,
  To point the term of human strife,
  And on the low dark verge of life
The twilight of eternal day.

'In Memoriam A. H. H.'
Alfred, Lord Tennyson

CONTENTS

PROLOGUE January 1976 1

ONE Sundial 5

TWO The Mouth of the River 25

THREE Mr Perhaps 50

FOUR Ailsa Craig 73

FIVE Schoolboy on an Elephant 94

SIX The Nights 113

SEVEN The Economy of Grace 135

EIGHT Balliol 161

NINE The People 194

TEN The Echo of Something Real 215

ELEVEN Kilmarnock 236

TWELVE The Single Life 260

PROLOGUE

JANUARY 1976

My mother once took an hour out of her romances to cast some light on the surface of things. I was just back from Rome and we stood together on the ramparts of Edinburgh Castle, watching the sky go black above a warship anchored in the Firth of Forth. Picture that time of day in the old city when the shop windows stand out and the streets of the New Town begin to glow with moral sentiment. She took my arm and we rested like passengers bound for distant lives, warm in our coats and weak in our hearts, the rain falling down on the stone.

'David,' she said, 'I'm going to give you some guidance that is more serious than the afternoon requires.'

My mother turned and I saw the gleam of old stories in her eyes. 'Always trust a stranger,' she said. 'In this life, it's the people you know who let you down.'

'You are a great tonic,' I said. 'If I go too long without exposure to your bad character I begin to grow affectionate.'

'An adverse growth, as your father might have said.'

'Quite so.'

When the light had disappeared and our hands were cold, we thought better of going round a pictorial history of the one o'clock gun, walking instead to a chintzy tea room at the top of the Royal Mile. The place smelled of wet carpets and Calor gas, and the counter was taken up with those three-tier cake stands, ornate and sad and heavy with scones. 'Lovely plates,' said my mother. 'Bohemian glass.'

We warmed our fingers round cups of tea.

'A person not willing to have their heart broken is barely alive,' she said, putting a piece of shortbread into her mouth. 'I don't mean you, David. You're a different case altogether.'

'Stop it, Mother,' I said. 'I'm not some whey-faced character from one of your books. Crazy-haired. Mad with grief.'

'I don't see why not,' she said. 'There's nothing wrong with grief. You've been through such a lot.'

'Rome put it behind me.'

'I don't know about "behind you". In my experience, nothing is ever behind anyone.'

'Oxford has vanished,' I remember saying. 'All that stuff. It seems so mysterious to me now. You know, Conor almost gave me a way of thinking. It was like the world was going to go our way at last.'

'It might still,' she said.

'We would fight all the spite and shame of the world.'

I told her I was looking forward now to a quiet ministry in Blackpool. 'Maybe that will be my tribute to Conor,' I said. 'Just working in an ordinary parish and greeting the faith of ordinary people.'

'You've always been addicted to sweet thoughts,' she said. 'But I advise you to put your faith in strangers. Sometimes it's nice to just be on the surface of things.'

'Not easy for a priest,' I said.

She paused to lick her finger and dab some grains of sugar from the corner of her mouth. Her watch said twenty past five and it gleamed as she reapplied her make-up.

'Just don't forget your way back.'

'No,' I said. 'I won't.'

People passed outside in the rain. I could see them stooped beneath their umbrellas, voyaging home, wrapped in privacy. 'I suppose you belong to Lancashire,' she said. 'But there is always a place for you here.'

'I know.' I lifted my cup. 'But here's to the south. We go where we must go to find the right weather, don't we, Mother?'

'Oh, yes,' she said. 'If we have the wings, that is what we do. Just keep your scarf round your neck and your phone numbers handy.'

'You're so practical, Mother.'

'I know,' she said, with a lipstick smile, 'but what else is there?'

I

SUNDIAL

One is never prepared for the manner in which home changes over time. That tea room was twenty-nine years ago. Scotland was my mother's world, and my years in Blackpool were spent in pastoral oblivion, a kind of homelessness which has followed me everywhere. Lancashire was the place where I grew up, my father's world, but serving there as a parish priest provided me with nothing much greater than the small comforts afforded in my line by the habits of duty.

I wanted to add something new to my mother's life. She had always been so original, so full of words, so ready with money, the distances between us being no bar to her encouragement of me, her enjoyment of our hard-hearted jokes. But she was growing old. I thought we might do more laughing together and visit the places she liked. The year before last, I came back and took charge of a small Ayrshire parish, to see her, to be close to her, though I can hardly say that the move was made in heaven.

Troubles like mine begin, as they end, in a thousand places, but my year in that Scottish parish would serve to unlock everything. There is no other way of putting the matter. Dalgarnock seems now like the central place in a story I had known all along, as if each year and each quiet hour of my professional life had only been preparation for the darkness of that town, where hope is like a harebell ringing at night.

It all began to happen on Good Friday. The rectory was pleasant and well-groomed, and my housekeeper, Mrs Poole, brought two large bowls of lettuce soup to the sitting-room table. I had just come back from the second service of the day, feeling tired, with a heaviness in my legs that made me wonder if I wasn't ageing rather badly. It is not always easy to know the difference between religious passion and exalted grief. I felt Mrs Poole was watching me and ready to say a number of things, but the light of the chapel still glowered in my head, willing me to regret the need for human contact and the niceties of lunch. Mrs Poole was in her most efficient mode and soon had me smiling.

After several months in Dalgarnock I noticed she was more at home in the rectory than one would have expected. She loved it there, loved what she called 'the feel of the house', and her admiration was particularly drawn to the presence of numerous clocks and books and second-rate pictures, the stuff of my own past.

'You've a bit of education up yer sleeve, Father. That's the thing. When people have been places you can just tell. What a house for pictures. You are somebody just like me: you like yer wee things round about you. Now, half the people you meet go on like their home is a prison. But when you walk in here, you see right away it's a place for thinking.'

'I don't know about that, Mrs Poole.'

'Oh, away ye go. A man like you knows how to think.'

She made a fetish of the house plants, speaking to them, paying tribute as she bent with the watering can to the good company they provided. She was a great enthusiast for the

6

environment, by which she meant the outside world, but the inside world was the domain of her greatest exactitude. Hours would come and go as she moved about the place, the dust a sign of some freedom she had barely known, the cluttered rooms full of corkscrews, prayer books, exhibition catalogues and seed packets seeming to her to indicate a peaceable universe very unlike the one she maintained in her house by the railway bridge.

'Mrs Poole,' I said, 'don't get me started on big topics. I'm looking for laughter today.'

'You've picked a fine day for it,' she said. 'There's a dirty great sponge of vinegar being presented to the Lord's face as we speak.'

'That's fine,' I said. 'But I need a glass of wine.'

'Bloody hell,' said Mrs Poole. 'When I was a girl, Good Friday was a day for closing the curtains and hanging yer head. Now you're all calling for the wine bottle. You'll be casting lots for the bloody cloak next.'

I spun my keys and looked up at the ceiling. A frosting of cobwebs sat lightly over the old chandelier.

'Did I ever tell you, Mrs Poole?' I plucked at my bottom lip and pointed up.

'What's that?' she said.

'This very chandelier was hung in my first set of rooms at Balliol. Can you imagine? A present from one of the Anderton aunts.'

'Heaven save us.'

'It's true. My aunt thought it was criminal for a young man to have to study under an oil lamp. I used to stare up at it during the night instead of writing essays on the English Civil War. It was even dirtier then. Can you imagine that, now? This very chandelier?'

7

'A right ticket you must have been, Father,' she said, 'with your chandeliers and all the rest of it. Very nice. As you lay there inspecting your fancy light, my sister and I, we were five years younger than you and working nightshifts.'

'Hard work. How dreadful. Was she cured of it?'

'Oh, aye,' said Mrs Poole. 'We were all cured of that soon enough.'

'I'll take your word for it,' I said, 'given the amount of muck on that chandelier up there.'

'Don't start me,' she said. 'There's work enough to be done. Too much work to be bothering wi' yer daft lights.'

'Get you,' I said. 'It's *Mutiny on the Bounty*.'

'Slave driver.'

'Yes, indeed,' I said. 'You wouldn't want it any other way.'

Mrs Poole was forty-two, but her attitudes made her seem older. Only when she smiled did one notice she was quite young. She had no college education, nor did she come from a background that supported her enthusiasms, but she had schooled herself with the kind of personal passion that verges on panic, and her mind absorbed and retained. This process had started years before I met her – with night classes in French, with cookbooks – but she always said that side of her had become important in her time with me.

'You just sit there quiet half the time,' she said. 'But I know you're boiling with arguments, Father.'

'Is that right?'

'Oh, piping! And don't be shy. There's a thousand things to discuss and hardly anybody to talk to.'

'Very good, Mrs Poole.'

My mother made the point that my housekeeper was like a heroine in Jane Austen: she would have distinguished herself in any class, yet her circumstances acted upon her like a series of privations she was determined to overcome. The fact made her unsteady sometimes but pretty much always likeable. She had little time for The Tongues, as she called them, the people of the town, and saw our friendship as an overdue reward and a lucky extension of her long dedication to self-improvement.

'I have finally found my job,' she said. 'And a person who knows how to put a sentence together.'

'Good stuff,' I said. 'Just don't forget I've a gangplank through there for people who yell about their rights.'

'Fascist,' she said.

'Uh-huh.'

'Roman soldier!'

'That's right,' I said. 'That's my job.'

She smiled and hooked a dish towel over her shoulder. 'That's enough of your cheek, Father. Come and have your lunch.' She swept a theatrical hand over the dining table in the manner of a far-travelled merchant presenting his latest silks. 'Quickly now. It's soup. *Potage de Père Tranquille*.'

'*Du Père*,' I said.

'Right. The best abstinence money can buy.'

'Goodness, Mrs Poole. Lettuce soup. There are monks and starving people who would thank you for this. Can we go wild and add a few bits of bread to the feast?'

'Suit yourself. Be my guest. If you want to remember Christ's agony by gorging on crusts, I can't stop you.'

'Just a few delicious dods of the old *pain de campagne*.'

'That's fine,' she said. 'I bought the organic stuff.'

Mrs Poole worked only two and a half days a week. She liked to smile at unpredictable things and gave the impression she showed sides of herself in the rectory that she couldn't show at home. Her husband Jack was a part-time gardener for the council. 'He just cuts the grass,' she said, as if to separate his efforts from the sorts of things we might do ourselves.

Mr and Mrs Poole appeared to live together in a state of settled resentment. She said they seldom went out and that he had given up on trying to make her happy. He wasn't the man she had married, apparently, and a thousand things had happened, she said, that made it clear he couldn't deal with responsibility. Even after the events of that year, I don't think I ever came to understand what Mr Poole really thought of his wife and the world she craved. But she may have been wrong to assume that his drinking was the biggest part of him, that he was, in some barely conscious way, a standard-bearer for the town's worst prejudices. Some might have called him a broken person, yet there was more to him, and more to her, than either of them would find time to recognise.

It was Mrs Poole's habit to see him as a failure. I think perhaps his biggest failure, in her eyes, was to seem to deny something very essential in her as they got older, something that might have made them more elevated and more sophisticated than the people around them, the people – 'his people', she would say – of whom Mrs Poole had come to feel perhaps too easily scornful, and whom he, Jack, had an equally natural ability to understand and to rub along with quite nicely.

'Yes,' she said once. 'Being one of them.'

'Don't be too hard on Dalgarnock,' I said. 'The people from here are no different from people elsewhere, except they probably have more to deal with and smaller means to do it.'

'You'll find out if I'm too hard on them,' she said, and I knew from the way she said it that she'd heard things against me or against priests in general or people from England.

Mrs Poole thought that Jack saw her new habits and interests as being pretentious and wanted to deny her an opportunity for personal growth. 'He doesn't know me,' she said. 'You know me better than him.'

'I don't know about that, Mrs Poole. I only know a few old prayers and a dozen facts about Marcel Proust.'

'That's you then,' she said. 'But it's not nothing. It's a damn sight more than most people round here. Most of those people wouldn't give you daylight in a dark corner.'

'Is that one of your native expressions?'

'That's right. They wouldn't give you the shine off their sweat.'

'Nice,' I said. 'Proust would be proud of you.'

'Shush,' she said. 'You know what I mean. You can't expect a priest to know much about life, but at least you've read a couple of books.'

'Whatever you say,' I said.

I could only assume Mrs Poole came to work to live another sort of life. As with all her jealously guarded, self-defining hours – the night classes, the environment, the afternoons down at the Red Cross shop – her time at the rectory was spent, at least in part, in solid opposition to her husband's view of her as a person gaining airs and ignoring the hands of her biological clock.

One day we visited the garden centre. It must have been a month into my time there in the parish. I had been telling Mrs Poole a thing or two about the older kinds of rose. We looked up some books, and it was decided that rose bushes were exactly the thing for the rectory garden, planted with care round the walls, each of us falling by degrees into a strictly imagined world of old fragrances. That day, Jack was in the children's playground next to the garden centre when we came out bearing our new plants. He didn't see us coming along, though I suspect Mrs Poole saw him, for she flinched and the small leaves on the bushes shuddered as we walked across the gravel.

'Amazing,' I said.

'Sorry?'

'That's actually a twelfth-century rose you're holding.'

'The weight of it,' she said.

Jack was sitting on the roundabout with a passive look on his face and a bottle of booze in a paper bag. We put the things in the car and then Mrs Poole went back to use the loo, while I sat behind the wheel and watched her mysterious husband removing table-tennis bats from a large blue bag and throwing them into the trees.

Before we'd started the soup, the postman came to the door and hammered on it with his usual disregard. 'Nothing gets your attention like a knock at the door,' said Mrs Poole, and she went out. I spent a moment playing a phrase on the piano, placing my foot on a dull brass pedal. Then I stopped and cocked an ear before putting Chopin into the CD player; I could hear very clearly what the postman was saying to Mrs Poole.

'How's yer English priest getting on then?'

'He's not English,' she said. 'He was born in Edinburgh.'

'Don't kid yerself,' said the postman. 'Yer man's as English as two weeks in Essex. Get a load ae that rug lying there!'

'What are you talking about?'

'That thing under yer feet,' he said. 'They didnae have that in Father McGee's day. That's a pure English rug, that.'

'Just go about your business and stop coming round here talking nonsense,' said Mrs Poole. 'This is a Persian rug.'

'That's Iran or Iraq,' he said. 'You want to get rid ae that.' As he laughed he sent a menacing splutter into the hall. 'There's blood in they carpets. Our troops are over in that place and they're not buildin' sandcastles. There's young men dying out there. You have to watch out for the Iraqis.'

I'm sure there's an essay in which Liszt writes of Chopin's apartment on the chaussée d'Antin, the room with a portrait of Chopin above the piano, and the belief of the younger musician that the painting must have been a constant auditor of the sound that once flamed and lived in that room, bright and brief as a candle.

'The postman?' I said.

Mrs Poole put a letter into its envelope and folded the whole thing in three. She creased it as people do who never file their letters, holding the stiff paper in her hand like a small baton. 'Aye,' she said. 'Just another of yer local idiots.'

'Isn't Good Friday a bank holiday? Don't they get the day off?'

'Not in Scotland,' she said. 'That's an English thing.'

She seemed more than slightly annoyed with the postman, as if his careless and brash way of talking had added some terrible degree of insult to the letter he had given her, the letter she now stuffed into the front pocket of her apron.

'Are you all right?'

She smoothed one lip against the other. 'In this country,' she said, 'they prefer to have an extra holiday on the second of January. They ignore Good Friday but they don't ignore the second of January.'

'Really?'

'Of course,' she said. 'The second is the day after New Year's Day, and they'd much sooner have an extra day with alcohol than an extra day with God.'

'You're very severe, Mrs Poole.'

'No wonder,' she said. 'The idea of a person like that being responsible for bringing the post.'

'He's just doing his job.'

'Don't be soft,' she said. 'He's an idiot. And you'd do well to recognise an idiot when you see one.'

Mrs Poole picked some lint from her skirt, and a moment of unease registered with her before she appeared to decide in favour of cheerfulness. 'This is more of your film music you're playing,' she said.

'It's the best thing in the world.'

'Oh God,' she said. 'We've got something good to talk about at last.'

'Yes,' I said. The swerve past the unmentioned letter was still there between us. 'I'm afraid I like the Nocturnes more than anything else. More than Bach.'

'Away ye go.'

We moved to the table and she straightened the cloth.

'I'm no expert,' she said, 'but I'm sure that's wrong.' She looked cheerfully combative. 'You might have to rectify it or else find a new cleaner.'

'A new cleaner who likes nocturnes?'

'That's right,' she said, enjoying her joke. 'You're such a dangerous snob, Father David.'

'No danger to you. You're the most gigantic snob I've ever met. I count it as part of my good fortune to have come across you.'

'I intend to become worse,' she said.

'Be my guest.'

'Only two and a half days a week, mind.'

I asked her again if she was all right, and she nodded into the tablecloth before lifting her spoon. She hoped it was fine to receive mail at the rectory.

'By all means,' I said.

She brushed her cheeks with the back of the spoon as if to

14

cool them and then said we should get on and have our soup. 'The stock is just right,' I said. 'The stock is perfection.'

She had no little regard for the small things, for the dominant note in a perfume – almonds, say, or vanilla – and she appeared almost girlish in her enthusiasm for finding the right shoes and dressing to her mood.

'You've got to make an effort,' she said.

'You'll see us all to our graves, Mrs Poole,' I said. 'You have more energy about you than any of us.'

'I've got that,' she said. 'But you've got the other things.'

I asked for a little of last evening's Alsace. 'Very sweet,' I said. 'It will cut through the taste of your soup.'

'That's not very abstinent of you,' she said.

'Even at this sad time, Good Friday,' I said, 'we must have gaiety. We must have gaiety at all costs.'

At first she said she wouldn't drink any, but then suddenly she changed her mind, bringing over a glass which she pinged with a fingernail. I filled it and she drank the glass in one go, lifting her napkin and dabbing the edge of her nose as if the napkin were a sort of accomplice.

'Is that all right?' I asked.

'*Parfait*,' she said.

'You have a nice tone to your pronunciation.'

'Thank you,' she said. And after a moment: 'Has France always been your favourite? I mean, of all the places?'

'Well, it's created some personable Englishmen.'

'What do you mean?'

'A little contact with France does an Englishman no end of good,' I said. 'But too much of it can make the French intolerable.'

'Is that a joke?' she said.

'Depends if you're English or French.'

'And what if you're Scottish?'

'Bad luck,' I said.

'God, you're a pain,' she said. 'One minute you're Scottish yourself and the next minute you're more English than Churchill. I'm sure I don't know what to be saying about you.'

'Well,' I said, 'here's some advice. Only say sweet things about me and you'll never go far wrong.'

'A pain!' she said. 'Maybe you're just a turncoat, and the war has turned you against France.'

'Perhaps,' I said.

Mrs Poole looked at me and bit her lip and said nothing, as if the matter was best forgotten and not looked into; then everything seemed to resolve itself as she asked again about the sweetness of certain wines. 'I would like to go some day to France,' she said, 'and see these vineyards.'

'Alsace is in the northeast.'

'Like Aberdeen,' she said.

'*Exactement.*'

A print of Bernini's *Apollo and Daphne* was hung so as to absorb the light from the window that faced the church. I saw myself buying the print long ago at the Galleria Borghese, a small purchase on a spring day after a walk under the pines of the villa gardens. Waiting for Mrs Poole to speak again, I looked at Daphne's anxious face and noticed her fingertips flowering into branches and leaves. The light was very subdued.

'I wish you'd turn that music off,' Mrs Poole said. 'It gets on my nerves. I hate all that watery music. I borrowed some of it from the library. God. It makes such a fuss of itself.'

'You just like to argue with me, Mrs Poole.'

'I do,' she said.

She smiled and then laughed as she poured herself another

inch of Alsace, her eyes flaring, willing me to argue my case.

'Poor washerwoman that you are,' I said. 'The famous Scottish education system barely left a mark on you.'

'Father, don't make me swear. Jesus is up on the cross covered in wounds and you're nearly making me swear.'

'You will never go to heaven.'

'It's mechanical.'

'You'll never be happy.'

'I'll never be sad, more like! Gluttons for sadness, you Chopin fans. Bedwetters.'

'Goodness, Mrs Poole,' I said. 'Strong words. I should say you were brought up in a bath of coal.'

'Born and bred. But I still know Chopin is dodgy stuff.'

'If it wasn't for Chopin his people would still be kicking up their heels in circles and baring their black teeth to the vodka jug.'

'And you a good whatsit – socialist,' she said, lifting the plates and doing a little victory sashay into the kitchen.

'Not in a long time,' I said.

There was a decent pause. I looked at the swirling carpet and felt ashamed of its cheap, nasty appearance, the purple and beige nylon a field of static electricity. 'Three months and we've still got that terrible floor,' I said.

I looked at the Bernini again and my eye travelled to a framed photograph beneath it on the mantel. It was me at school in my black tie and blazer, a bare hawthorn tree standing behind on the hill above Ampleforth, its branches seemingly shaped by the wind. Next to that was a picture of an elephant rising on its back legs surrounded by workers from a Yorkshire factory. I looked up as Mrs Poole came back. I could see she was happy with the progress of our talk.

'Sorry,' she said, looking down at two new bowls, the redness high in her cheeks. 'Here's the pudding. It's a bit so-so, I'm afraid.'

'Never mind,' I said. 'Good things are temporary.'

The light at the window reminded me that I must soon be off to the school. I wanted to tell her I wasn't half as serious as she thought. I wanted to say that neither of us needed especially to believe what we said. But something in her and something in me made actors of us both when we were together, and I couldn't admit how much I looked forward to being with the young people at the school, just so as to lose myself and to fall in with whatever they were doing. I tried to joke with her but she would always bring me back. She believed my teases were just pauses between big pronouncements, and she wanted them more than anything, the pronouncements, as if I owed them to her.

'So what are you saying?' she said.

'Nothing,' I said. 'That I like music with a sigh in it, that's all. The Nocturnes are hymn-like.'

Mrs Poole lifted a pencil from a pot on the bookshelf. It was idly done, how she examined the pencil, stroked its length and then pressed the point into the fold of flesh between her left thumb and forefinger, before licking another finger and erasing the mark.

'Oh, who cares?' I said. 'It's all just a way of going on.'

'Lovely!' she said. 'I've got you going now, haven't I?'

'Yes, you've got me, Mrs Poole. But I won't argue with you today. I'm in too good a mood and I've got tasks.'

She smiled. 'That's right,' she said. 'Tasks. But I'm glad we have time for our wee conversations.' She wiped a spot from the table. 'I won't say I very often agree with you.'

My father always said one wasn't a man and knew nothing of life until one could read the local newspaper from cover to cover and find every item interesting. Everything from the church news to the prices of used cars, from the legal notices to the births, marriages and deaths. I was very small, but I clearly remember him reading the *Lancaster and Morecambe Citizen* with a bone-handled magnifying glass, enlarging the specimens of print – even in the house he showed his love of science, his capturing eye – to discover the inner pattern and the secret of life.

Yet I can't quite see his face. It appears to me in dreams sometimes, like my own face but tougher, his high forehead signifying an easy and proud domination of family routines as well as some unspoken understanding of the world's troubles. My father was a surgeon and he took a surgeon's interest in what might be called the near certainty of outcomes. He was an educated man of his generation: more interested in habits than in character, more given to thought than declaration. Such men are apt to remain a mystery to their sons, but I know my father believed in preparation, he believed in the profes-sional approach, and, when it came to the consideration of life's priorities, he liked to quote Samuel Johnson on the notion that there was nothing too small for such a small thing as man. That was his unbending rule.

He hated chaos and impropriety. People who failed to make their beds in the morning were reprobates to him, and those who failed to pay their taxes were worse than murderers. One had a duty to polish one's shoes and give up one's seat. It was crucial to know when to shut up and when to tell the truth about oneself. His standards were not especially high, just especially precise and rigid, giving one the impression that a netherworld existed beyond shoe-polishing and bed-making, a region he had come to know about in his life's travels, a terri-ble hell for people who did not know how to live and who had no gratitude. He doubted the arts and anything remotely 'airy-fairy,' content to live, as he did, in a world of concrete objects and brown English likelihoods. I'm sure he would have come to find my mother and me quite intolerable. He wanted simple proof of everything, the weather, for instance, or the existence of God, and my going into the priesthood would have seemed to him, like my mother's novels, a grand and unnecessary bid for an idealism too proud to accommodate the facts.

Yet he wasn't morose. He was excited by his life. He enjoyed getting up in the morning and kept a woodpecker clock by the bed, a Swiss contraption that shocked him out of sleep at 5 a.m. He had leather carpet slippers ready on the floor, which he wore for the journey to the bathroom, a gleaming place where everything waited in good order, foreign soaps, tooth powder, his shaving things and a bottle of cologne. Every small element of life fascinated him and he wanted to get it right. The kitchen was a laboratory and so was the garden. It was always clear to me, even as a boy, that my father was the type to believe that human beings, even if not capable of it, should be ready to have an influence on everything around them and be conscious all the time of how to live and what to do.

Once a swallow's nest fell from the eaves of the house. My father gathered us together in the front room. He made us sit quietly by the window, watching the unfolding drama, seeing if the chicks inside the nest would be rescued or abandoned or stolen. In the end it was all too much for him. He brought the nest inside and taught me how to feed the chicks with a dropper. Two of them died, but one survived, and he put everything into the life of that bird. He took a pencil and pointed to the bulging purple skin that seemed to cover the bird's eyes and he showed me the place where its heart was beating.

'We have interfered,' he said. 'But that is what people are meant for – interfering. That is what we must do.'

'Why?' I said.

'Because we are human beings. Speed the plough. Search the galaxies. Find a cure for smallpox. That is us.'

'Will the bird live?'

'It may do,' he said. 'It may fly to South Africa with our help, if we can fix its bastard wing.'

I smiled, but that's what it's called: the bastard wing.

'It may die,' he said.

'Oh,' I said. 'Is that possible, after all the time we've spent? And you're here. Not many birds have their own surgeon.'

'It's possible,' he said. 'But, David, haven't we learned a great deal about what it takes to keep a thing living?'

Mrs Poole gathered a heap of newspapers in her arms and carried them outside to the recycling bin by the front door.

'All these trees,' I heard her say. 'Some day people will open their eyes to what they're doing to the world.'

Sitting at the table, I thought of an old man who had come to ten o'clock Mass that morning with his usual bags. He was a town councillor years ago, apparently, but now he just came to Mass every other day with bottles of sweet cider secreted in plastic bags along with a number of newspapers and library books. He always wore a raincoat that was faintly charcoaled with age and he sat in one of the side chapels, under the crucifix, reading the *Morning Star*. Once I saw him at a table towards the back of the Lite Bite, a café down the road. The bag containing the cider was jammed under the formica table and a dish of lasagne sat going cold at the centre of his papers and his scribbles.

I spoke to him that morning. His name was Mr Savage. He

often seemed ready to be spoken to, though few people went near him, leaving him alone with his scribbling and his tea. He was one of only two people, the other being Mrs Poole, who told me to watch out for myself in that town. I just smiled at his comments. He seemed like an aged version of some people I had known in my youth, and I liked him for that. He told me he took holidays twice a year with a company called Progressive Tours, always to places like Cuba or Vladivostok or Dresden.

He came up to me after Mass.

'Why no altar-servers?' he said.

'We seem to have lost them all,' I said. 'My predecessor, Father McGee, hadn't taken on any new altar boys for a while. We had an elderly gentleman who was serving morning Mass but he's not in good health.'

'I've seen him, yes.'

'Young people are busy, I suppose.'

'You know what they're like now,' said Mr Savage. 'They'll want a few quid before they'll agree to do anything.'

He smiled and I saw he had the most perfect teeth. I wanted to ask him if he'd had them done in Poland, where all the dentists are said to be cheap and where Progressive Tours might still go.

'It's the dictatorship of the proletariat,' he said.

I asked him if he was a Marxist.

'Naturally,' he said.

'And yet you come to Mass?'

'It's the auld alliance. Uncle Joe and Jesus Christ.'

'Oh,' I said. 'I've not heard that view expressed for years. It was something we used to play with in my youth.'

'Aye, well,' said Mr Savage. 'There's them that plays and them that stays. You're missing half your theology, Father.'

*

22

I caught sight of myself in the mirror as I stood up from the table, the old dog collar feeling rough and my suit too warm for the day. Something in my discussion with Mrs Poole had stirred me, as if I might find a way to dispel boredom and burn my routines. Was I hoping for something the minute I stood up? I reached down the side of the piano and opened a rosewood box that lived there, finding hymn books and loose sheet music, materials from my old parish, much of it dusty. I leafed through the music, took a few sheets out and placed them in a folder before turning again to Mrs Poole.

'Have you got everything?' she said.

I checked my pockets, feeling an assortment of pens and mints and small notepads. My breast pocket had a secret fold containing a duplicate of my mother's credit card. I tapped the pocket and knew it was there. Mrs Poole stood by the sofa rubbing her hands together against the non-existent cold, and I tried to look casual.

She laid a round basket filled with bottles of Baby Bio on the sofa. 'These are for the rubbish,' she said. 'You keep sneaking bottles in and the plants don't need fertiliser.'

'I'm sure it's very evil, Mrs Poole.'

'Too right,' she said. 'Evil. Those chemical companies are trying to turn everywhere into Kansas. I saw a thing on the telly.'

'Maybe you should be putting all the TVs on the rubbish tip.'

'You can laugh,' she said.

'I have no opinion.'

'That's right. You have no opinion. TV's all right in moderation. Maybe if you watched the odd bit of TV you'd know more about the world.'

'I'm sure you're right.'

'You'll say anything to keep me quiet,' she said. She rattled the small bottles in the basket and pursed her lips. 'It wouldn't do you any harm at all. But I have to grant you, books are more friendly.'

I waited a second or two.

'It's good that you come here,' I said.

I saw something, a momentary stiffness, perhaps, that seemed at the time like a grade of panic, and I thought to cancel it by placing a friendly hand on her shoulder.

'None of that now,' she said. 'No banalities, please. It's not the house for that sort of thing.'

'Right you are,' I said.

She grinned and I saw the good nature return to her face, though her hand was trembling as it reached out for a tin of polish.

'*Film* music,' she said.

'Oh, shush,' I said. 'Go about your business, woman.'

'*Au revoir*,' she said.

Mrs Poole put the polish under her arm and said nothing more as she walked across the carpet. The day was very fine. She chewed a fingernail as she reached the back of the sitting-room, and she paused there, looking out through the large window at the rose garden and a blackbird drinking from the sundial.

2

THE MOUTH OF THE RIVER

Dalgarnock is a junction parish on the Ayrshire coast, about thirty miles outside Glasgow. The river now goes to the sea, but when St Ker first arrived there in 682 AD, the river went in the opposite direction, flowing through Ayrshire's bracken woods towards the lowlands of Lanarkshire, where the tributaries of several Scottish rivers gather in green, heathery lochs, and where home-remembering salmon and handmade arrowheads can still be seen glinting in the shallows.

St Ker was a monk on Iona and the famous annals say he left the Abbey consumed with gout and the whisperings of God. He is thought to have journeyed into the Irish Sea and crossed the inland dark in a skin-covered boat. Arriving in the night to find nothing thereabouts, and half-starved, he cursed the river at the place of Dalgarnock, but the river changed course to outwit the curse and has flowed ever since to Irvine Bay.

An empty explosives factory marks the skyline of Dalgarnock, but the better part of the town seems to be given over to black and white council houses with windows the size of bibles. Behind the houses there are shops and schools and a wasteland of gorse crowding yellow to the sea. At the furthest edge of the town, next to the late-night petrol station, a graveyard is filled to the edge of a quarry with Protestant bones. You pass the graveyard and its plastic flowers if heading by road towards the old commercial centres of Irvine and Prestwick, Ayr and Kilmarnock, the town where Robert Burns published his first work.

Bishop Gerard was a friend from my seminary days in Rome. Some years older than me, he worked back then for the English-speaking section of the Congregation of Bishops, and I still recall with some nervousness those Glasgow words and phrases murmured through the grille of a confessional box at the church of Santa Maria sopra Minerva, a Gothic construction next to the Pantheon. Gerard came from the Calton area of Glasgow. People said he was tough, dutiful, harsh even, and he certainly had a fund of stories about the Connollys of Drum – his Irish progenitors, a race apart – and would take second place to no man in his admiration for Celtic Football Club. But my experience of Gerard was different. To me he seemed continually buoyed with plain spiritual grace and a love of the sacred, and he never held my childhood in England against me, not in any very serious way, though I recall that he chose not to visit the English College in the via Monserrato and never failed to scoff at our considerable fondness for cricket.

'They say you English seminarians walk differently from other people,' he said. 'The Romans can tell you a mile away, before you open your mouths, just by how you walk. They call it *il passo nordico*.'

Once he was back home and Vicar-General of the Glasgow diocese, Gerard wrote me frequent letters about what he called, with no particular respect for reality, 'the steady progress of holy matters in the land of footballing excellence'. He never failed to keep me in mind whenever he found impertinent jokes against French wine or English literature. As was intended, I spent my pastoral career in Lancashire, most of it in Blackpool, and by the time I wanted the transfer to Scotland my old friend was the Bishop of Galloway. When I petitioned him for a parish, Gerard seemed to think long and hard before offering me Dalgarnock, a decision, I like to think, made mainly in order to present a challenge to my liking for freshly cut violets.

I wonder if he knew what he was doing. It would be fair to say the town had a suspicion of strangers. No matter. It was the beginning of a new life. Driving over the moor at Auchentiber that first October evening, I saw Dalgarnock Abbey and the town below it emerge out of the darkness like burning matter in a dream of constant renewal. I tasted sea salt coming through the open window, I turned off the radio, and immediately thought of the Balliol drinking song. Versions of myself fanned out and danced before the headlamps, and I pursued them, these furies, the window open to the ancient world and the town glowing orange and alive down there at the centre of its own embers. I turned off the headlights to see the place better and then turned off the engine, rolling down with the handbrake off to a town that appeared to know its own past.

It was the ruined abbey that struck me most. You could see it from every point in the town, each face of the clock tower telling the wrong time and the stones underneath heaped together in memory of a Reformation that had never stopped. The south transept was nine hundred years old. It was broken down but still powerful, magisterial, emboldening. Even the moss on the fallen stones had dignity. The tower was erected in the nineteenth century after the original collapsed in a storm. My first day in the town, suitcases still unpacked, removal men on the way, I went into the tower and climbed up to the open top. The stone steps were covered with the remains of dead birds, skeletons lying in their sprigs of feathers. Death had made the birds into their own tombs, each like a nest, their departed selves now shaped like their former dwellings.

We come from a long line of Catholics. It still feels vaguely presumptuous to speak of 'our' ancestors. I think of them as my father's people, the Andertons, those Lancashire monks and martyrs whom my father admired less for their undying faith than for the commanding way they had tried to take hold of life. He would speak of John Rigbye, son of Margaret Rigbye née Anderton, who was hanged, drawn and quartered in London in the year 1600 for refusing to join the state church. 'He was better than a saint,' my father said. 'He knew the things he had to do.' Then there was Thomas Anderton, Prior of St Edmund's in Paris between 1668 and 1669, who wrote *The History of the Iconoclasts*. 'These people had learning,' my father would say. 'They weren't afraid to get up in the morning.'

Their names were everywhere in my childhood. They fell like unsettled dust from the roof beams and attics of ancient memory. There was Laurence Anderton who wrote *The Protestant's Apologie* under the pseudonym John Brerely. There was Robert Anderton, a student at Brasenose College who acknowledged Elizabeth I but said he would not oppose the Pope and was later executed for his trouble on the Isle of Wight. The Anderton name is often to be found on the recusancy rolls, and when I was five or six my father would sometimes take me by the hand through the graveyards of Wrightington, Ince Blundell or Hindley. I can still see dragonflies hovering over the grass and darting between the stones.

One of my last memories of my father is on such a day, at a graveyard outside Wigan. 'You see,' he said, bending down at a grave and scraping the stone with his fingernail. 'Anderton. Cotton-mill worker, it says.'

'Not the one that got executed in London?'

I remember him making a friendly frown and his blue surgeon's eyes swallowing me and the graveyard, its trees and its toadstools too. I can see him so clearly with his good hair and the pale sun at his back, my father reaching out for my wrist and squeezing – it seems now – for all the years that he wouldn't know me.

'We didn't only die for God,' he said.

The Mother Lodge stands in Main Street. It is a rather gaunt building of reddish local stone. Dalgarnock people call it the 'Number Nothing', for it houses the oldest Masonic establishment in Scotland, Lodge No. 0. Members are wont to defend the title against the claims of the Edinburgh lodges with reference to compelling medieval hearsay and land rights going back to the foundation of the abbey.

My first winter in the town, a group of men were standing outside as I passed. Some of them had grey hair fairly shining with pomade, and they chewed gum and wore training shoes, each man seeming to be in preparation for some kind of cardiovascular event. They began to laugh as if to communicate how stupid it was for a Catholic priest suddenly to waft past them in the street wearing his dog collar, but their smiles turned sinister when I lifted my hand to wave back and return the smile, as if war songs suddenly echoed in their blood at the sight of my insulting friendliness.

The men at the door of the Mother Lodge made me feel as if the sight of me was hurting their eyes. Some younger ones came out of the door behind them and froze. I stared for a few seconds. 'Good day,' I said, and though I seldom really hear the tone of my own voice, I heard it then, sounding, I'm sad to say, not unlike the Lord Privy Seal.

'On yer way!' said one of the youngsters.

'I beg your pardon?'

'Away ye go, ya papish scum.'

The older men retreated to the top of the steps, as if the matter was now out of their hands and out of their league. But one of them, a rather distinguished-looking gentleman, seventy-something I'd have said, a venerable statesman with white hair and ruddy cheeks, leaned forward and winked at the younger fellow. 'That'll do fine,' he said. 'We don't want any kinda trouble here.'

'Don't worry, auld yin. I think he's got the message.' He looked again. 'That's right, I'm talking aboot you, ya English bastard.'

He glared at me. He was wearing a Rangers football top. I was surprised by what he said and how he said it, but I suppose my surprise would have insulted them further. The older men seemed friendly with the younger ones but also somewhat embarrassed by them. It seemed possible to me that something had changed lately in terms of how those people inhabited their great beliefs and prejudices. The younger men growled like people rather sure and rather proud of their injuries, and this man in the football colours – his drunk eyes, his thin, begging laughter – appeared instantly to assume the wisdom of common authority. The younger men had an eager proximity to violent action, as they sometimes do, and this alone was enough to crowd the old men's moderation into silence.

'Go on,' said the blue top. 'Fuck right off. We don't want you here.'

I felt so mortified I almost laughed, just as one might when a mood of contentment gives way to sudden embarrassment. No one had ever spoken to me like that before: a priest gets used to being respected and sometimes pitied, but never in my life had anyone made me feel so vulnerable and so disliked. Something in the man's face had seemed to represent ancient grievances, and his hard eyes and his balled-up fists had spoken of some vast and unknowable capacity for rage. I swear it was new to me in that narrow street, and I walked back to the chapel feeling hurt and disjointed and confused, thinking perhaps I knew less about other people and less about Dalgarnock than I ought to know.

The Church of St John Ogilvie stands at the top of a lane opposite an abandoned railway station. They built the chapel in the 1930s to appease Irish labourers who had come to work at the local iron foundry, and their own schools followed soon after. During those first months in the town, I suppose it shocked me how lazy the Catholics were, especially given the efforts of their industrious ancestors, but then, in such matters, the tribal element will often eclipse the spiritual. It turned out that Dalgarnock's small community of Catholics – much like their opposites – were enslaved to the denominational impulse: few of them regularly attended Mass, none sent their boys into the priesthood, yet they loudly swelled with sectarian pride. Northern Ireland was just across the water, and what Dalgarnock had was a briny dilution of Ireland's famous troubles, without the interest in votes, assemblies or breakable guns. Hidden in the trees across from my church, smothered in part-time grievances, there stood a windowless hut painted royal blue, in which the band of the Dalgarnock Orange Order chose to rehearse each Sunday morning.

I blamed Mrs Poole's soup for the heartburn. I felt an empty, dyspeptic scorch as I drove to the school, like a rising argument at the centre of my chest, and I found there were no Rennies in the glove compartment. Then I thought maybe it was the white wine, a nightmare for heartburn, though you couldn't fault the freshness of a good and well-made Alsace, the taste of Easter and crushed flowers.

The headmaster at St Andrew's, Mr McCallum, was a God-fearing alcoholic of the old stamp. The pupils called him Fuck-Face. He drank in his office and seemed to live in fear of the changing times, also in dread of the nuns who taught geography and French. Generally speaking, he would display the defensive meekness of the professional drunk, but now and then his disorder would express itself in a wonderful display of bad temper. But McCallum was kind, asking me if I'd like, as a historian, to give the occasional lesson, an offer I found obscurely flattering. I never taught the curriculum, of course, the curriculum being useful only for the half-hearted cultivation of barely obedient idiots, so I took the chance to talk about Pugin and William Byrd to the senior students. They seemed to enjoy it well enough, so long as you let them drink their fizzy drinks throughout the lesson and didn't give them homework.

One got the impression the staff believed very strongly that education was a matter of bitter entrenchment as opposed to any sort of managed revelation, and they seemed in cahoots with the children when it came to the sorry victory of rights over responsibilities. Stupid children are always aware of their rights, and so are stupid teachers: they share a belief in the supreme relevance of what they think themselves and wield these opinions like home-made weapons in the war against self-improvement. The staffroom at St Andrew's was worse than the playground, the domain of idle bullies, a place of pecking orders, where the ignorant and the disappointed daily stalked the carpet tiles, fully in love with their petty jealousies and three sugars. The classrooms were both garish and dirty, which doesn't aid the spirit when one is leading on the poetry of Gerard Manley Hopkins.

It should've been a holiday, but it seemed most parents would do anything to avoid having their children at home an extra day, including sending them to the Kissing of the Cross. I bumped into Mr Dorran at the edge of the sports wing. Dorran was Head of Music and very short, always wearing needlessly ugly ties over his junior shirts. Not for the first time, I wondered if he had become a teacher in order to feel like one of the world's naturally tall people. He certainly swaggered among the pupils as if his chance to be big had finally come. I also noticed he had the beginning of a moustache.

'Ah, just the man,' I said, placing the crucifix and some other things on the register table.

'Hello, Father David,' he said, trying to dodge me with an armful of violins. 'I'm awful busy. This was supposed to be a day off.'

'Of course,' I said. 'Just a word in your small ear.'

(I see now that in many ways I was not wise. Dorran smarted.)

'If it's about the music, you must spare me.'

'Not a bit of it, Mr Dorran,' I said. 'I made a request of you at the beginning of Lent. Let us not have any more of these rubbishy hymns. There is no one else to whom I can address these remarks. You are the man in charge. Rubbishy hymns, horrible words. What are these hymns about sunny days and being happy? Where do they come from? In the new term, can we not progress a little to . . . well, to proper music?'

'Excuse me, Father,' he said. 'Those hymns have been used in Scottish schools for quite some time. They are very popular. The pupils like to sing them.'

'They also like to sing Eminem, Mr Dorran, and we shan't

be introducing that to the Mass just yet. I gave you the music. I didn't hear any of it at the Mass for the beginning of the Easter holiday. Could you not manage "Cross of Jesus"? It being Easter. "Cross of Jesus"?'

'I don't know it.'

'Music by John Stainer, 1841–1901,' I said. 'Words by William Sparrow-Simpson, 1860–1952.'

I squeezed some sheet music between his instruments.

'Please don't do that, Father. I won't be patronised in this way every time I see you.'

'Mr Dorran, I'm not asking for the "Stabat Mater".'

'Yes, you are!' he said. 'In the context, *yes, you are.*'

What can only be described as a look of utter hatred suddenly crossed the good man's eyes. He flushed and plucked a string on one of the violins, as if to mark the taking of a bold decision. 'Has it ever occurred to you that you don't belong here, Father David?'

'Well, of course, Mr Dorran,' I said. 'I've never been sure I belong anywhere in the world. Perhaps you'd take pity on me therefore and spare me the terrible agony of having to listen to seven hundred impressionable young people singing "The Beautiful Month of May".'

'That is typical arrogance,' he said.

I could see Mr Dorran was fighting to restrain some coarser instinct. He looked at me as people do when they think they see through you. 'Can I remind you,' he said, his jaw slackening, 'this is a comprehensive school. You may find it difficult to imagine just what that means, Father. It is a *com-pree-hen-sive.* We have to make certain allowances here. This is not Eton College.'

'Heaven forfend,' I said.

'Pardon?'

'That really would be something to worry about.'

'You know what this town is? It's an unemployment black spot. I don't think you understand what has happened here. The factories are empty. The churches are empty.'

'Ah, Mr Dorran,' I said. 'But the heart is full.'

The Head of Music conducted a symphony of derision into a single sniff. 'You should take a leaf out of Bishop Gerard's book,' he said. 'He comes here with the crook and everything else, but you know what? He sits down at the piano and plays Boyzone to get the pupils' attention.'

'Yes,' I said, 'but Gerard has a much larger range than I do.'

Mr Dorran looked at his tired shoes, as if he might find there an instant companion for his piteous feeling.

'Good afternoon, Father. I have a group of musical illiterates awaiting instruction in the finer points of Johann Sebastian Bach.' And with that he was off down the corridor with his rick of broken strings.

My contact lenses slipped during the school service. The smoke from the burning incense stung my eyes and the lenses were lost for a second in the sudden dampness, making me see the congregation for a moment like rows of creatures under water. The children stood in their lines of blazers and uttered the prayers as if they were chanting the seven times table, which they were, without the satisfactions of either pattern or precision. I had to ask Mrs McCourt to be my assistant at the Kissing of the Cross when it became clear that every other pupil was chewing gum. She stood with a look of great piety before the cross, holding a paper towel, stopping the offenders as they knelt down and relieving them sorrowfully of their once sugary fragments. Each halted pupil behaved as if it were an added ritual, giving up the contents of their innermost selves. 'Behold the wood of the cross,' I said, 'on which Christ died.'

Children tend to like the Crucifixion, not the veneration of the cross so much as the driving in of the nails and so on. It appeals rather directly to their obsession with cruel and horrible images. Good Friday was a version of *Nightmare on Elm Street* to most of them. They liked the spectacle of Christ being scourged with metal-tipped whips; they admired the nails being hammered into His hands and the sponge of vinegar going up and the spear being driven into His side as the dark clouds rolled above and the constant mother wept at the base of the cross. You could see it in the children's eyes. They found it amazing, the drama of brutality, the soreness, the cracked limbs, and they were never so silent as when Christ's agony was given to them in vivid pictures.

After the service, when the pupils and teachers had poured out of the hall in a wave of sudden laughter, eye rolling and phone start-up jingles, I went to the second floor to talk to a group of fourth-year students doing an after-school project on world religions. I stopped in one of the empty corridors, the tiles on the floor shining up, appearing almost to speak of historical scuffing and departed concerns. The more robust teachers called it the Social Sciences corridor: it began at the stairwell with Classical Studies, a room presided over by Mr Muir, a young Catullus fan with a marked disaffection for all events that had shown the bad taste to occur after the year 300 AD. The next room along was Modern Studies, a non-subject much preferred by shirkers, encouraged by a nice woman called Susan who admired China. There was a run of English classes piled with tatty copies of *Lord of the Flies*, a number of geography rooms decked with charts about soil erosion, and singing out, close to the end of the long corridor, was Mr Platter's Art class, a room festooned with terrifying teenage approximations of the work of Joan Miró.

That day, Good Friday, I stopped in the corridor to look at the walls. They presented such a contrast with the oils of former abbots at my old school, those prints and architectural drawings framed and hung so handsomely next to the big hall. In contrast, the walls of this Catholic comprehensive were replete with old photographs of the working poor, sepia-toned, white-lighted, each figure a smoky spectre from the plates of Adamson, Annan or David Octavius Hill. From the Classical Studies rooms to History, 'Unloading jute, Dundee Docks' and 'The forge at Sumerlee Ironworks, Coatbridge'. Dotted between them were photographs of cobblers (tie-wearing, waistcoat-snug, side partings, young) sitting in rows at the Loch Street Co-op in Aberdeen and 'Girls in the dyeing room at Templeton's Carpet Works, 1910'. From English to Geography were cold, industrial prints showing the building of the Forth Road Bridge, and between Geography and Art, 'The new liner *City of New York* takes shape at Clydebank, 1886', 'East coast fishwives gutting herring, 1900', 'The men of Cumnock Colliery, 1912', 'Cleaning fleeces before baling, circa 1870' and a larger one, smudged and grey: 'Workers at William Blackie and Co.'s book bindery at Glasgow in 1932'. The people in the photographs had the solid bearing that only history affords. Arms folded, working overalls creased and blackened, eyes sharp, they lit out from a known, dead world, no longer unhappy, no longer curious, but ghosts in that long corridor children now pass down on their way to a better time.

The pupils were waiting in World Religions. They hung over their desks as if they had just been dropped there from a great height, looking like their limbs confounded them and their hair bothered them, and several chewed the frayed ends of their sweaters in the style of caged animals attempting to escape their own quarters. They tended to wear uniform, though each pupil had customised it with badges and belts and sweatbands; you felt they had applied strict notions of themselves to the tying of their ties and the sticking up of their shirt collars. The small energies of disdain could be observed in all this, and the classroom fairly jingled with the sound of forbidden rings and bracelets.

They had already been given a talk by Sister Pauline, who apparently spoke quite passionately of her attempts to gain the canonisation of Mother Mary Joseph, the founder of her order, and another group had gone on a visit to the central mosque in Glasgow.

'It was mad,' said one of the girls. The threads of her school badge had been unpicked: once upon a time the Cross of St Andrew, it was now a flare of orange fuzz on the top pocket of her blazer, like a sacred heart. 'Totally mad,' she said. 'We had to wear these mad as shit scarves and stop talking and everything.'

'And shoes,' said a tall boy next to the radiator. 'They had a thing for shoes by the door. Yer no' allowed shoes. No' even trainies. Guys went into one place and lassies into another. It's mad. You're no' allowed to mix.'

'What did you learn?' I said.

'They chop off women's hands for nothing,' said the girl.

'They eat bulls' cocks,' said the boy. 'Telling you. They eat anything.'

That was the first time I met the pair of them, Mark McNulty and Lisa Nolan. They called him 'McNuggets'. I never knew him as that, though I would come to know him well enough.

'I don't know why we had to go there,' he said. 'It's all suicide bombers and everything. You're jeest walking down the street and next minute people are blown up and dying every-where. Jeest for walking down the street. It's totally nuts.'

As this was said, the mouths of most of the other pupils twitched into a smiling complicity. Giggles erupted. Friendly swipes were given or received. A smaller boy with a cold called Cameron seemed to take his own view. 'That's no' right,' he said. 'That's jeest prejudiced.'

'Shut it, Ca-Ca,' said Mark.

'My name's Cameron.'

'Shut it, Cameraman.'

'Come now,' I said. 'What else did you learn?'

'It felt creepy,' said Lisa.

'That's not very thoughtful,' I said.

'It's true, but,' said Lisa, looking for support.

'Check this out,' said Mark. 'It stank. They're all . . . thingmi. Whit's it called? Asylum seekers.'

'You can't let them say that, Father,' said Cameron. 'They are jeest being totally ignorant.'

'It was on Fox News,' said Lisa. 'My da watches it.'

'That's jeest crap,' said Cameron.

'Language,' I said.

'Whatever,' said Mark. 'Don't ask us if you don't want to know. We went to the place. It was a total dump. They throw acid in people's faces if you don't agree with them. That's some crazy shit.'

'There's no evidence for that,' said Cameron.

'Dry your eyes, Cameraman,' said Mark.

'Aye, shut up, Cammy,' said Lisa. 'He puts on this big act. He's always dropping science about shit he knows nothing about. He does it in Modern Studies as well. Like, "I love for-eigners."'

'Stop Xeroxing me, bitch,' said Mark. 'I'll walk Cameraman down by myself, no problem. All his shit about camel jockeys.'

'Please,' I said. 'I won't have names in here.'

'Awright, Father,' said Mark. I saw him winking at the girls over my shoulder; I saw he knew how to use his brown eyes. 'But you've got to admit,' he said, 'terrorists are terrorists.'

'They're not terrorists,' said one of the other boys. 'They just believe in their own religion.'

'Exactly,' said Cameron. 'These people, many of them, their ancestors were building temples, inventing things. You know, making carpets and stuff, when people in America and in this country were still running aboot in the swamps.'

'Aye,' said his friend. 'It's Christians that are responsible for most of the world's greatest atrocities.'

'Get a grip, Eval,' said Mark. 'It's not Christians or Jews that go flying planes into people's offices.'

'No, you get a grip, McNuggets,' he said. 'It's Christians that put people into gas ovens. It's Jews that bomb people out of their own houses in Palestine . . .'

'Oh, get lost,' said Lisa.

'No, you get lost,' he said. 'It's Americans that burned babies in Vietnam. It's Catholics that put bombs into bloody chip shops in Northern Ireland.'

'Exactly,' said Cameron. Mark stood up.

'Shut it, Cameraman,' he said. 'It's no people from this country that drive planes into people's offices. It's no people from here that take folk hostage and cut their heads off. It's no Americans that gas their own folk. Why don't you and yer wee boyfriend there just go and live together in fucken Gayland or wherever it is you get yer ideas from.'

'That's quite enough,' I said. 'We won't have that kind of language in here. Do you understand?'

'Whit language?' said Mark, his face crimson. 'The Scottish language?'

'No,' I said, 'that's fine. Let's just do without the expletives.'

'That is our language, Father,' he said, smirking and including us all in the wealth of his joke. Lisa looked at him through her clumpy mascara and smiled. It was clear that Mark was the hero of the form. Lisa did more than smile: she glowed through her cheeks; she loved him.

'Any road,' she said, 'I hated that mosque place we went to. They're jeest into killing people for nothing.'

'That is not very tolerant,' I said, feeling quickly unctuous. 'The people you are speaking about, those terrorists, are, I believe, a small minority, and the people at the mosque wouldn't hold those views.'

'They're always going to those countries,' Mark said. 'Weird places in the Middle East where they learn about bombs.'

'It may be just a violent minority,' I said.

'It's all violence in those countries,' he said.

I tried again. 'Civilisation takes many forms, and, as Christians, we must use our faith to help bring peace to the lives of those people who have none.'

'Not just peace,' said Mark. 'More than that. Democracy.'

Old political notions tugged at me, 1960s notions, but I thought there was something in what Mark was trying to say.

'Perhaps we have a duty in that direction,' I said. 'Many people think so. But we mustn't indulge in insults by saying these people are only terrorists. There are many good people. They have beautiful traditions.'

'But we did it in English,' said Lisa. 'They chop women's heads off for going with men. They bag them up and wipe them out.'

'That wasn't in English,' said Mark. 'You saw it on Fox.'

'Shush, McNuggets,' she said, blushing. 'It was me that told you about it.' Lisa had the quick temper that often elicits admiration among young people. 'You dogged that class.'

'My da told me,' he said. 'They just want to get weapons and do in all their enemies, and you've got to say "no way" to that shit.'

'These arguments are interesting,' I said. 'As Catholics, we often find that mercy is the key to our dilemmas. You went to the mosque in Glasgow. These people do not see God in the same way we do ourselves, but they are part of our community.'

After a while, some of the pupils put on their coats. There were buses to catch and suppers to be in time for, but Mark and Lisa seemed in no hurry to go home. It ended up just being the three of us, and their talk grew ever freer, even more rude, as if the extracurricular atmosphere had bled into one of immunity and licence. Except when quoting their prejudices, they spoke of their families as if they were enemies and spoke of the future as if it could never come quickly enough, a fixed site of retribution, where no one was boss and beer was freely available.

I pointed out of the classroom window at the middle of the sea. 'That's Ailsa Craig over there,' I said. 'Have you ever been out there?'

'To the rock?' Mark said. 'Paddy's Milestone. Why would anybody go out there? It's just an old rock covered in bird shit.' I looked past the coast to where the island rose like a lilac pyramid in the fading light.

'Because it's beautiful, Mark.'

'It's always been there,' said Lisa, walking over to the window and pressing a new stick of gum into her mouth.

'Exactly,' I said. 'You've both lived here your whole lives, haven't you? What, fifteen years? And Ailsa Craig has been out there every day. Don't you wonder what it's like?'

'I know what it's like,' said Lisa. 'It's boring.'

'No, you're boring,' I said. 'There are no people out there. Just a world on its own in the middle of the sea.'

'No government,' said Mark, looking out.

'No nothing,' said Lisa.

'It's a bird sanctuary,' I said.

During the short time we watched it from the school window, Ailsa Craig became several degrees darker until it folded into the dusk and a small light blinked at the base of the rock.

'So what do you like, Mark?' I said.

'Celtic,' he said.

'So that's your tribe. A football club.'

'It's no' a tribe,' he said. 'It's a tradition. Oh, man. Did you see the Liverpool game at Anfield? We're in the semi-final of the UEFA Cup for the first time in thirty-three years or something. That game. I'm telling you. That was bitchin'. Totally awesome. To beat Liverpool on their own soil.'

'I used to like Liverpool,' I said. 'Not the team. I don't know anything about football teams. I liked the place.'

'That's why he's so happy,' said Lisa. 'He thinks Celtic are going to win the European Cup.'

'The UEFA Cup,' said Mark.

'Whatever.'

'We could do it, by the way,' said Mark. 'Martin O'Neill could do it for us. Henrik Larsson could do it. You know what? That Liverpool game was the best night of my life. No kidding. When that guy came on at the beginning and sang "You'll Never Walk Alone", that was it. Every fan in the stadium held up their scarf. Just a sea of colours. Pure magic. We drew with Boavista. If we beat them in the return match in

43

Portugal we're in the final. I'm telling you, this could be the best year we've ever had.'

Lisa rolled her eyes. 'Paul Lambert,' she said.

'That's right,' said Mark. 'He's awesome. Even I would shag him.'

'Excuse me,' I said. 'Language. That's quite enough of that.'

Mark was a danger to himself and others; you could tell by the way he narrowed his eyes and screwed around with his hair. He knew how to insinuate himself into people's worries about themselves, and he did it with his eyes and his hands, as well as with his words, the kind of sharp and brutal honesty that passes for charm with some people. 'Father,' he said, 'in your whole life have you ever had sex?'

'Stop it,' I said.

'You've got to answer,' said Lisa.

'I'm not answering,' I said.

'Come on,' said Mark. 'Get over yourself.'

'Get over myself? Is that another one of your American television phrases?'

'Right. Whatever. Come on, Father. Is it yes or no? Have you ever had sex in your whole life?'

'You're very disrespectful,' I said. 'And I'm not in the business of answering a question like that.'

'That's awesome, man. He has!' said Lisa.

'I know he has,' Mark said. 'If he hadn't he would just have said "no". You're busted, Father. It's "yes".'

'Don't be so idiotic.'

'Don't sweat it, Father,' he said. 'We're all human.'

'I have my doubts about that,' I said.

'That's right,' he said. 'Like Arabs.'

We talked about other things, or they talked and I nodded, the young people's views proving less interesting to me than

44

the liveliness with which they were able to express them. It all left me doubting my basic honesty but also feeling giddy and hopeful and slightly breathless.

During my time in Dalgarnock, it had begun to cling to me: not faithlessness, which I haven't suffered since leaving Oxford, but a large private sense of wanting to depart from the person I had always been. I could see it happening: one sort of world was colliding with another, and that evening I wanted to join their world and embrace their carelessness. That's what I wanted to do. I wish I could say I knew their kind and beheld all my errors, but what I knew about that pair, Mark and Lisa, was only what I wanted to know. They were very young and ready for life.

A smell of pine came from the corridors. The cleaners were knocking off for the evening and the janitor came with his grumpy face and his chain of keys. 'Got to lock the doors now, Father,' he said. 'It's been a long day. Don't let these ones keep you.'

Maybe I felt refreshed by their badness; maybe I knew them all along, those two, and fell out of step with myself in recognition, knowing they might keep me from boredom with their loose talk and their chaos. The boy rose from the desk and eyed me, then he yawned. I later noticed that Mark would begin yawning every time there was a pause of more than two seconds in his adventures. He was never attentive to anything that didn't involve himself directly and had no sentiment beyond that relating to the fortunes of Celtic Football Club.

'You're a good laugh,' he said. 'You don't get eggy over a bit of chat. No' like them dicks.' He nodded out to the corridor and the invisible teachers now home in their kitchens.

'Thank you,' I said. 'It's rather diverting for me to hear the opinions of young people. Especially on current affairs.'

'Diverting, is it?' he said, grinning. 'You're awesome.'

The only American poet I cared for in my childhood was Wallace Stevens. He wasn't terribly Christian, not like the others I read, but I loved the colour of his thoughts, the way the earth was to him a paradise of green umbrellas and red weather rather than a place of obscure punishments. My mother gave me *Harmonium* for my twelfth birthday and I don't suppose I understood the poems at the time, but I've been thinking about them ever since, and I begin to see that the search for happiness is all we have. To sit in a park and listen to the dogs barking; to sit in a park and hear church bells: are we not always present, always human and always religious according to our faith?

Those poems are made for the earth-loving young. I remember my delight at what they suggested, the world outside with its stars and palaces, its teacups and oceans, and my mother and I chuckled over his titles: 'Stars at Tallapoosa' – 'there is no moon, no single, silvered leaf' – and 'Hymn from a Watermelon Pavilion':

> You dweller in the dark cabin,
> To whom the watermelon is always purple,
> Whose garden is wind and moon.
>
> Of the two dreams, night and day,
> What lover, what dreamer, would choose
> The one obscured by sleep?

It was Mark and Lisa and me. We laughed in the car on the way to the Blue Star garage. The young people were so completely themselves that they wasted no time on reserve, and so we drove round the edge of the town as if we'd been companions for years, and it seemed right that I was with them and not with anybody else or thinking about the past. That was my folly: the past was actually present in every word and grin.

'Call me David,' I said.

'Call me Cardinal,' said Mark.

Lisa was tapping out a rhythm on the back of the headrest. In the car park of the school, in the light coming from the houses, we had seen Mr McCallum, the headmaster, throwing up beside his car. He was partly hidden by the trees, but we saw him bending down and we stood back.

'Did you see that?' said Mark. 'Fuck-Face was puking down the side of his crappy Volvo. What a pisshead.'

'Don't,' I said. 'You must have pity.'

'He's just an old tosser,' said Mark. 'Hates me anyway. They all hate me. Don't they, Lees?'

'Aye, they hate him,' said Lisa. 'But he is horrible, though. Don't you think so, Father?'

Mark laughed. 'You are trippin', baby.'

I just laughed too. 'Don't be listenin' to her,' he said. 'The only thing she knows aboot is hip-hop and she's a crack whore.'

'A what?'

'The original Scottish coochie,' he said. 'Nasty!'

'Ignore him,' she said. 'You don't even get crack round here. He's just talking rubbish. He thinks he's a Jamaican hip-hop gangster.'

'Steady on,' I said. Mark rapped on the dashboard and laughed and gave me a soft punch on the arm.

'*Steady on*,' he said. 'You're cool.'

I asked them both if they'd really had such a difficult time on the visit to the mosque. 'Damn right,' said Mark. 'Those people just want to hurt people. They's mad as shit.'

'They hate our way of life,' said Lisa.

'You definitely got that from the telly, bitch,' said Mark, turning round in his seat and smacking Lisa's head.

'Bite me,' she said.

I looked over towards the shore as we pulled into the garage and could see only darkness stretching across the water, the lighthouse on Ailsa Craig blinking its cold warning over the bay.

'America is out there somewhere,' I said.

'At least in America they have good music,' said Lisa.

'Too right,' said Mark.

'And films.'

'Too right,' he said.

I gave the pair some money and they went into the garage shop to buy things. I could see them inside, larking about in the aisles and picking up stuff they didn't need. Mark shook hands in an elaborate way with the guy at the cash desk: his colleague, I presumed, as Mark had already said he worked in the garage at the weekends.

I saw myself in the rear-view mirror. What was I doing? What was I doing *here*? My hair was grey and my eyes tired. It's amazing how you wake up grey. We start by thinking grey hair is somebody else's story, a crowning jest in the lives of the contented and the wise. Then you wake up grey yourself, realising you happen to be neither contented nor wise, and that grey hair is nature's revenge on the complacency of lustre.

What was I doing?

The kids were chuffed and preening in the confectionery aisle, gagging for fizz, keen for trouble, scenting the latest chance, each one a selfish fool made charming by the power of the moment and the yellow strip-lights. The car wash was idle. I wound down the window and looked through it, feeling the sea air.

Grosvenor Square. The people linked arms in the afternoon and the horses charged forward, police helmets flying. A hippy offered a bunch of flowers to one of the officers and was beaten to the ground, and we sang our songs and the future was a dream.

Mark and Lisa were laughing into the garage's microwave oven. In their arms they held slabs of chocolate, bottles and magazines, and I watched them for a while from the car and saw myself at the blurred edge of their existence. This was the great present: maybe the saddest place of all.

'Goodnight then,' I said, the sense of Easter as real to me as their laughing eyes and the condensation on the windows of the Blue Star garage. I drove off before they could see I was gone.

Each man has his own way of betraying himself. For so long I had known myself only in prayers, in silent shadows and in dreams. Say I was longing for disaster. Say I was a victim of the moment, the perpetual now. But driving along the coast road I began to feel less obscured by those years of determined avoidance. I felt alive. There was no moon up there to manage the occasion, no stars to make a feast of the sleeping shore, but I know I felt peaceful as I drove the car over the bridge and past the abbey with its wrong clock faces marking the night.

3

MR PERHAPS

My mother was someone who enjoyed the paradoxes of experience. 'Children like the taste of sweets,' I once said to her in the garden at Heysham. 'Of course,' she said. 'But do sweets like the taste of children?' She met my father when he was working at the Eastern General Hospital in Edinburgh and was immediately, she said, in love with his moral beauty, the kind of thing that Edinburgh girls of her class and generation were educated to look out for.

'Didn't you just fancy him?' I said years later, after another florid retelling of the story.

'No,' she said. 'He fancied me. I fancied spending my life with someone of that sort of quality, which isn't the same thing.'

She said she knew all about the Anderton ancestors. The whole business appealed to her passion for history's approval; she wanted to feel included in the great debates and sacrifices of the past, and I suppose the burgeoning romance-writer in her had an instinct for material. When he got the job at Lancaster Infirmary, and his own past loomed to swallow us up, the past of England and his own people, as well as daily life in the small village of Heysham, she thought it could only be a good thing.

'Honestly,' she said. 'Your father was the only person I'd ever met who truly knew how to live his life. He wasn't perfect. But he knew what it took to be happy. He used to walk down that Lancaster canal as if it were one of life's unbeatable pleasures. He'd carry a guide-book. He'd check the provenance of chimneys. That's your father. He knew what to do.'

'But did you love him?' I asked.

'I miss him every day,' she said.

There came a time in Dalgarnock, in May or so, when my friendship with those reckless young people suddenly deepened. On Lisa's sister's wedding day I was thinking of my mother and father while arranging my vestments. The patter of rain was heavy on the sacristy roof, but none of the great elements could damp down the noise of laughter and bawling coming from inside the chapel, where the families had gathered for the service. Babies cried out in the pews, folded in young arms, both parents and children rather pink, compact engines of untold wants.

I opened the window above the sink and watched the rain. It brought the smell of other parts of Scotland, bogs and glens and open fields, the parts of Scotland I had read about in my mother's books, where history occurred and ruined cottages still stood to account in a smirr of rain.

White chasuble, I thought. *White stole.*

I put the garments over my head and wetted a comb under the tap. With the teeth of the comb I sought my parting and trained my hair into neatness. Looking in the mirror, my body heavy and stately with the old priestly stuff, I saw a child: myself as a child in my first dedication to the performing arts. My eyes' blueness was undiminished, stronger even, but the light in them was dimmed just then, as it might always be, by the knowledge of what could hardly be seen. I had got to the ridiculous age when one looks to see what one has found in the universe. That Saturday in the sacristy, the day of Lisa's sister's wedding, the noise of future happiness touched the glossy walls and slipped through the gap under the door, and I gazed into the mirror and saw something frozen and not quite resolved. The young lady and the man from Kilbirnie were soon to be married, and good for them. They meant to be happy. Even their stupidity was brave. I saw my own eyes and how old they seemed. Those eyes had looked on many things, but I couldn't be sure they'd ever seen oneness.

Yet there had been moments. There was Florence. I stood once at the window of a hotel on the Piazza Santissima Annunziata, the Duomo very clear and Giotto's clock tower puzzling and beautiful in the haze of the morning sun and the honey-glut feeling of the hour. I remember everything one could see from that window: a cypress tree in a lone garden, a house with green shutters, a bicycle parked against an ancient wall. The church bells sounded out in great, intemperate rondels, and birdsong – chirrupy, urgent, nervous for events – rose up from invisible places. The sound of all this made a mystery best suited to that exact time and place. It was simplicity too, like the Fra' Angelicos that filled the former monastery of San Marco round the corner from the hotel, their lightness, their spirituality, carrying at the same time the reality and the unreality of life, offering the young a perspective on belief.

That morning in Florence there was a wedding down below. I saw them coming through a door in the old wall, past the bicycle, through the fog of bells; they all seemed to be wearing greens and yellows, most of them talking and laughing. Then came the old men wearing straw hats and children silent in short trousers, one of them climbing on the bicycle, waving, smiling. The bride and groom had become one person and one force for good under the green shutters. I saw him kiss her and nothing was absent. Not just then. Above the clock tower a dozen swallows were tumbling and circling the peaks, and my eyes fell from the birds to the young couple kissing in the courtyard. The beautiful day would dress them and the night undress them. Music played in the distance. And just then, at the open window, a hand touched my shoulder and I reached up for it without turning, and I knew he was speaking Shakespeare through a smile, as he often did in that summer of love.

> Blame not this haste of mine. If you mean well,
> Now go with me and with this holy man
> Into the chantry by: there, before him,
> And underneath that consecrated roof,
> Plight me the full assurances of your faith;
> That my most jealous and too doubtful soul
> May live at peace.

People want to applaud in church nowadays. One simply lets them. ('Pragmatic, pragmatic,' Bishop Gerard says.) The boy marrying Lisa's sister stood at the altar with wet-looking, gelled hair and bore, together with his best man, a mischievous smirk dabbed round with aftershave. They had the sort of cosmetic freshness that follows hard on the heels of debauchery, and the congregation buzzed that morning with repressed jokes. There were giggles when I asked for any reason why this marriage might be put asunder, and the service ended with applause and cheering of a sort that might be thought, on a rainy day, to have taken too little account of the perpetual suffering of Christ, whose journey to Calvary was depicted at intervals on the walls of the chapel. At the rear of the line of tanned youths coming to Communion was Mr Savage, the old communist, who shuffled towards me with his plastic bags. This time he asked for two hosts, one after the other. 'I can't do that. You're not hungry, are you?' I whispered.

'No,' he said. 'Just tired.'

The bride's mother saw the old man coming out of nowhere and she looked confused and then faintly repelled. I saw her examine the back of his raincoat and then point him out to a group of the men, as if to ensure that he couldn't harm the proceedings. She did it swiftly with a single painted finger, as if she recognised his type and hated his coat. I watched him for a second over her shoulder as he walked to the door and stood in the shadows. 'That was just beautiful, Father,' she said, staring at me somewhat manically for a second. It occurred to me she looked like someone who had taken lessons in smiling. Her face was orange and her hair quite yellow. 'You gave oor Helen a great send-off. Okay. Now. You'll come to the reception, won't you? We've set you a wee place at the table.'

'I don't think so, Mrs Nolan. It's very kind of you, but I have a great deal of parish business to get on with.'

'Oh, away ye go,' she said, giving me a gentle shove. 'It's a Saturday. You'll certainly be coming along. Are we no' good enough for you, Father? I'll have none of that nonsense now. Come to the reception and have a wee dram. I know we're no' your type. But just for me. It's no' every day a person sees their oldest lassie getting married.'

As she spoke her plump words, I caught sight of Mark and Lisa over her shoulder. Mark was wearing a black tie. He saw me looking up and made a quick, friendly nod, as if proposing that I acquiesce to whatever Mrs Nolan was asking of me. 'Of course,' I found myself saying. 'Of course I'll come. That would be splendid.'

Rice was sticking to the umbrellas and pinches of confetti

floated in the puddles. The faces of small children appeared; they had different haircuts, the children, but the same eyes, and their voices rose in anticipation of a challenge and an opportunity.

'Scramble!' they shouted.

I watched them from the tinted dark of a hired limousine, the best man throwing handfuls of silver and the children diving onto the gravel to pick up the coins.

'Look at the state ae them,' said Mr Nolan, the bride's father. 'A buncha piranhas. You'd think they'd never seen a coin in their lives.'

'It's one of your Scottish traditions?' I said.

'A good one,' he said. 'When I was young, we used to scour the town looking for weddings, just to get in on the scramble.'

The car moved off down the lane with a beep at the crouching kids and a squeak of upholstery. 'You were born in Dalgarnock, Mr Nolan?'

'Born and bred,' he said. 'And I'll tell you something for nothing: it's no longer the place I grew up in.'

'How so?'

'I'll tell you how,' he said. 'There used to be plenty of work about here. Good jobs. Coal mining for one, and a big steelworks over the river. That ICI place used to employ thousands, making paint, and, before that, it was Nobel, making explosives. Men worked in those places for forty years and at the end of it the Jobcentre was trying to turn them into Avon ladies.'

Mr Nolan was a youngish man, still in his forties I'd have said, but his delivery was hardened and wise seeming, his attitude somewhat elegiac, as if life had already shown him its uselessness.

'Is that right?'

'You're damn right it's right,' he said. 'Humiliating. That's yer global economy for ye, Father. Experienced tradesmen start working in pet shops, and that's the lucky ones. Half of them have never worked since they got their apprenticeship papers. And these younger ones leaving school? Well, they wouldn't want jobs even if there were jobs to give them. Talk about lazy.'

The car was being driven up the coast road, the other passengers cooing about the bride's dress or things being nice, but Mr Nolan seemed to grow more surly as we passed the dual carriageway and the new houses. 'This was all fields,' he said. 'Now would you take a look. It's all houses for people who aren't even from here. Incomers, Father. People from Glasgow or England or worse. Interlopers. You know they're even packing those bloody asylum seekers into those boxes?'

'Places do change, don't they, Mr Nolan?'

'Aye, well. I'll tell ye, this place has changed for the worst.'

'Oh, for heaven's sake put a smile on your face, Dominic,' said Mrs Nolan. 'You'd put years on a person, the way you talk.'

'Well, it's all true,' said Mr Nolan. 'He's as well to know the truth. This used to be a good place to rear children. Now, it's just an open-air asylum. People used to have sports days and Highland games or whatever else out on that grass. Scottish country dancing. You name it. Now it's all Indian restaurants and Christ knows what else, and no jobs for the locals.'

'Just ignore him, Father,' said Mrs Nolan. 'He's always in a bad mood when he knows he has to part with a shilling.'

'I'm sure that's not the case,' I said.

'Oh, it's true all right,' said Mr Nolan.

'I'm sure you've heard all the great sayings about the Scots, Father Anderton,' said Mrs Nolan.

'I simply ignore them,' I said.

'Well, you shouldnae,' said Mr Nolan, 'because they're all deserved. I'm getting more tight-fisted by the week, is that not true, Denise?'

She just laughed at the window and clouded it. She thought her husband and I were deep in conversation, but I saw her lift a finger and draw a heart on the cloudy window and then wipe it clean.

'And I love a drink,' he said, disarmingly. He stared into the fairy lights around the edge of the car's interior. 'I can honestly say I like a good drink more than I like any of my children.'

'Dominic!'

'Well, it's a fact.'

'Today of all days!'

'Never mind,' he said. 'The Father doesn't mind a wee bit of the truth, do you, Father?'

The hotel had tartan carpets and too many balloons. Each table in the reception suite carried several bottles of Frascati surrounded by net bags full of sugared almonds. Mr Nolan gave a speech saying he wasn't losing a daughter but gaining a son. The best man gave a speech saying the groom had lost his virginity round the back of a disco called Caspers, to a bus conductress twice his age. The groom's riposte included the observation that the best man was a 'bammer', whatever that is, along with the point that he first came to admire his new wife because she was a 'mentalist'.

In my own, unscheduled speech, I tried to get into the swing of things by quoting Robert Louis Stevenson on the idea that marriage was a sort of friendship recognised by the police – titters into coffee cups – and then used scripture to argue that matrimony was a sacrament that deepened the couple's union with Christ – yawns – before raising one of the toxic glasses and taking my seat to cries of 'Olé, Olé, Olé.' A certain Auntie Mary was sick into a bag of wedding gifts. A certain Uncle Alan threw a punch in the direction of a certain Uncle Stuart, which missed but instead hit a curtain and cracked the panel of light switches behind it. Mrs Nolan complained to the hotel's function manager that the galia melon hadn't been cold. The bar ran out of ice just before the Guinness taps went down, but by then the band had appeared at the edge of the dance floor and the newlyweds were dancing to a song called 'Three Times a Lady'.

'Enjoying yourself, Father?' said Mark.

'I wouldn't go *that* far,' I said.

'This party's great, man,' he said. 'Totally mad.'

'Is that good?'

He cuffed my shoulder with the knuckles of one hand.

'It's cleared up out there,' he said. 'The rain's off. We were just outside. Have you seen the bogs in here? Right fancy. We bought these.'

We were on the carpeted stairs next to a fire extinguisher, and people were pouring up from the downstairs bar. I remember looking at him and thinking how sharp he looked, his tie loose and the skin on his face so clear and fresh. He was showing me a handful of square packages: red-coloured condoms. 'Check them out,' he said. The stairs were cloying with the smell of aftershave and dry smoke. I reached my hand down behind me and felt the cold, soothing roundness of the fire extinguisher.

'Are you trying to shock me, Mark?' I said.

'Do you know what they are?'

'No,' I said, 'but I have a suspicion they might be very evil indeed.'

'McNuggets, stop ribbing him,' said Lisa, coming up from behind and leaning on both our shoulders.

'They are *ribbed*,' said Mark, howling with laughter. 'That's what it says on here.'

'Father, are you having a nice time?' asked Lisa. 'That was cool, what you did today. My sister's a bitch actually.'

They both laughed.

'Well, she is. But never mind. It was nice. Now I've got a room to myself, that's all I care about, so it is. And I keep the stereo.'

'Excuse me, Lisa,' said Mark. 'If you don't mind, I've just been showing Father Anderton these rubber johnnies.'

'Oh, yes,' I said. 'I was very shocked.'

Lisa took a condom from him and pressed it into my hand. 'Now he's holding one!' she said. In that second I saw there was something a little vicious about Lisa; she didn't really care what happened in the world around her, so long as she found something to thrill her. 'I've got the key to their honeymoon suite,' she giggled.

'Hey, motherfucker,' said Mark, 'stop telling everybody.'

'We're going to put loads of johnnies all over their bedroom. Do you think that's a good idea, Father?'

'Very good,' I said. 'Just don't tell the Bishop.' I dropped the thing onto the carpet and didn't look down.

'Or the Pope!' said Mark.

A group of boys came up holding pints. 'Check them out,' said Mark. 'Ties and everything. Totally fucked up.'

The lagered boys seemed unsure what to do at a wedding. Each just stood around in his shiny black shoes. Their way of talking kept jolting me back to another time: they spoke like redneck Yankee soldiers from the 1960s or film mobsters, or was it black people they'd never met except on music videos? Two of the boys nodded to Mark, and he turned to me and lowered his voice. 'Don't go yet,' he said. 'See you out the front in half an hour.' One of the boys spoke into Mark's ear and then the whole group disappeared into the Gents.

I went to the bar in the reception suite. I'd noticed there was a general apartheid at this sort of wedding: men drank at the bar while women sat with other women at the tables, passing cigarette lighters back and forth and occasionally squirting perfume on one another. The noise level seemed to grow and the night leaned backwards.

'Look, Tommy,' said one of the men. 'There's your Jean. Holy Christ. They're all up for the Slosh.'

'What's that?' I asked.

'Your man here doesnae know the Slosh,' said a man with razor burns down his neck and a sodden tie.

'It's a dance that women do at weddings,' said Mr Nolan. 'Don't worry yourself, it's a Scottish thing.' He looked up as he said this and a slight gleam of hostility showed in his eyes.

'A Scottish country dance?' I said.

They laughed.

'Not really,' said a bald man with glasses. 'It's a west coast of Scotland thing. Or maybe an American thing. This side of the country is closer to America, Father. We've got their Trident missiles. We've got their air bases. We've got their telly programmes. And we've got their dances.'

'It's no' American,' said Mr Nolan. 'It's a Scottish dance. It's a working-class kind of a thing.'

'Oh, I see,' I said.

'But I don't suppose you know very much about the working classes now, do you, Father?' he said.

'I'm a product of the 1960s,' I said. 'We assumed we knew everything about the working classes.'

'Aye, Father,' he said. 'But you don't know your authentic Scottish *pro-le-tariat*, do you?' He said this through half-gritted teeth.

'Well, Mr Nolan. My life hasn't perhaps been as sheltered as you may think.'

'Oh, "perhaps",' he said. 'Look, fellas. It's "perhaps". Perhaps his life hasn't been quite so sheltered. Hey, Mr Perhaps, maybe your life's not been so sheltered as we think.'

One of the men handed me a glass of whisky and I put it to my lips and fed off the fumes for a second or two.

'People like you,' said Mr Nolan, 'people that talk like you. Posh arseholes from England . . .'

'Come on now, Dom, that's out of order,' said the man with the glasses. 'You don't talk to a priest like that.'

'No,' said Mr Nolan quite calmly. 'It's just us talking in private here. Forget everybody else. You don't mind a wee heart-to-heart discussion, do you, Father?'

'Carry on, by all means.'

'By all means,' he said. 'Perhaps I will.'

He took a long drink from his pint and looked up. 'Middle-class arseholes from England, pardon my French. You think Scotland is a playground for shootin' and fishin'. You think it's all fucken kilts and haggises and crap like that. You think it's folk songs and single malts and Hogmanay and the fucken Isle of Skye. Well, it's nothing like that. And it's no' hairy-arsed warriors wantin' to die for freedom either.'

'Come on, Dominic,' said another man. 'It's no' half as bad.'

'I'm no' sayin' it's bad,' he said. 'I'm sayin' *their view* ae it is bad. We've been listenin' tae it for hunners a years. They think we're a novelty act up here, just a bunch a people no' worthy ae the same kinna respect these people take for granted when it comes tae themselves.'

'Well argued,' said the bald man, his eyes wide, his moustache soaking wet and his face seal-like in its beseeching dumbness.

'Respect isn't a thing you just get,' I said, 'like free school milk. People earn respect by their actions. And sometimes by their words.'

'And what, Mr Perhaps,' said Nolan, 'if yer actions are limited by yer circumstances? What if yer thoughts urnay really yer ane? What happens if the state is organised tae undermine yer language?'

'That's paranoid,' I said. 'You've made a silk purse out of your grievances, Mr Nolan.'

'Now we're talking,' said his friend.

'You people come up here and buy houses and land. Not you. It's no' you I'm talking aboot. You're just a priest. But people like you. English people. Or else people from fucked-up places who turn up here without as much as a working radio. They want the world.'

'You're no' being very consistent, Dom,' said the friend. 'Either you don't like rich folk or you don't like poor folk. Make up your mind. Sounds to me like you just don't like anybody very much.'

'Inverted snobbery,' I said.

'I don't like people very much,' said Nolan. 'That's part of my charm. It's part of the national charm, is that not right, Father? You must have discovered that by now.'

'Whatever you say, Mr Nolan. It's your day.'

'That's right,' he said.

'It's your daughter's day.'

'Uh-huh.'

'And it's your country.'

'Ye better believe it.'

Nolan drained his glass and gasped as if to recognise that the taste was refreshingly horrible. He stroked his chin, looking around at the others in the room with a softening contempt.

One could have sworn Nolan felt sorry for people who had the misfortune not to be in his shoes. He played the part of the dyspeptic father, the cynical husband, but I'd bet you anything he enjoyed the spectacle of his life in that town, the constant drama of his dislikes, his role as a man coming down hard on strangers and phoniness, all the while, I suspect, more strange and more phoney to himself than he ever thought possible. Such men have pride in their roles, yet they also hate the way things have gone, forever conjuring former worlds in which individual performance ceded to the collective habits of the community. That world had disappeared. Nolan knew it had disappeared and he didn't seriously mourn it. He liked to cast a cold eye on the present, though he, in fact, was the present, the coldness beholding itself.

'Our Lisa said you help her and her pals,' he said. 'Up at the school. She said you go places and that. Good for you. But jeest watch that lot. Oor Lisa could run rings round a matador.'

'She's very sweet,' I said. He looked at me with pale pink eyes. I thought we might be friends in a different world.

'Perhaps,' he said.

The man with the wet moustache leaned against the bar and exhaled his warm breath in my face. The women were still up on a dance floor entirely free of men. 'So, you'll no' be doing the Slosh then, Father?' he said, smirking at his watch.

'I'm still not sure what it is,' I said. 'An American-style barn dance for west coast of Scotland people who hate having Trident submarines near by and aren't hairy-arsed warriors or haggis-eaters but who hate the English middle classes? Sounds fun.'

'Get lost,' said Mr Nolan.

*

The people who worked the shore were employed to tear out the mussels, leaving the petroleum-coloured shells in a mound against the seaward side of a low granite wall. The beach was strewn with rubbish of every description: one could see glass twinkling in the moonlight and hear the faint rustle of bags at the edge of the sea. The smell was so high it reminded me of the French poet's lily that soaks up blue antipathies. I looked behind me at the hotel, the disco lights, the sound of people becoming themselves again. Two young girls were lying on the bonnet of a car, drinking and talking. They soon staggered across the road dripping with bottles and handbag straps, their continuous laughter swallowed by the hotel doors, leaving us standing at the edge of the car park around the orange glow of Mark's cigarette.

Mark had approached me from behind as I stood in the cold. He seemed high on something but just smiled when I asked him what he'd taken. During my time with Mark and Lisa, around the housing estate or at the school, in playgrounds or at church events they had come to in search of trouble, they often smelled of glue and spoke to me as if I were a natural enemy of authority. They spoke of stolen money and air pistols and homemade cider. They went out joyriding at night while pretending to sleep over with friends. Over the months, I began to know worse things about them, how little they cared about life, how dehumanised they could be, yet I know I did nothing to oppose them. I gave in to every aspect of them, every aspect of myself. I watched them as one might watch people in a film, because he was beautiful, because I liked the way they seemed to think of me.

Late one night, Mark and Lisa appeared at the rectory in the company of a feral-looking boy they called Chubb. They stood in the chapel lane throwing gravel up at the window. I could hear them laughing as I came down the stairs, and when I opened the door, I saw full bottles of milk stood in rows across the path.

'What's this?' I said.

'Milk bottles,' said Mark. 'Just me and my homeys. Do you need any milk?'

'No, I don't. Where are they from?'

'People's doors,' said Lisa, giggling. 'We raided all the doors for milk and now we don't know what to do with them.'

'That's childish,' I said.

'It's funny,' said Mark. He looked defiant. 'It's gonnae be hell for them in the morning wanting their cornflakes. Can you imagine it?'

'Just about.'

'Can we come inside?'

'Certainly not. Take those bottles back where they belong.'

'No chance,' said Lisa. 'We need to sit down. We're tired.'

Rather bold in himself, the one called Chubb put his cold hand out for shaking when Mark introduced us.

'What kind of name is Chubb?' I said.

Lisa broke the seal on one of the bottles and started pouring milk down the drain at the edge of the path.

'He's good with locks,' Mark said.

The new boy wore a grin that showed his sharp little teeth.

'It's nae bother, Father,' he said. 'Just a wee laugh with the milk bottles and that, but no harm done, know what I mean?'

'It's theft,' I said. 'You should take them back before people wake up and notice they're missing.'

'Talk to the hand,' said Lisa.

The three seemed luminous in the chapel's shadow. When I returned upstairs I could hear their laughter in the distance, then the smashing of bottles over the road where they had stopped at the bus shelter. I changed into my clothes and drove out to find them on the estate, the four of us ending up on the steps of the school playground, just sitting together and smoking, talking about drugs that people used to take in the 1960s, the youngsters boasting about all the things they didn't care about. They expressed their hatred of teachers and their liking of me, drinking milk, and me drinking milk along with them, forgetting the time. In the houses people were sleeping, not missing us, and Mark reached over and wiped my mouth with the sleeve of his jacket. 'You've got a moustache,' he said.

They loved to practise driving in my car at an industrial estate situated in some fields next to the dual carriageway. Mark would twiddle through the radio stations until he found one that sounded illegal and black.

'This tune is butter,' said Mark. 'Eat it up.'

'I love this one,' said Lisa.

'Not too loud,' I said.

'God, I wish we had urselves a bottle of Tanqueray,' said Mark. 'Gin and juice and we'd really get our swerve on.'

A lot of empty factories up there, places where the young people could shout and their voices would echo from one end of the shed to the other. All the glass was broken. Our favourite used to be owned by a company that made denim garments. I think it was called Blue Bell. Anyway, we went there several times, and I can still see us sat down, smoking on the oily ground, Mark tossing lit matches across the shed, and Lisa dancing or jumping or running the length of the building, sometimes coming back with handfuls of metal buttons, the ones you get on blue jeans, which she found in some corner and gave out as tokens of her love.

That was how our friendship grew: nights like that. They fought in front of me and they sang stupid songs; they cursed

and argued and we drove places in the car or ate chocolate that
Mark had stolen from the Blue Star garage. Perhaps they knew
me, in their careless way, much better than I did them. Their
desolation seemed greatly addictive at the time, and I sat waiting for them to bring me into their world.

'I could teach you how to do the internet,' said Chubb.

'That would be very kind,' I said.

'I could get you a cheap laptop, as well.'

'There'll be no need for that.'

The wedding night, Mark and I walked to the pier. He told
me an endless story about the best man being drunk and
locked in a room. I lifted my head and saw Ardrossan Castle
standing bare and open on the headland, a window up there at
the top, the dark wind rushing through. I imagined Mary,
Queen of Scots appearing at the window, her eyes scanning the
wrong horizon for France, her fierce, feeling eyes dropping to
the sands, the stretch of beach now coloured with disco pinks
and sapphire clouds from the hotel. We walked back to a car
Mark held the keys of and sat inside with the music thumping
behind us.

'It's no' fair,' said Mark. 'Why do you get to drive?'

'We're not driving anywhere,' I said. 'We're sitting.'

'I got the keys.'

'You're too young to drive a car.'

'That's what everyb'dy says. If you can drive you should just
drive. I could get a job driving.'

'You could get a better job than that,' I said.

'Doubt it.'

The car had a terrible scent of vanilla air-freshener and
something else, something bad. At one point Mark twisted
round and gave an exasperated sigh. 'Jesus Christ,' he said,
'that's completely out of order.' I turned round in my seat and

saw a dead, deflated bird lying on a blanket of wet newspapers.

'What's that?' I said.

'A dead seagull,' he said.

'What's it doing there?'

'One of the boys,' he said, smiling. 'I bet you it was Chubb. He'd be trying to wind Lisa up. This is his idea of a good wind-up.'

'But how did he get in here?' I asked.

Mark rolled his eyes. 'He's not called Chubb for nothing. He can get himself in and out of anywhere you like. Cars are no problem tae him. And he knows this car well enough.'

The bird was lying with a cold eye lighted in the dark. Its neck was soaked in blood. There was, to me, something terrible about its presence and its dirty feathers. 'That's really wicked,' I said.

'Yeah,' he said.

'Not like that. Not your sort of wicked. It's just a terrible thing to do to a living creature.'

'It's bad news, yeah,' he said. 'Some of the boys. Not my pals. Just people who live round here. It's sick. They fish off the pier and sometimes they – man, this is sick – they put chips on their hooks and cast them out to the birds, and sometimes the seagulls bite and the sick fuckers reel the gulls in and hit them with bottles.'

'You are joking, Mark.'

'No. They leave the dead ones at the pier or they throw them into the water. It's bad news, isn't it?'

'I can't believe it.'

'Chubb and the boys probably found this one. They put it here for a laugh. That's what they're like.'

We sat quiet for a moment inside the car's shadows. Mark

began speaking again, but there was a new tone. He was recounting an experience, something that had happened, and he sounded altogether new as he said the words, speaking from somewhere I hadn't known and that caused him to tighten his slack manners. He spoke of being a child and going to the Auchenharvie baths. He spoke of one day in particular. It was raining that day – black clouds, he said, a long boring afternoon – Dalgarnock feeling strange, a place that seemed far away from the world. At Auchenharvie it was warm, and he said he felt great under the chlorinated water, seeing the white legs of other swimmers.

'Only white?' I said.

'Aye,' he said. 'Black people don't go to the swimming baths here. There are no black people around here anyhow. If there was, they wouldn't go to the swimming.'

'Why not?'

'How should I know?' he said. 'Black people don't like the swimming baths. They don't like dogs either. The chlorine burns the back of your throat. People dive for their rubber bands. The tannoy says: "Would swimmers wearing yellow bands please leave the pool now." The skin at the ends of your fingers gets wrinkled if you've been swimming too long. There's always shouting at the baths, and it sounds as if it's echoing inside you when you're under the water and watching the legs and swimming down.'

'Yes,' I said.

'I was sitting on the edge of the pool when I saw him.'

He was talking about his father. He remembered him coming from the changing room and standing at the metal steps. He was way fat, Mark said, the fattest man in Ayrshire. 'He knew I was coming to the swimming,' he said. 'He must have known I'd be there.'

'He didn't see you?'

'I saw him. Everybody saw him. They were all staring. He looked about and it was noisy and people were laughing at him. Doing the backstroke and laughing at him; diving in right beside him and laughing.'

Mark's father just swam through the jeers and the splashing. And Mark slipped into the water, held onto the side and dipped his face so that only his eyes peeped out of the pool. 'It was horrible,' he said. 'My dad was being shouted at and he just did the breaststroke. Even just swimming like that, because he was so fat he made waves that rolled right across and splashed my head. His face was bright red but he didn't seem bothered. I just hid from him. Imagine that was your dad.'

Mark spoke of the noise he could hear as he swam down into the depths of the pool and saw his father's body passing above his head. Like a shark's view of a passing boat, I thought. Mark got to the steps, climbed out and went to the changing room. 'I was shivering next to the lockers for ages,' he said. 'I wanted to go back and get him.'

'Why didn't you?' I said.

'They were all laughing at him.'

Even in the dimness of the car, I could see there was a look of defiant hurt in Mark's eyes. 'He used to be quite a sharp guy,' he said. 'He had all the cool gear before everybody else. He got a trial to play football for Kilmarnock one time. He used to read books and that.'

After a moment I clicked off the headlights and looked up. Stars were beginning to show above Arran and we breathed out. I thought of the distance and listened to Mark speaking, and after a while I forgot the scent of the dead bird. 'I'll take you and Lisa over to see Ailsa Craig,' I said. 'If you want to.'

'To the rock?' he said. 'Is there a boat?'

'I'm sure I can use my influence. If you want to.'

'I'd like to see it,' he said. 'Just the once.'

'Then leave it with me.'

'You're mad,' he said. He flicked a lighter on and off for a minute or so and tapped on the dashboard. 'Some people would think it weird, wouldn't they, a priest and a young guy sitting in a car?'

'I'm sure they would.'

'Well,' he said, 'that's their problem, isn't it?'

I wished suddenly that I had a good glass of wine to take away the taste of the meal and the conversations. There are days when you realise you haven't enjoyed one lovely thing, then when you do have it, as I had the company of Mark for that hour, you want something to complement the pleasure, to raise it further and make it last.

'Okay,' he said, 'I'm going back to the wedding.'

I asked him to take that thing with him, the dead bird on the back seat, and he complained before lifting it up in the newspapers and walking to the sea wall to dump it over.

'Shit, that was horrible,' he said.

'Yes.'

'Quite a cool joke, though.'

'If you say so,' I said.

He took the keys and walked away from the car, Mark going ahead, while I came behind and hesitated before crossing the road.

'Look,' I shouted, and he turned round with a strange, pleased smile on his face. Mark always seemed as if he were humouring others while gaining in his own estimation. There was never any telling what really mattered to him. I was standing at the kerb looking up at the sky and I pointed to a place above the sea.

'Look at that,' I said.

'What about it?'

'Out there,' I said. 'The bright one is the North Star.'

'Cool,' he said, before skipping up the steps of the hotel and making as if to disappear into the universe beyond the doors. He looked round in the final second and creased his brow and smiled again. 'I wonder if you can, like, see that from America,' he said.

4

AILSA CRAIG

Mrs Poole once told me something one couldn't forget. She was making her bed at home one day and found a piece of paper under the mattress, dug in deep beyond the valance on her own side. The paper had writing on it, a solitary line across the middle of the page. She said the ink was faded and the writing was in Jack's hand. Her husband always wrote in capitals, and he used those poor pens that came free at the betting shop. It made her wince to remember it, but the words were very clear:

I DON'T LOVE YOU ANY MORE

She sat on the edge of the bed, she said, for what seemed like hours, with the piece of paper on her lap and the house looking at her. She stared at it until her vision began to go in and out, and then, standing at the window in what she called a state of shock, she wondered how long she had slept on that terrible message and why he had put it there. To make the nights more bearable for himself? To send a message through the sleeping hours to a person he couldn't speak to with honesty? Was he drunk? She told me she stayed in the bedroom considering all these things, and others too, before finally asking herself whether the great boldness of his feeling might not in fact have faded with the ink.

Her story came back to me one morning in the rectory when she handed me a letter. It said 'Crosshouse Hospital' across the top. I can't recall the letter's exact words, though I know it was badly written. It said something about steroids not performing as expected, about genetic factors, something with regard to the growth of cells, and the word 'purpura', which stuck in my mind because of its oddness and beauty. She said the letter explained what the consultant had said to her. 'I haven't told Jack,' said Mrs Poole. 'God forgive me, but I can't tell him. I don't want sympathy, and he'll just give me sympathy and that's not what I want. Do you know what I mean, Father?'

'Yes,' I said. 'I think I do know.'

She had held onto the letter for a number of weeks and now her hand was shaking as she took it back from me and wiped her eyes. Over her shoulder, through the landing window, the oak trees were showing large green leaves and the early morning appeared to broaden over the fences. She had breast cancer and something in her kidney; she spoke of an operation, of convalescence and time off work. The way she spoke brought to mind an instant panorama of snow-topped chalets and sanatoria. I thought of a bald-headed Nijinsky practising his famous *entrechat* in the Alpine evenings.

'They are trying things,' said Mrs Poole, 'but these drugs don't do anything.'

'You'll need peace and quiet,' I said.

She looked puzzled and seemed to struggle for a moment to find her bearings at the foot of the stairs.

'Give it time,' I said. I knew then it meant nothing to say such things, but the right words escaped me. I looked down at my rucksack by the door and was overwhelmed for a moment by the smell of furniture polish.

'Life's short,' she said.

'Come on, Mrs Poole.'

'It's been coming to a head these last three months,' she said. 'And God knows where I'm headed now.'

The school bus was beeping outside, but I asked her if she would like to say a prayer, and she said she would. So I dipped a hand into the water font and we sat on the stairs and said three Hail Marys. We stood back up and I could see a person wearing a baseball cap through the frosted glass of the porch door. I hugged her and said that God would find a way, and her shoulder softened as I placed it under my chin, a smell of figs and almonds rising from the wool of her jumper.

'That's just as good as a prayer,' she said.

It never escaped me that Mrs Poole considered my general tactility to be yet another aspect of my falseness, and it seems now, when I look back, that she reproached herself for responding to it. I believe she observed the impossibility of sexual interest on my part, but we each found it hard not to play sometimes the parts of man and wife, even if only for vivid moments engraved more with pain than pleasure. Only once that year did I stop inside my own thoughts to consider her differently. We had gone to Glasgow to buy chairs from one of those superstores, and we passed through the aisles on either side of a massive trolley, stopping to look at lamps and bookshelves and little bedrooms with bunk beds that accused us with their multicoloured pillows.

'They have such nice things nowadays,' she said.

For a brief moment that day, I had thought of the children we might have made together and the father I might have become. I saw myself lifting a child up to the top tier of that plywood bunk bed; I saw myself pulling up the duvet, kissing the child, and Mrs Poole standing at the door with a mug of tea in her hand and the child's trousers under her arm. How absurd. It is the only time I have ever thought of fatherhood. I believe it was the impossible colours and the atmosphere in Ikea: it kindled a notion of another life, a life of domestic contentment and heart-shaped lights. It must have touched Mrs Poole too, because we went downstairs to a lunch of meatballs and chips and she told me the story of her only son.

'He lives with my sister, Irene,' she said. 'I don't know if that was the right decision, but it was the decision I made. He is a good-looking boy. I don't see him much. He has his three cousins and he calls them his brothers and Irene is good to him.'

'But why?'

'Simple,' she said. 'I couldn't bear to bring him up with his father the way he is, the drink and everything.'

'That was the only reason?'

'That's a big enough reason. It is to me anyhow. Jack talks like he loves families. But he only likes them at a distance. He doesn't actually know how to be in a family. So that was it. I wasn't having the boy suffer from all that, a father who didn't know how to be a father, a family full of disappointment and blame. So my sister took him.'

I closed my hand over Mrs Poole's, and she let it rest there for a second, moving her fingers in compliance.

'In life,' she said, 'you've just got to do what you can to improve the situation.'

She pushed the lunch plate away from her that day. She bent into her shopping bag to examine a packet of night lights she had bought and never mentioned her son again.

The young people were banging on the rectory door.

'Hurry the fuck up!' shouted Mark.

'Really,' said Mrs Poole. 'You shouldn't let those youngsters speak like that around you.' I opened the door and Mark was smiling amid all his stripes and hoods.

'Morning all,' he said, tipping his cap with a stick of lip balm. His appearance was always very sudden; as soon as he presented himself all the oxygen seemed to be swallowed into the vacuum he created. I could feel Mrs Poole becoming rattled at my side.

'I hope you crowd are going to behave today,' she said. 'It's a treat, Mark McNulty. Do you realise that? Father David is taking time out of his own work to give you all a nice time.'

'Definitely, Mrs P. A day off school and everything.'

'It's Mrs Poole to you.'

'Whatever.'

'Okay,' she said. 'Just mind yourselves.'

Before joining Mark in the lane, I went into the sitting room to lift my mobile from the piano, and I spent a minute listening to my messages. One was from Father Michael, the priest at St Margaret's in Irvine, telling me about a restoration and repairs meeting the following week. The second was from my mother. She always spoke to the answering service as if she were giving a small public speech, uttering things very deliberately and quite formally, seeming never to believe that the only likely listener was me. She said something about the goodness of a certain Lebanese red wine, reasonably priced, that she'd found in the buffet car of a train and which was now available in half bottles. And she asked whether I might want to join her for a morning at the Royal Botanic Gardens, where some interesting new items had just appeared in the glasshouses. After listening to these messages, I scrolled down my inbox and found three texts that had come from Mark a day or two before. They had come roughly forty minutes apart:

'80,000 Celtic supporters in Seville. First final in 33 yrs. Come on da Celts! Come on da Bhoys!'

'Kissing telly. Larsson scores. Estadio Olimpico total uproar. Please say prayers. Have 2 win.'

'We got beat 3–2 in extra time. Did u say a fuckin prayer or not? Hail, hail the Celts! We will never walk alone.'

Lisa Nolan clapped her hands as we passed Ayr and began singing in that show-offy, reaction-dependent way of hers.
'All the ladies in the house, yeh, yeh! All the ladies in the house.'
'What are you talking about, Lisa?'
'I'm singing my thang, Papa,' she said, laughing. 'All the babies go crazy when I get my milkshake on.'
'You do talk some infernal rubbish,' I said.
'She's the money,' said Mark.
'Too right, nigger,' she said. *'All the ladies in the house!'*
On the way to Girvan to pick up the boat for Ailsa Craig, I tried to read a book at the back of the bus, while the four youngsters – Mark, Lisa, a boy called Colin and a girl with black nail varnish, Michelle – talked about chemist shops and their contents, each of them assuming I wasn't listening or couldn't understand what they were talking about. But I kept my head down and took in every word.
'Don't be daft,' said Mark. 'They keep them in the drawers. You have to ken what you're looking for. Diazepam under "D". Always in a big grey plastic jar.'
'Same as Valium,' said Colin.
'Yellow but,' said Mark. 'The Xanax comes in packets.'

Lisa was swigging from her can. 'They're called Roches,' she said.

'Like on a joint?' Colin asked.

'No, you fucken idiot,' said Mark. 'That's the name of the firm that makes them. The big factory in Dalry.'

'Tell him about Phenos,' said Lisa. I saw him rolling his eyes, indicating to her to keep her voice down.

'Phenobarbitone,' he whispered. 'Make sure you get the 60 mg. And try for Napps. What's their right name?'

'Dunno,' said Lisa. 'Morphine something.'

'Or look on the shelf,' said Mark. 'Try and find Codeine Phosphate Syrup. It's mad. Comes in a litre bottle.'

Lisa laughed towards the ceiling of the bus and put her hand over her mouth. 'Watch for Ritalin,' she said. 'It's as good as E but speedier. Watch. Sometimes it's in a locked drawer.'

The janitor turned the radio down and his eyes appeared in the rear-view mirror. 'What's all the whispering for?'

'We're not doing nuttin,' said Lisa. 'Nothing,' she added.

'You better not start any of your carry-on today,' he said. 'I know what you two are like, and if there's any carry-on during this trip, I've told Father David just to call me and I'm taking you right back up to the school.'

'I hope you're a good swimmer,' said Mark. The janitor craned round from the wheel and bared his teeth.

'I'm warning you, McNulty. This is supposed to be a nice day. Any crap from you and you're in deep trouble.'

'Awright,' said Mark. 'Keep your wig on.' He turned his amateur smile on me at the back of the bus. 'He's always like that. We're going to have a good day out, aren't we, Father?'

'That's the intention,' I said, putting the book down. 'You reckon you're a bunch of gangsters. We'll see how brave you all are when you're halfway across the sea.'

79

'Up shit creek without a paddle,' said Lisa.

'Language,' I said.

We began our descent to Girvan harbour and could see the rock standing out there at the centre of the morning like a golden bell, half-submerged in the waters of the Irish Sea. 'It looks much bigger from here,' said Mark.

A mile out from the harbour, the boat seemed to glide forward on the breeze and Mark was leaning over the side, trailing a finger in the green water. 'Careful,' I said. 'The boat could suddenly tip and we don't want to lose you just yet.'

'Let him go,' Michelle said. 'He'll just sink to the bottom like a stone and nobody will miss him.'

'No, he'll float like a McNugget,' said Lisa. She leaned against the rope and shaded her eyes. She pointed downwards. 'Father,' she said, 'are there many boats down there? I mean, shipwrecks and stuff?'

'Thousands,' I said. 'These coastal waters are rough in the wintertime. We couldn't cross. The waves would come right over the boat, and you wouldn't be smiling then.'

'So it's like one big graveyard,' said Mark. 'Down there.' He stabbed a finger through the surface. 'Just a graveyard of old ships and that.'

'Sadly, yes,' I said. 'Going back to before the Age of Improvement, when coal ships travelled these lanes. Merchant ships bound for the East Indies. And smugglers. This coast was bad for smugglers two or three hundred years ago.'

'Drugs?' said Mark.

'Brandy more like.'

'Cool.'

The journey to the Craig was ten miles, but each mile brought slow-forming changes in light and perspective; it felt as if the boat was moving through the grades of perspective itself, the red roofs at Girvan now low on the horizon and the rock beginning to crowd our vision moment by moment until the senses themselves were enlarged.

'It's like travelling inside a painting,' I said to the group.

'Except we're real,' said Lisa.

'Keeping it real,' said Mark.

An hour seemed to go in perfect peace, the skipper moving the boat over the sea and the unknown graves below, the young people talking their reams of nonsense, opening their smiling faces into the breeze.

'It must've been mad,' said Mark eventually. 'In Vietnam or, like, the Falklands. Going out in a boat knowing people could start shooting at you any minute. Totally mental. And you'd have, like, a machine gun rigged up here to get the bastards.'

'Don't start up about wars,' I said.

'The Bay of Tonkin,' he said. 'Or San Carlos Bay. Gunners giving it da-da-da-da-daga-daga. Argies falling about all over the place and getting theirs. Dumb fucks. Imagine it, but. Dead Argies everywhere.'

'You weren't even born,' I said.

'I've read about it,' said Mark. 'It was totally mad. The troops sorted them out all right.'

'The poor penguins,' said Lisa. 'Mr Harris in History said hundreds of penguins got blown up down there.'

'Get a grip,' said Mark. 'You always get casualties in war. Who gives a fuck about penguins?'

'People died,' I said. 'People die in war.'

'But it's cool,' said Mark. 'Friggin' sort out all those crappy dictators and stuff. That's how it should be.'

'It's a terrible business.'

'Necessary though,' said Mark.

'Sometimes necessary,' I said. The others were taking in the immediate world around the boat, the volumes of water and the diminishing land behind our backs. Lisa was sitting on the deck in bare feet and was busy pressing the buttons on her phone. 'When I was about your age I wouldn't have agreed with you,' I said. 'In those days it was the fashion to hate all wars. More than fashion: we really believed it and it seemed to us the government was corrupt. That's how young people used to think. Now you're all more gung-ho than any government.'

'But you like it,' said Mark. 'You're just as bad.'

There are people who notice the power of themselves in any conversation. They won't be put down, and their steady gaze can come to bare one's nerves and cancel one's resolve. Mark was like that. I don't know if I've seen it in anyone so young before, or so small-minded, though there comes a point in life when all young people seem capable of knowing things one could never fathom. Perhaps his mother had adored him too much, for Mark behaved as if the world was invented just for him, and his face was serene enough to convince anyone who looked at him that things would be all right if one stuck close. I think in our hearts we believe that beauty is a very sincere kind of knowledge: we fall for the wisdom of beautiful lips no matter what they are capable of saying. Mark knew it. He knew it the way a bird might know where to fly in winter. He might have known nothing else but he knew people needed the youthful, vivid certainty of his presence, and it didn't matter to him then, as it would one day, that this fantastic power was set to fade into nothing. We noticed when he opened his eyes and shaded them from the sun to look at us, because they brought something of the sun down with them, to include us, to let us share in his own warm rays of assurance.

82

'You like it,' he said again, 'us taking a stand against evil. Fuck peace. You've got to take a stand.'

'To some extent, perhaps,' I said. 'But not always.'

'It's like football,' he said. 'You've got to have your team. You want them to win. You want that more than anything. You get to the stage you'd do anything for your team. Me, I would do anything for Celtic.'

Jellyfish floated past the boat, opening and closing. Everyone seemed to be thinking their own thoughts, then Mark broke through the silence to tell a story. 'The night of the Liverpool game at Anfield,' he said, 'my da actually opened his mouth. He's usually got nothing to say to me and nothing to say to my ma, but my ma was out selling tablet . . .'

'What's that?' I said.

'Rubbishy fudge,' he said. 'She sells it round the doors. Anyhow, he pushed the sofa in front of the telly. He brought out crisps and that, sweeties and ginger he'd bought off the van, and he said for me to sit down and watch the game. He usually hates people around him. He just sits in his chair and smokes.'

I could picture Mark's living room as he spoke. Near the beginning of my time in Dalgarnock I had gone to his house. I didn't know Mark at the time but his mother came and asked me to speak to her husband about his depression. She explained it had been going on for a long time and that he wouldn't have anything to do with doctors. 'Maybe you can get through to him,' she said. 'It sometimes takes the priest.'

When I came to the house it seemed to me Mr McNulty didn't want a priest or anybody else, but he was polite, terribly overweight, sitting in the armchair Mark talked about and saying he was fine. He was just going through a funny stage, he said. I remember the fire with imitation coal and the stack of video tapes, the large, gold-framed photograph of a baby who sat on a furry rug and the table at the back of the sitting room crowded in the middle with sauce bottles, vinegar, a jar of beetroot. 'You have a nice way with words, Father,' he said. 'Are you English?'

'I was born in Edinburgh,' I said. 'That's my mother's city. She met my father there and they got married and had me. Then we all went to live in Lancashire. That was his territory.'

A strange smile – same as Mark's, now that I think of it – appeared between the mounds of his cheeks and he lit a cigarette. 'Lancashire,' he said. 'Never been to Lancashire. I like Ireland.'

Mark's father spoke a little about his own father. He showed me some cigarette cards the old man used to collect, and he referred to his life with the vague piety, I thought at the time, that we deploy when discussing the lives of people we wish we had known better. In fact, it reminded me of the way I sometimes talked myself. 'They say he was a very good sort,' said Mr McNulty. 'An old lady was ill once, just up the road from where we lived. She couldn't eat. And my dad went up there and sat by the bed for hours, squeezing oranges into her mouth.'

'Very kind,' I said.

'Aye. That was the measure of the man. He always had plenty of things to do. He kept an allotment.'

'And what sort of father are you, Mr McNulty?'

The question was coarse, but I asked it with a view to perhaps opening up the question of the man's unhappiness. He just looked at me. 'Did my wife ask you to ask me that?'

'Not at all,' I said. 'I would like to help you.'

He smiled and lit another cigarette.

'Doctors and priests,' he said. 'Good men.'

'I try to do the odd thing with Mark,' he said. 'It's not

always easy to think up things to do, but I take him to the swimming. There's a braw pool at Auchenharvie. We've been there a few times.'

Seagulls followed the boat, nipping in closer, tilting on the wing, as if they too were listening to Mark's story about the Liverpool game. 'I really wanted them to be the European champions. The Lisbon Lions all over again, just like 1967. My da usually just gets a few cans and sits them at his feet for a game. He doesn't want anybody in the living room. And that night he said, "This is your history." He made me a shandy and he said: "This is what your people fought for."'

Lisa and the others just nodded. They seemed to understand. 'My da and my uncle cried at that game,' she said. 'They cried at the start and they cried at the end when we won.'

'We were a European side that night,' said Mark. 'Half the English national team were running about in red shirts – Owen, Heskey, Gerrard – and we'd never gubbed Liverpool in a European match before. And what a feeling among the Celtic support. You could see the fans giving it full pelt in the terraces. The songs. Don't get me wrong: Liverpool have brilliant supporters, but the Celtic crowd are different.'

'Why's that?' I said.

'Because they've had to fight their way up,' said Mark. 'They fought to be accepted, a Catholic team in Glasgow and then in Scotland and then in the world. It's a community, intit?'

'But that's true of Liverpool too, isn't it? Those people have had to fight their way up.'

'That's what I'm saying. They have brilliant supporters. It's just, with Celtic, there's something a bit more.'

'And what happened at the house,' I asked, 'when you were watching with your father?'

'When Thompson scored, it was a free kick, okay. Not far

outside the box. It was like this.' Mark motioned with his foot. 'Larsson skipped over the ball and Thompson blootered it and the wall just crumbled. I'm tellin' ye: the wall fell apart, players jumping up and turning sideways to avoid the ball hitting them, and instead of hitting them it fired right into the back of the net. One–nil. I was jumpin' up and down in the middle of the room and my da was smiling from ear to ear.'

'That's awesome,' said Lisa.

'He went to get up. It's a bit of a hassle for him sometimes, getting up. He tried, but then I just bent down and grabbed him and cheered. He said, "That's yer Liverpool for ye. It went right through their bloody legs. What a goal. Get me another beer frae the fridge, we're gon tae the semi-final."'

We were silent for a moment around Mark.

'It was weird,' he said, 'because I don't think he likes me.'

'Nonsense,' I said. 'Of course your father likes you.'

'It's nothing to me,' he said. 'But what a night for Celtic. You've got to have your team, Father.'

'I suppose so.'

I looked back to see Scotland, the woods that fringe the headland and the green breast of the hills. From our position it seemed nothing could ever reach us or force us back, and we passed into a strange proximity with the advancing island of Ailsa Craig. More than an island, it seemed like a testament to physical endurance, this place, this lonely rock less than a dozen miles from the coast. It could have been the Aegean. It could have been the Bay of Bengal. But it was a golden spot on the Irish Sea, and we sat in the open boat as it moved into the shade.

Before we reached the jetty, I asked the youngsters to stop talking and listen to our place of arrival. There was nothing

86

around us but the sound of birds. 'Are we the only people here?' whispered Lisa.

'Yes,' I said. 'We are alone here.'

'That's weird,' said Mark.

I lifted my rucksack and the group ran ahead, shouting and cavorting up the incline that leads to the Garry Loch. They made their way in a gaggle of soft punches and Americanisms, hollering into the distance or back down to the water. That was their way, but still, leaving the skipper and the boat behind, I felt the value of their young voices tumbling down the rock. For a short time that day, we were a nation on the island of Ailsa Craig, them and me, under a sky so blue it made all dreams seem continuous. Lisa sat down next to the loch and picked at some marsh marigolds sprouting from a border of moss.

'How old are you?' she said.

'Fifty-six.'

'That's mental. Fifty-six. So what happens when you retire? Is there, like, a home for priests?'

'No,' I said. 'You just go somewhere. There's always a lot in the world to be getting on with.'

'My dad,' she said, 'he hasn't worked since I was about two or three. They closed Massey Ferguson. They made tractors. That's where he used to work when he had a job.'

'What does he do now?'

'He does the Lotto,' she said. 'Nuttin else. He gets on my mother's nerves. She works cleaning the school and he watches Sky Sports.'

'What do you want to do?' I asked.

'I want to be, like, a make-up artist. For films and that. Or like on magazines. You know, like where they go to places with models and they put clothes on them and somebody does the make-up. That's me.'

87

She looked over the water. Ayrshire was a series of green curves and grey houses: it looked like a place of certainties. 'I'll tell you something,' said Lisa. 'I'm not hanging about over there.'

'No,' I said. 'But I thought you didn't like foreigners.'

'Aye, but I don't care. I'd like to have loads of shoes.'

'What else?'

'I want to go out and that,' she said. 'Buy a car and a good stereo. You have to admit: that would be totally awesome. Gucci sunglasses. I want a pair of Gucci sunglasses.'

'Right,' I said. 'I'm sure you'll have that.'

Lisa stroked her shiny leg with a marigold and smacked her lips. She suddenly looked up at me as if she hadn't seen me before. 'Father,' she said, 'you have wasted your life, haven't you?'

The island was real to me in the way that memory is real, a place almost too solid and transfixing. 'I don't think so,' I said. 'I believe in God. That has been my life.'

'It can't be,' she said. 'You could have been having a good time and you've wasted it.'

'That's not true, Lisa. Not from my point of view. We have different names for it, but I've lived according to my faith.'

'What is your name?'

'Sorry?'

'Your real name. What is it?'

'David Anderton.'

'So what's wrong with just being him?'

I stood up and spun a stone across the loch to make it jump. 'It must be quite boring,' she said, 'being Father somebody and having to go on like you're good all the time. Nobody else does. And then you end up here, in Bumblefuck, UK.'

'I am him,' I said, and I knew my voice was quiet. I was

88

searching to say something permanent. 'Faith and good works,' I said. 'It's not *your* idea of a life, but it is mine.'

'Whatever,' she said. By that time the others had run over the verge and were panting beside us. 'He believes in God,' said Lisa, with a wide smile on her face.

'That's freaky,' said Mark. 'Him a priest as well.' I made a comedy face and put out my hands to him, advancing like Frankenstein's monster.

'God is the supreme Spirit,' I said, 'who alone exists of Himself, and is infinite in all perfections.'

'Call the cops!' said Mark, backing off. 'That is some scary shit.'

'God had no beginning,' I said. 'He always was, He is, and He always will be.'

'Get off,' he said. 'He's freaking me out.' We laughed and made our way over the rock, and we saw a cormorant rise from the reeds in the middle of the loch and fly off.

'He's a good laugh,' I heard Mark say behind me.

'He's wasted his life, though,' said Lisa.

'Don't say that,' said Mark.

'Why not?'

'Just don't.'

'Oh, bite it,' said Lisa.

Up there, west of the summit, a pillar of basalt rock called Kennedy's Nags conceals a cave once popular with smugglers. We found a path leading down to it, and I laid the rucksack at the mouth of the cave. The young people were shouting football slogans and other stuff into the darkness. They were startled to hear their voices coming back, and some of them ran inside. 'The walls in there are thick with bird shit,' said Mark.

'And markings,' said Lisa. 'Did people live here?'

'Some people tried to,' I said.

'What?' she said. It was hard to hear each other's voices for the screeches of gannets overhead. Thousands of them, swooping and perching with their yellow eyes troubled. 'The markings on the cave wall are quite ancient,' I said. 'People tried to live here. Apparently, two stone coffins were found in there several years ago.'

'*Apparently*, he said,' said Mark. Lisa giggled.

'You're so posh,' said Mark. 'The way you speak. The stuff you come out with. It's right posh, the way you go on.'

'Do forgive me,' I said. 'Perhaps I should annihilate my aitches and start saying "ken" instead of "know" or talking like one of your hip-hoppers.'

'See what I mean?' he said. 'You're a riot.'

We could still hear some of the others hollering into the cave and shouting oaths. 'Come on!' I said. 'Lunch.'

'What in Christ's name is that on there?' said Lisa.

'Roasted pepper,' I said.

'You must be joking,' she said. 'I'm not eating that.'

Mark and the others ate the food I'd prepared, lifting it out of the rucksack with pained but silent looks. Then they started agitating about a small apple-juice bottle filled with red wine. 'What is it?' said Mark.

'Valpolicella,' I said.

'Is that wine? Oh please. Just a swig.'

I gave him the bottle and he glugged until I pulled it away from him. Then he started dancing and fooling around. 'Telling you, man,' he said. 'When I start earning some money, I'm gonnae smoke Dutch Masters and drink Cristal till it runs out. I'm talkin' me driving the lowriding Lexus. That's how it's gonnae be when Chubb and me are your superstar DJs.'

Lisa was near the edge and I told her to come back. Then she screamed and said it was horrible.

'What's the matter?' I said. She came running back over the crags. Her face was red but I couldn't hear what she was saying for the noise of the gannets. Her eyes were full of tears when she reached us, and she struggled to get her words out.

'Horrible,' she said. 'Over there. At the bottom of the rock where the nests are. There's rats! I saw one of them with a tiny bird in its mouth, a puffin or something.'

'What is it with you?' said Mark. 'It's a bloody bird sanctuary. All about nature, Lisa. What did you expect?'

'Shut it,' she said. 'I don't expect fucken rats to be eating birds right in front of me. Baby birds.'

'Give her a slug of booze, Father,' said Mark. 'She's got her finger on the trigger. Give her a few slugs.' I passed her the cup, and she smiled into it and took a sip and said it was okay. I could see Mark had smoke coming from his hand, the one he held down the side of the rock.

'I can smell that,' I said. 'Mark, I'm not stupid. Put it out or there'll be trouble.'

'It's only a wee joint, Father,' he said. 'Come on, it's our day out. Nobody's bothered.'

All I said was that I refused to argue, and I told them I was going up the top to get the view. It was stunning up there with the breeze coming up a thousand feet from the water, the light now sparkling for miles in every direction. I could hear the young people laughing and shouting just below. 'You're great, Father,' one of them shouted over the grass.

'Whatever,' I said.

To the west one could see Belfast Lough and the coast of Ireland rising up in the clear afternoon, and on the other side, Scotland was quiet and complicit, its blue hills sheltering Ballantrae and massing southwards to circle Loch Doon. Further off, there were greyer hills and one could see the grades of distance, how the clouds seemed smaller and lower by degrees, until the smallest hung over England, I suppose. I sat down to take stock, while the voices of the young people came nearer over the grass. I looked back and saw Mark walking with Lisa, his arm crooked round her neck, and he bent down and kissed her with practised ease as they walked.

Above our heads, the gannets shrieked and cut through the air in their many hundreds, small feathers falling on my hands. I sat there and could feel the heat of the youngsters behind me. 'Oh, Father,' said Mark, his voice all cracked and ready for experience. 'It's totally mad up here. Look at the water. You can see the fishing boats. It's mad. Everything looks so wee from up here.'

'It's all perspective,' I said.

I could taste the wine in the corners of my mouth. As the young people darted over the grassy summit, laughing, teasing, smoking and speaking their important nothings, I thought back thirty years to Lake Bracciano. In the summer months, we used to gather our togs and travel out from Rome to the mineral hot springs, the English seminarians spouting water from their mouths and dodging eels. You could see medieval castles on the lakeside. I remember the one at Anguillara Sabazia and the sense of a noble, unchanged world radiating through the town with its high scent of rosemary to reach us out on the lake.

On the summit of Ailsa Craig, I left the young people in a huddle with their mobile phones. They were pointlessly texting each other, and I smiled over my shoulder and made my way down to the water. Heather burst through the rocks, and my hair was thick with air as I leapt the last metre to the beach. A life is a long time not to think of oneself undressing for another person, and the vividness of the thought held me back for a moment at the edge of the sand as I took off my shirt, my trousers, my socks. The water was very cold. Even now I can feel its slimy wetness burning my legs, inching over my private parts and hugging my waist. Then I dived, the water engulfing me in a shocking, sacramental way. Every part of me loved it. I was no longer cold, merely excited and refreshed by everything, the lifting sea and my love of it, the immense generosity of the waves as I swam out from the shore. And swimming there, I wished suddenly that I could give some of this water to my dead father, let it flood through the doors and windows of our former house, diluting the water from the pipe that burst the night he died and giving fresh life again to the rooms and all our things. There was nothing frozen about the water and everything about it signalled life. I plunged down and opened my eyes to see the blackness there, and for a second it frightened me and I wanted to cry out in the private dark. But instead I swam further down and seemed to master the moment with its strange miracles of thought.

I faced the shore with the sun in my eyes. There was no citadel, no church bells or Lazio evening, but I saw the young people clambering down the rocks and shouting the odds. I couldn't hear what they were saying but I could hear them laughing and see Mark jumping up and throwing my shirt into the air. The beach was all light and Ailsa Craig was a great thing at the young people's backs. They stood waving their arms, and with their hands around their mouths, they shouted their loudest over the water. I floated on my back, an orchid of the sea, my breath quick and my heart calling out to the sky before I turned again, swimming down through the water like a person escaping his skin, becoming again a boy with splayed fingers, feeling my way through the beautiful world of salt.

5

SCHOOLBOY ON AN ELEPHANT

It was winter when my father died. I could hear voices down-stairs, the voice of my mother, my father saying something in reply, the kitchen cupboards opening and closing. Frost glittered on the windowpane; I worried about a teddy bear's ears taking in the cold and took him down from the ledge. My mother brought a hot-water bottle and she kissed the tips of my fingers: that was our code for going to sleep. Comfort has a smell. It has a sound. Something then like roasting chicken and a voice on the radio talking about Berlin, the sound of my parents laying down cutlery. Before closing my eyes, I placed the bottle between my legs and saw a Spitfire diving through the darkness on a yellow thread.

They think my father's heart must have given out on the landing. There was certainly no shout and in the morning they came to the house and covered him with a grey blanket. I saw the latter stages from Mrs Ainsbury's flat above the Post Office; she brought Bourbon biscuits and told me to come back from the window. She kept saying, 'Everything will sort itself out,' but I knew it never would. My mother was away for hours and I was still holding the hot-water bottle in my lap from the last hours of my previous life. It turned very cold, and eventually she came back and walked slowly up the Post Office stairs. 'Your father was good at mending other people's hearts,' she said. 'But he couldn't mend his own.'

We weren't finished with my father. I had barely even begun with him and I had questions too, things he could tell me about bikes and God and enzymes and the Himalayas. My mother tried to stroke away my perplexity with a hand both soft and heavy. In my memory, those hands are a portrait with a gallery of their own: they trembled for months when she opened a letter and shook when she lifted a cup of tea, her soothing drink, each sip appearing to water and brighten her eyes. We couldn't go home for weeks after that because of the burst pipe and stayed in the spare room at the Post Office, my mother crying most nights, a long clock ticking in the hall and me sitting on the carpet turning a coin from one finger to another. It was a half crown given to me by Mrs Ainsbury: 1950, it said. George VI in profile. His straight nose was cut into the coin and I could inspect his jaw, his neat ear and his beautifully combed hair, all handsome, all silver, all mine.

One saw the larks in the spring of that year in Dalgarnock, climbing the sky above the rape fields that edged the town. I was taking confessions in the chapel as people from the Legion of Mary performed their cleaning tasks among the pews. A copy of the catechism sat next to me on the wooden bench. It was coarsely worded, I thought; all the better I had Cowper's poems on my lap.

> I sometimes think myself inclined
> To love Thee, if I could;
> But often feel another mind,
> Averse to all that's good.

95

How frugal and true a sentiment for a Saturday morning, when the church smelled of faded incense and a familiar boredom had taken up residence in the fibres of the carpet and along the empty pews. I find my lips move more when I read nowadays, and my distinguished educators would blush to see me over the tattered poems. As this thought occurred, the curtain on the other side of the confessional went back and I knew it had to be them, Mark and Lisa. I knew it from the rapid swish of the curtain, the joke silence, the dunt and clump of heavy shoes.

'Please forgive me, Father, for I have sinned,' he said. 'It's been a hundred and fifty years since my last confession.'

'Go on.'

'I'm afraid my mother and me, we killed my father last night. She smoked him with a gun right in front of me. And then I put a few slugs in him, just to make sure. He refused to get out of his chair and we had to do it. We killed him and we ate him for dinner. There's plenty of him left. He's in the fridge. Anyhow. I ask for God's forgiveness and promise not to eat any fat bastards again. Also, Father: I had sexual intercourse with a bus. It was very frightening.'

'It was a single-decker,' she said.

'Yes, Father, a single-decker. It was giving me the come-on for ages. Big red bus. Brazen it was. Well. Eventually I gave in to temptation and had it off with the bus in broad daylight. God forgive me.'

'You're very silly,' I said.

'How many Hail Marys for shagging a bus?'

'At least a thousand. And another thousand for ganging up on your dad. You must learn to suppress your appetites.'

'We're bored,' said Lisa. I could hear the smack of chewing gum and smell something like hairspray.

'I've got house visits,' I said.

'Bite it,' said Mark.

'Aye,' said Lisa. 'Can we no' go on a wee drive up to Glasgow? Come on, let's go up to Princes Square. Totally awesome. Mark's fed up. He had a fight with Chubb last night.'

'A fight?' I said. 'What about?'

'Just stuff,' said Mark. 'I got burned. He's a thievin' bastard.'

'Aye,' said Lisa. 'He is so.'

They could talk. Later that day I saw Lisa stealing soap from a cosmetics shop on Buchanan Street and Mark had watches in his pockets. 'Don't steal when you're with me, Mark,' I said. 'If I see you stealing, then I'm leaving you here and that's the end of it.'

'That's hardcore,' he said.

'I mean it.'

'You won't leave,' he said, casually.

'What makes you so sure?'

'You're not the leaving type,' he said, leaning into my arm and putting his hand on the small of my back.

There were protesters wearing gas masks in George Square. I sat on one of the benches to watch them for a while. They stood under a statue of Robert Peel, and my eyes got lost in the style of them and the chants they were making.

'What you staring at?' said Lisa.

'Shut it, bitch,' said Mark.

'Fuck you, nigger,' she said.

'He's just watching all the mad hippies and their daft protest. Those people just want Saddam Hussein to run the world.'

One of the banners said: 'Say No To Religious War.'

'Don't be stupid,' I said to Mark. 'They have every right to protest if they don't agree with what's going on.'

'What do you care?' he said. 'You hate Arabs just as much as me.' As he spoke, he was lighting matches from a box and flicking them over the back of the bench.

'I don't hate anybody, Mark. And let me tell you something: you don't know the first thing about me.'

'Awright,' he said. 'Keep your wig on.'

'You don't know me. Why would you say I hate Arabs?'

'Because you let us talk nasty about them.'

'That's got nothing to do with me.'

'Right,' he said. 'Just fuck off then. I'm starvin'.'

He put a lighted match inside the box and the box flared up before he closed it. After a second, he opened the end of the box again and sucked out the smoke, inhaled, then blew it out of his mouth before chucking the spent box into a puddle. He walked off.

'He's angry,' I said.

'Naw,' said Lisa. 'Don't worry about him. He flies off the handle all the time. Let's go to Burger King.'

I looked for a second or two at the people in the masks and their colleagues giving out leaflets by the stone lions.

'It's a bit pathetic, isn't it?' said Lisa. 'For a protest.' I said nothing and stood up to go off and find Mark.

'Let's go back to Fraser's after this,' said Lisa, spinning a line of chewing gum around a purple fingernail. 'My mother works in there on Saturdays and I love stealing from the places she works.'

I handed her a five-pound note. 'Here,' I said. 'The two of you can go back to Dalgarnock on the train. This is not what I had in mind for a day out. You're going to have me strung up.'

'Don't get eggy,' she said. 'We're just havin' a buzz.'

I felt vaguely humiliated and unstable as I walked to the car park, and I stood for a while in the concrete stairwell, urging myself to be brave and leave them behind. Then eventually I walked back to the burger place where they sat at a table sucking on straws.

'Hiya,' said Mark.

My mother's life became solitary after my father died, and the solitude was productive. She said she didn't have the gift to make other people's lives orderly, and I think I understood that, keen in my own way to emerge from my father's death as a changed person. She began to write her best books. At first, she rented a farmhouse on the outskirts of the village, turning it slowly into the kind of place that better suited her own talents. The other house had really been all about my father, everybody happy to live by his clock and be instructed by his taste, yet my mother had always possessed her own more colourful vision of how to furnish and decorate her life, everything in time growing exuberant, her books no less than other things. As for me, I was always a secondary husband, a little adult, and after his death she took my complications for granted, allowing me to go in whatever direction I chose so long as it didn't put a drag on her own dear plans for survival. I hope I don't sound bitter. We each had a right to our share of bitterness, but we didn't go along with much of that, simply ordaining one another with the freedom thereafter to live whatever lives we were capable of imagining.

I asked to go away to school. It was my decision, and I think it saved our friendship. My father's higher selfishness had put a check on my mother's more local kind, and I don't think we could have been happy playing house together. The way we managed things, her eccentricity grew in step with mine, and we came quite to admire one another's jokes and to save parts of ourselves up for one another in a way that has never changed. There was never any of that weeping at the end of the holidays. She didn't go in for those displays of devoted motherhood or the guilty bursts of attentiveness that so characterised the holiday antics of my school chums' mothers. We would each have been instantly embarrassed by anything of that sort. 'Darling,' she said, 'you've been very entertaining. You've got your bags packed. Off you go to Yorkshire now.'

'Goodbye, Mrs,' I'd say.

'Okay, then. Off you go,' she'd say. 'And don't make me use up any clichés. I need them all for my books.'

We'd laugh. And that was that.

My childhood gave me a strong sense of unreality, of stories and myths being better than facts. I suppose this made me a natural Catholic but a less than natural person. Anyhow, I admired the miracles and rituals, the business of the Assumption. It all seemed to give texture to life and to the hunt for goodness, and I loved the stories and thought they were beautiful – the Last Supper and the pieces of silver, the raising of the dead, the loaves and the fishes and the water into wine. I liked the Galilean weather and I liked the feel of old England too, the England of martyrs and illuminated manuscripts. The lives of the saints were my myths of adventure and transformation, my Hercules and Achilles, my Apollo, my Minerva, not stories so much as ethical testaments, consummate portraits of suffering, death and redemption, to enlarge the soul and brighten my daily efforts.

I stood at the library window and could hear the sound of plainsong traversing the halls and spreading out there in the fields. The school to me was a community not so much of excellence as of total sufficiency. But most of all it is the tone of the monks that remains, for me, an idea of exactitude and sportsmanship and continuity with the medieval world that seeped by hours and by years through the older buildings to change the character of the boys. We are supposed to have had it tough. But I don't think so. It was the world outside that seemed tough to us.

There is said to have been abuse at Ampleforth, and the newspapers can now produce individuals who recognise the gleam of lust on every friendly face from the past. I'm sure the individuals are right: there was evidence that some of the monks were troubled and troubling in that particular way, and early Masses in the crypt may have been difficult for some of the boys. But I cannot give in to the notion that the school was a hotbed of abuse, partly because 'abuse' did not have the currency in our minds – perhaps in anybody's mind – that it now enjoys on a worldwide scale. I would never seek to excuse the hurts that lonely men are known sometimes to enact upon their juniors. Yet the school was paradise to me, a heaven spotted with frailty. I can't bear witness to the horror stories because, to me – perhaps another of my blindnesses – Ampleforth was a merciful place and a truthful one. It gave me the means of forgiving others before I sought to be forgiven myself.

I was in St Thomas's House, and if you were brisk enough to ask the housemaster, Father Victor, what one was expected to learn at Ampleforth, he would go quiet, gently refuting suggestions about maths or Latin, concealing his hands in the sleeves of his black habit – we called the monks 'crows' – and smiling at the suggestion that it was our purpose there to learn to love and serve God. The crows were always rather sedate. 'You are here to learn to behave beautifully,' Father Victor would say. The library was my lair of choice: I liked the books, certainly, in which the elements of life coalesced with the beauty of language, but I also liked the desks and the chairs, the great, wooden solidity of the school furniture, each item carved by a venerable carpenter called Thompson, whose signature, discernible everywhere, came in the form of a small oak mouse.

I felt very temporary as a child. I may always have felt that way, but Ampleforth had a way of making one feel more fixed in the world, more indelible overall. Part of that feeling must have been Yorkshire – one never forgot that the school lay in a valley bordered by moorland and drystone dykes, and, further afield, mining pits and lime kilns – but it must also have been the soft hum of reliability that came at all times from the Benedictines, who seemed to know the world, and not only this world. Every boy at the school, whatever his attainments, whatever his plans and whoever his parents, came to be marked by a certain unobtrusive quality. A good joke was more impressive than a powerful idea. The plains of indecision were more attractive than the wilds of passion. Ampleforth wasn't like other English public schools: we hated ruthlessness, we liked ease, and we followed the monks in feeling that being a little absent was infinitely better than being too present.

I wrote only once from school for money. I was preparing for Gormire Day, 5 June, the day when everyone in the school went up to the Gormire Lake for picnics and games. It was traditional to make your way by whatever conveyance you could manage: a great many went by bike or by bus; Fletcher and Leishman, my best friends at Ampleforth, once went by milk float; legend said that a group of Durham boys had once gone by pony-and-trap. It was the greatest single event of my schooldays, Gormire Day 1959. I imagined I was carving a perfect day out of marble. I begged my mother for money, and she was good enough to consider it an excellent investment.

Billy Smart's circus was in York, with its herd of fifteen elephants. The beast I chose was an old, tolerant-eyed animal named Birma. I wrote letters and my mother wrote letters; it came to seem to me a production out of Genesis, and a truck was hired, special feed was arranged, permissions were sought and hastily denied and then warily granted.

'How clever of you to think of it,' my mother said. It must have cost a fortune, yet it was the sort of expense my mother could approve of. Her gift has always been to avoid the conventional view, especially when it stands in the way of the grand or ridiculous act. My mother wanted to repay me for the originality of my impulse, and we spoke the same language. I think she enjoyed knowing my father would have called it outrageous, and, on the appointed Friday, she came to York so that we could go and see the man about the elephants, which were marched that day from York station to the field where the circus took place. I remember the handler asking my mother if Birma was to be hired for educational purposes. 'In a way,' she said, 'that is very much the case. But also for romantic purposes.'

'Is it a wedding?' he said.

'Again, in a way,' she said. 'Not a wedding, but certainly a marriage. My son is being married to the joys of the modern imagination.'

'Right you are,' said the man, though he must have thought we were lunatics. 'I'll be there to lead him off and look after his feed.'

'Thank you,' she said. 'There's a bonus for good cheer.'

'Right you are.'

He told us Birma was the star of the fleet. We watched him at the railway station, his giant feet on the road, people gazing up and jostling one another for a better view. I liked his eyes. I liked his silence. The handler spoke of the animal as if it were a friend that nobody understood. 'When the guvnor brought him over,' he said, 'he had to spend a year in quarantine in Edinburgh Zoo.'

'In Edinburgh?' my mother said. 'What a nice thought. That must have cheered up his chops somewhat.' She laughed towards me. 'You're practically cousins, you and Birma,' she said.

'Thank you for this, mother. You are a sport.'

'Any time,' she said. 'Any time, for the collective beasts of Edinburgh. You know how patriotic I am.'

All in all, our researches proved equal to the exquisite thrill on Gormire Day, the wonder of Birma waiting at the top of the hill festooned in feathers and satin armour. It seemed so right to mount an elephant and rise in my white shirt above the dry Yorkshire road, my long-lashed vehicle all tassels and bells in a glorious rapture of unacceptable pomp, the gypsy smoking his cigarette and leading us all the way to the Gormire Bank. People left their bicycles by the roadside and cheered. The sun cracked through the trees in flashes and points of light. Birma the elephant raised her trunk and hooted into the Hambleton Hills and the monks surrendered their vote at last to the sheer madness of it all.

'I m-must say,' said Brother Joseph, 'm-m-most singular.'

Brother Joseph was master of the day. He'd known of my plans and said it was probably the greatest wheeze since 1857, when Thomas Hodgson, the schoolmaster at Kilburn, got his boys to cut out a giant horse on the side of a hill and paint the ground white: the White Horse of Kilburn. During those five slow miles on the back of Birma, I saw the locals' faces looking up and shining with delight. The working class was another thing back then. They had a culture. They didn't have their gold chains or their cable television; they had their work, their interests, their families and no very obvious sense of spite or entitlement. The monks had a long history of going into those villages with pastoral zeal, and the people admired the Benedictine style of balance – order, prayer, discipline, self-denial, or self-indulgence as it's sometimes known – but here was a new style of balance altogether, David Anderton as imperial traveller, passing the good people of North Yorkshire on the back of an elephant, mill workers and bottle-factory operatives stopping to wave from the roadsides of Oswaldkirk and Oldstead, sending me off in a rain of makeshift confetti on the road to the Gormire Bank.

Mark McNulty was no friend to the flammable: he loved fires, and I never saw him without a box of matches on him. I suppose he took them from the garage where he worked, along with the occasional inch or two of petrol for making bombs to throw into the trees. I could imagine the trees on fire and see his warm face glowing with pleasure.

'Maybe you should become a fireman,' I once said.

'No way,' he said. 'My job is to keep them in work.'

One night in May, I saw him playing records at the Dalgarnock Youth Club. He was with that sinister friend of his, Chubb, the one with the pimples and the sharpened teeth, both boys wearing hooded jerseys. I had gone along that night at the request of a social worker, Miss Path, to give lessons in backgammon, but before going off to the classroom set aside for board games I drifted over to the turntables.

'Whiddye 'hink?' said the Chubb fellow.

'Sorry?'

'The decks. Whiddye 'hink?'

I looked at Mark. The noise was too much but it wasn't the

noise so much as the boy's impenetrable speech. Mark leaned over the turntables.

'He's saying: "What do you think of the decks?"' We got the club to buy in a proper set of decks to play the records on.'

'Oh, excellent,' I said.

'Aw. Massive choon. Totally gallus, man.'

I smiled and shook my head at Mark. 'What did he say?'

'He said the record he's just put on is very good.' Mark let out a little barked laugh and we both stared at his friend. He was holding one headphone to his ear and rocking his head from side to side, pushing a record with two fingers on the turntable, baring his insane teeth. 'He's gone,' said Mark. 'Just mad for it.'

'Thus us totally bangin',' said Chubb.

As he bent over, I could see a length of rubber tube hanging out of the pocket of Chubb's jersey. I think Mark saw me looking at it and he stuffed it out of sight as he leaned over to lift a record sleeve.

In the games room, later on, Mark and Chubb arrived with red faces, snapping their fingers and scanning the room with busy, alert eyes. I was playing a very slow game of backgammon with two giggling girls, but I saw the boys going over to a table by the window where a quiet boy was playing Monopoly with a handicapped girl. Chubb kept leaning down and saying things to the girl. She shrugged him off but he kept at it, and every time she turned, Mark would drop another small piece from the board into her cup of orange squash.

'You can play each other now,' I said to the girls, and I ushered Mark and Chubb out of the room.

'I didnae dae any'hin',' said Chubb.

'He didn't do anything,' said Mark.

'Enough,' I said. 'Yes, you did. You were tormenting that poor girl in there and I won't stand by and watch that.'

'Naw I didnae!'

'No, I didn't,' said Mark, smiling.

'Stop it,' I said.

I took them down the corridor and we found a room where they were showing videos of old football matches. 'Ya beauty,' said Mark. I stood at the back of the room while the two boys commandeered the television and the pile of tapes, finding Celtic ones to put on. 'Fast forward. Watch this goal,' said Mark. Chubb seemed to dance under the TV light.

The roar of football fans filled the room. I suppose it must have been for music lessons in the daytime. There were instruments standing in the corners and a trolley of percussion things. After the second goal Mark was leaping up to kiss the screen – 'Come on, the Celts!' – and his friend was shaking a tambourine and beating it with his elbow. At one point they stood face to face in front of the flickering game. They clasped one another's hands and moved in a circle, each with his own touch of menace, scuttling round like two scorpions in love.

'That's mental,' said Chubb.

I walked them to the pizza shop along the road, or I walked and they rolled on their skateboards, occasionally grazing the kerb with the edge of the boards or flipping the boards into their hands and walking for a while. Mark said he wanted Lucozade, and Chubb wanted a bag of chips.

'Have you got any money?' said Mark.

'I wish you'd spend it on something healthier,' I said, handing him some coins and turning away. They smelled of petrol.

'Let's hang out together one night,' he said. 'Just me and you, without all these dweebs.'

'These what?'

'Dweebs, jerks, idiots, tubes. Call them what you like. I'll show you Mark McNulty's Dalgarnock. Just you and me.'

'We'll see,' I said.

'I'll text you.' He said this walking backwards into a pool of yellow light falling from the pizza shop.

They seemed to belong to the brilliant colours of the shop. The rows of sweets and cigarettes looked down on them, and Mark pointed at his shoe and did an imitation kick beside the silver fryer. Yet as I walked away, I looked from the corner of my eye and saw that everything in the shop looked suddenly white, as if a polaroid were being consumed from within by its own unaccountable fire. The shop was unchanged, but my mind was filled with potential dramas involving those youths: the smell of petrol, the length of tubing, their love of matches, and the flashing lights of the television set a half hour before, burning over the boys' heads, making haloes around them, before reaching my face at the back of the class.

Brother Joseph ran the Wednesday film at Ampleforth. There were no videos back then, so a blue van would come to the gates of the school midweek with canisters from the lending library in York. Brother Joseph's great passion was *film noir*. He liked all those American movies starring Richard Widmark, stories told in shadows and Chicago accents, always involving guns and poverty, loose women and redemption, and I still see Joseph's youthful face shining as he stood at the edge of the long passage, the light from the projector picking out his oiled hair, his pale cheeks, the look in his eyes the very picture of intentness. One Wednesday night, it must have been around 1961 or '62, we sat in rows watching a film with Marilyn Monroe and Clark Gable, *The Misfits*, and Joseph was saying it wasn't what he expected. 'It's a John Hu-Huston film,' he said.

'What does that mean?' I said.

'It usually means b-bad guys. Guns. *The M-M-Maltese Falcon.*'

We walked out into the quadrangle after the film. Brother Joseph's subject was meant to be geography, but he preferred to speak about books and films. He didn't bother that much with physical reality, except to remind me, that night, lifting his long hand with its bitten fingernails, that the ridge behind the school was called the Beacon and up there one would find the Monk's Wood, the graves of the Ampleforth monks. Joseph bent down and lifted something from the grass. 'Look,' he said. 'R-r-radishes. This area was p-p-ploughed until about t-ten years ago.'

'Why?'

'The war effort, young f-fellow,' he said. He handed me the radish and I immediately took a bite. 'You're very brave,' he said. 'These things can be p-poisonous.' He smiled.

'No,' I said. 'It's good. Tastes nothingy. Well, it tastes of nothing with a touch of pepper.'

'Good, Anderton,' he said. 'You have d-d-d-discernment.'

Joseph's superstitions had colour and fear in them. He thought blackberries could poison babies after a certain time in the season. He thought lilac was an unlucky flower to bring indoors. He hated daffodils, and he thought nettles and dock leaves told a story about uncertain minds, quoting Chaucer on the subject, *Troilus and Criseyde*: 'Nettle in, dok out, now this, now that?' Brother Joseph was the first person I knew, the first who wasn't my mother, who used the miracles of art to help one to live one's life. He did it naturally. I came to think that all those movies of his, all those stories and superstitions, only aided his religious feelings, somehow enlarging the scope of his belief. He told me that night in the quadrangle that his father had flown in the war and that it made him feel sick to imagine it. My tongue was thick in my mouth and viscid with liquorice.

'Sir,' I said, 'I want to ask you. What is more important to the world, ethics or taste?'

'What a g-grand question, Anderton. Have you b-b-been hovering under the clock-tower staircase again, in the library? I mean, are you de-de-devoting your afternoons to the F-French novel?'

'It came up the other day.'

'Yes indeed,' he said. 'It will come up every day. Well, I th-th-think you ask the question because you know the answer.'

'Ethics,' I said.

'Good boy for saying so, b-but that is n-not what you think. That is what you f-f-fear.'

'It is what I believe.'

'Very g-good. You will go far. And yet, I am not asking what you be-believe, but what you feel.' I knew in that moment there was something fine and wasted about Brother Joseph. The hills were dark blue and ignorant against the sky. 'Young Anderton,' he said, 'don't worry about the answer. The question is the b-better part. You have your own answer. I believe a minute ago you detected p-p-p-pepper in that radish.' He walked away for a moment and sniffed the fields.

'Sir,' I said, 'why aren't you out in the world?'

'Sorry?'

'You like films and things. Why are you here? Why not out in the world making films or being an actor?'

'I am an actor,' he said, very quietly. He stroked his head with an open hand and walked onto the grass. 'Being a person of faith,' he said, 'is just like being a m-m-movie actor. Friend of the dark.'

'It's nice out here, isn't it?' I said. 'Cold, though.'

I fell asleep that night thinking about Brother Joseph and his father who flew in the war. I thought of the movie and wild horses in the Nevada desert, and I dreamed of radishes that made one invisible to the naked eye. Several years later, Brother Joseph fell in love with a boy at the school and was removed. They say now he should have been removed long before. He's one of the names now mentioned in the annals of the unspeakable. All I know is the Wednesday film was never the same after he disappeared, and I always looked out for his believing face, right at the edge of the film projector's long and flickering beam.

Sometimes I curve my hand round a candle, or reach for a book, and I see the Amplefordian who exists in that simple action. The school may have given me a defective sense of my own merits, but it also gave us a style, and I never saw that style so clearly until I moved among the young people of Dalgarnock, those youngsters who lived, each one of them, as if community were only a club for resentment or a background against which to measure and prove their superior powers. My school's mysterious sense of unity may have been a romantic conceit, but it worked to make us want to know an existence larger than ourselves, to see a manner of living and thinking and speaking to which we all might subscribe. We would have denied these values, but they live in the heart. And one day we wake in a strange place and find we know those values most intimately by their absence from every scene except the scene in our own heads.

It was Father Victor's job to come and direct the boys from the railway station after the summer holidays. York Station: a long poem of steam, late arrivals and violet evenings, where advertising hoardings spoke of other people's choices, Bird's Custard and Capstan Full Strength, the tracks down there like blades set to cut open the future and bring us forward to meet it. Years later, I heard Father Victor recall that we boys came back from our summer holidays and found once again our natural unity. 'The Irish boys came into York Station speaking with Irish accents,' he said. 'The Scots came from the north speaking Scottish. The West Country boys arrived speaking just like that, and the London ones came out of the station talking like East-End Charlie. But you know what? The boys were like plants whose stalks bend involuntarily towards the sun, and by the middle of the following day they all spoke more or less the same way. That is what the school was like, and that's what young people were like back then if you didn't trample them.'

6

THE NIGHTS

The weeks of June had been especially busy with weddings and funerals and school visits. The church hall was barely empty a single evening that season. My garden was rather outstanding, the work of Mrs Poole and myself during our more green-fingered moments. We had left the work a little late, though Mrs Poole, once we started, got down to cutting the blooms with her usual surfeit of devotion. I'm sure it was on one of the garden days that I first noticed her wincing as she bent down among the stems; from the landing window I saw her standing with a pained look on her face and a gloved hand held to the middle of her chest. Mrs Poole's privacies seemed so severe at times that I chose not to ask her about it then, but all the hours we worked on the roses I weighed up the state of her health.

I have a love of old roses more than anything, especially Damask – Madame Hardy we grew, and Ispahan – with their sweet, musky perfumes, their great thorns and intricate memories of Persia. The sun in Scotland is never great for Ispahans, but they came through well enough that summer, with the sort of freshness that heralds its own ruin. Mrs Poole said she preferred a good old Roman flower: the Rosa Mundi, red with white flecks and a renovating scent of spices.

'Do you know . . . ,' I said.

'Probably not.'

'No, but do you know the Empress Josephine's famous garden at Malmaison was almost entirely Gallica roses?'

'Well,' said Mrs Poole, 'we must do better than the Empress Josephine. Even if we only have this poor soil to handle.'

At the back of the garden, beyond the sundial, we had several Centifolia roses that never blossomed. Perhaps our garden disappeared too early for these ones to show, but we tended the bushes carefully, Mrs Poole saying one day she had read a book which specified these flowers, Fantin Latour, to be those often used by the old Dutch and Flemish masters, the ones they preferred to paint and bring to life. I appreciated that, but we could never bring our own bushes to life, not in the time we were there. And we could see from early on that they were not flourishing. 'It may be too shady,' I said, 'on account of the wall. Perhaps I should use something to help them along.'

'Nothing chemical,' she said.

'Just a little to get them going.'

'No,' she said. 'I'd sooner stop the garden than begin using harmful stuff out here.'

'I'm going to shove in some pesticide when you're not looking,' I said.

'You dare.'

'So what about nutrients for the back wall, then?' I said. 'These bushes are costing a fortune and they don't look promising.'

'Put a banana peel in the soil,' she said. 'And better manure. We can take a trip out to the farms and get it free.' She would often put her hands at the base of her spine, as if to prop herself up.

'Maybe you shouldn't bend down so much, Mrs Poole,' I said. 'Just until you're feeling better.'

The days seemed to pass along with a certain idle grace. I hadn't seen as much of Mark and Lisa, and it was all quiet morning Masses, Benedictions at Nazareth House, concerts, christenings and diocesan meetings at the bishop's house in Ayr. I must have been lulled by it all, for I paid too little attention to the changes in Mrs Poole; week by week, she lost touch with that old sense of herself, turning slowly away from the garden, from French and her former enthusiasms.

'What's the story?' she said on one of her Fridays.

'Well,' I said, 'I've sacked the organist.'

'That's a sure sign of age,' she said. 'You're now going around sacking people. It'll be me next.'

'Don't be like that,' I said. 'Though his Philistine views were similar to your own when it came to the organ music of Thomas Tallis.'

'Dark stuff,' said Mrs Poole. 'Wailing music for those who have trouble putting a smile on their faces.'

'What's smiling got to do with it?'

'You might well ask,' she said. 'But we'll be enjoying no lessons in the matter from Thomas bloody Tallis.'

I could see it was going to be one of those days when Mrs Poole felt less than her best and blamed everybody.

'Now what am I doing with this rhubarb?' she said.

'Stewed,' I said. 'I thought we agreed on Monday. It's in the *Fruit Book*.'

'Strictly speaking, as you might say,' she said, 'it's not actually a fruit.'

'It's a pre-fruit,' I said.

'Semi-fruit,' she said. 'It says here: "The Greeks called this medicinal rhubarb *rha barbaron*, because it reached them via foreigners, barbarians, down the river we call the Volga and they called the Rha." The leaves were toxic.'

'That's not the English kind,' I said. 'We only use the young pink stalks.'

'Who's "we"?' Mrs Poole said. 'Would that be the royal "we"?'

'Oh, shush,' I said.

Mrs Poole began laying pieces into a pan and squeezing an orange over them and a sprinkling of sugar. I opened the kitchen door and breathed in something of the garden bushes, took a trowel from the windowsill and turned some soil in the border. Back inside, Mrs Poole was placing the pan on a large flame. 'Even the English kind has medicinal qualities,' I said. 'You should eat lots of it. Do you no end of good.'

'I don't think rhubarb's the remedy,' she said, without looking up.

'Maybe it's the bitterness,' I said. 'We always think bitterness is good for us. Wouldn't you say?'

'I don't know anything about it,' she said, folding the dish cloths over the oven handle.

'It's true,' I said, 'that rhubarb contains a lot of oxalic acid, and that can adversely affect the absorption of calcium and iron. You ought to watch out for that.'

Mrs Poole walked into the sitting room with a small silence gathering in her wake. I knew I had a tendency sometimes to get things wrong with people, saying too much, placing myself too centrally in other people's worries about themselves, as if the worry might naturally take second place to my superintendence of it. Mrs Poole had a way of making a room obey her weather like nobody else. 'Would you come through here, Father?' she said. And when I went into the room she was standing beside the piano biting her nails. 'I know you're trying to be helpful,' she said. 'I know you're trying to be kind. But you must stop talking to me about remedies and cures. It's offensive.'

'I don't know what you mean,' I said.

'Yes, you do. In some way it makes it easier for you, doesn't it? It makes it easier to make light of what's happening and pretend I've got some . . . some stupid ailment. That's just the sort of person you are, Father David. You think manners and conversation can get us round anything at all. But the truth is . . .'

'Mrs Poole . . .'

'The truth, Father David, is that I have cancer. Not just one but two kinds. That's that. The truth is you will have to pay me off soon because I am not going to . . . And God knows what will come next.' Her voice was even stronger perhaps than she had meant; its force engulfed the calm of the sitting room.

'I understand,' I said.

'It is not your job to *understand*,' she said. 'It is not your job to make things smaller than they are.'

'I'm sorry if I have seemed to do that.'

'You do it every time I see you,' she said. 'And I expect more than that from you. I expect you to help me prepare.'

Standing there listening to Mrs Poole, I remembered a speech she had made, a speech about death that had come to seem like a premonition of her illness. She was happier in those first months of my ministry, relieved almost to be spending time with someone who was ready to be amused by her and find her interesting. We were out in the garden and she was knocking frost off some useless-looking bulbs.

'People don't listen,' she had said. 'Or they don't remember. And you do both, Father David, at least some of the time, so I'm telling you something important. If you're around here I want you to make sure I get a green funeral. I don't want a wooden coffin and I don't want a headstone. Do you hear me? I want to be part of an ecosystem. Do you know about that? There are places where they put you down in a cardboard box and plant a tree. That's it. That's all I want and I need you to make sure it happens. Do you hear?'

'Where is this place?'

'I've got it all written down,' she said. 'It's near Kelso. I put the information in a tin where the insurance policies are kept. The cupboard in my kitchen, above the kettle. A woodland burial it's called. I couldn't suffer to have anything else done around this town.'

'Happy subject for a cold afternoon,' I said.

'Never mind. You take care of it. It's the best thing you can do now if you care about the environment. Plant bodies.'

She had stuck a bulb into the soil. 'It's all the rage,' she said, smiling. 'Some people get buried under vineyards.'

'I've never heard of that.'

'Aye,' she said. 'It's a good one, isn't it? Live a bad life, become a good vintage.' We laughed as I leaned into the path to lift the secateurs. Mrs Poole's efficiency seemed easily to stretch from the matter of patting down the soil around the cheap bulbs to contemplating her own death. 'Some people go for a thing called Eternal Reefs,' she said.

'What's that?'

'It's mainly in America. In Florida. You know what they're like over there in America. They make a block out of your ashes and attach them to a live coral reef. See what I mean? They make you part of the sea after you die.'

'That's extraordinary.'

'Aye,' she said. 'The waves coming over ye. But it wouldn't work here. Can you imagine it in Ayrshire? That sludge boat out of Glasgow's only just stopped running every day. Do you know it was carrying 3,000 tons of sewage out there and dropping it just south of Garroch Head?'

'Really?'

'Since 1914! Every day!'

'And they would just drop the sewage out there?'

'Certainly,' she said. 'Two boats as well. Every day out there dumping the sewage. The European Union put a stop to that environmental disaster. But you wouldn't want to be a bit of coral on the west coast, that's for sure.'

'I don't suppose.'

'No,' she said. 'It's the woodland burial for me. Promise me you'll see to it if you're around here when my time's up.'

'I don't think that's at all likely, Mrs Poole. But, of course, I promise.'

I was reminded of this during our talk in the sitting room, her dark-circled eyes serious and unrelenting, each rimmed with sudden antipathy and staring at me from her position on the piano stool. 'I know you are afraid of death, Father,' she said. 'That must be a wee bit unusual in a man of the cloth. You fear death. You don't have any feeling for risk at all, and that's your problem.'

She took out a tissue and wiped her nose.

'It's because you haven't lived enough, Father. You haven't risked anything in life.'

I sat down on the sofa.

'That is not right, Mrs Poole. I have risked many things. A great many things. The person sitting here is the sum of their failures.'

'There's no need to be so dramatic,' she said. 'You're such an actor when you don't have to be.'

'Forgive me,' I said. 'I just want to help you.'

'Well, if you want to help me then *help* me.'

She got up and went round the room dusting shelves and plumping cushions. 'You have changed,' she said. 'You don't sit and read now like you did when I first knew you. I found that quite nice, to see a man reading a book and improving himself. Jack would never do that. He's not a stupid man, but he's like a lot of people round here: he couldn't be at peace with himself for the length of time it takes to read a book. He's not got the patience. It's all gab, gab, gab with these people – they never stop – and it's silence that embarrasses them, not stupidity or anything like that. Jack can talk. He rings everybody up when he's got a drink in him. He'll phone Irene. I tell her just to put the phone down on him but she's a nice person, my sister.'

'But you don't phone?'

'Not much, no. I don't have the words for them. But Jack does. It's part of the old charm. He'll phone Australia and all sorts. Cousins he hasn't seen for years. I wouldn't know what to say to them.'

'We have our talks in here.'

'That's different,' she said. 'This has been a thoughtful house. But you have changed, Father. You don't prepare for your Masses any more. You don't listen to the parishioners. The people in the geriatric ward at Ravenspark say they haven't seen you for four weeks.'

She turned to look at me.

'You've been such a . . . such an inspiring person, Father David. Just in the way you lived. The way you appreciated things.'

'I've not gone anywhere, Mrs Poole.'

'Maybe you have,' she said. 'I was just upstairs. What's that hair gel doing on the bathroom shelf?'

I wanted to sleep but I couldn't. I stood at the bedroom window at two in the morning. My mother often found her characters at such times, peering into the dark to see those children of history, Mary Queen of Scots in a scarlet pinafore, playing on the floor as her French mother wrote letters in the upper apartments of Stirling Castle. Mary, the daughter of debate, would raise her arms to her mother, and the lady of Guise would bend from her desk to lift the child and wipe the tears from her eyes. My mother's nights were empty of sleep but filled with beautiful craft.

The fog was low on the ground, full of yellow lamplight, and it moved like an Old Testament menace through the streets of Dalgarnock, clouding the houses of the sleeping town. Late in his life, Chopin came to Scotland and played at the Merchants' Hall in Glasgow, more than half empty that day, though a miracle occurred to lift his spirits: Princess Czartoryski, his former pupil, came from London to make something light and grand of the Scottish rain. Chopin wrote a letter from Scotland that strikes me now as having the texture of my own memory. I found the words written on the flyleaf of my Penguin Ovid.

'One day,' he wrote, 'after I had played to them and some of the Scottish ladies had sung their songs, they brought out a kind of accordion and she began playing on it the most dreadful tunes with the utmost gravity. Those who know some of my works say to me in French: please play me your Second Sigh.' (The English edition of the Two Nocturnes Opus 37 was entitled *Les Soupirs*, 'The Sighs'.) 'I love your bells,' Chopin reports them as saying. 'And every comment ends with the words *leik water*, which means my music flows like water. And they all look down at their hands while playing the wrong notes with feeling.'

I was thinking of Chopin that night and looking into the lights when my phone began to buzz on the windowsill like an angry bluebottle. It was a text from Mark. 'Finished work. Whassup?'

'You should go home,' I texted back.

Him: 'Get lost. It's Saturday night.'

Me: 'Sunday morning.'

Him: 'Whatever. Me panelled. Going for a walk. Meet me at the Lugar tunnel in 25 if you want.'

The lane was wet and the night cold. I opened my umbrella, turned my collar up and walked past the library and the bowling green, where tall trees sheltered the well-tended grass. Mark was already there when I arrived; the dark included him. I made him out by the orange glow of his cigarette. The Lugar tunnel connected the old parish with the housing estate, and Mark lorded it there that night in dead silence, like a border guard at the edge of some mystifying country. He smelled of petrol and spearmint gum, and the ground beneath us crunched with broken glass. 'Welcome to Provoland,' he said.

'The what?'

'The Provos. The Provisionals.'

'Don't be ridiculous, Mark,' I said, breaking a piece of glass with the point of my umbrella. 'You've never been to Ireland. What has the IRA got to do with you?'

'My blood's been to Ireland,' he said. 'It started across the water, so don't go all English on me. You have to watch yourself around here with all these Orange bastards.'

'This is Scotland,' I said. 'Haven't you got enough problems without importing fresh ones from Northern Ireland?'

'Get a grip,' he said. 'You're a visitor here.'

'The town's not that bad.'

'Cop on,' he said. 'Five of the pubs up there are Ulster Volunteer pubs. I know your head's in the fucken clouds, Father, that's where it's supposed to be. But what kind of place do you think this is? Do you actually know where you're living? Are you blind or what?'

'Maybe I am,' I said. 'It's dark enough.'

My duties had shown me just about every street and cul-de-sac on the housing estate, and I must say the place chilled me. The fearful black and whiteness of everything was so overwhelming; the dead quietness of the squares in the afternoon, where cars were infrequent and dogs appeared sovereign in the alleys. Most of the houses were exactly the same, inside and outside, except for those which had been purchased from the council, an achievement often marked by a neon-coloured front door or a wall built round a garden of blue gravel. People lived and died on the estate without moving more than a few feet each day. The council planted shrubs that the children destroyed. There was nothing beautiful and nothing of human history on the estate, just an immoderate acceptance of life's low standards and a desire for state benefits and babies.

Mark seemed drunk and his tour past the playgrounds and the towers with their vandalised entry buzzers gave me a rather giddy feeling, a notion that I was living several lives at once. The chip shop was closed but the pavement outside smelled of vinegar and of curry sauce. We didn't see a single person, but the stars were bright. 'Mark,' I said, 'even when you're out by yourself around here, do you ever feel watched?'

He looked at me, his pupils large.

'No,' he said. 'There's nobody here.'

Under the railway bridge, there was a concrete bench popular with Mark and his friends; they used it as a place to smoke and hang out while watching the trains go past. There was a wall, and blackberry bushes crowded the verge between the wall and the tracks: the leaves were green but the dark fruit was some months away. 'It's great here,' said Mark. 'The best place in the world.'

'It smells of pee,' I said.

'Aye,' he said. 'People just take a slash here if they need to. Like, nobody's going home for a pee if you can just do one here and that's it done. It's awesome. Just standing here. It's quiet, intit?'

A cider bottle stood by the wall. Mark lifted it and poured some onto the ground and swiped a finger through the pouring liquid. 'Magic,' he said, putting the finger in his mouth. 'You have to watch out. Some ae the fuckers will jeest pee in the bottle.' He seemed to brighten and become higher under the bridge, dancing with the bottle as I tapped the iron girders with my umbrella.

He passed the cider. 'Have a few slugs of that,' he said.

I took the bottle and drank from it, feeling for a while that we were not answerable to anyone but ourselves. A large drystone wall on the other side of the tracks was inhabited by starlings. I could see them begin to stir in the holes in the wall. Mark laughed and swayed beside me, the birds missing nothing, the time growing good with the taste of sweet cider in our mouths.

There was this perfect moment, I tell you, deep in the sapphire gloaming of the outgoing night, against the stone bench and under the bridge, when a goods train passed before us and we raised our voices and yelled like lunatics under the noise of the train. Nothing will stand in the way of that moment, when he looked over at me and laughed out loud and began shouting as the iron trucks scudded past in the gorge beneath the blackberry bushes. In the roar and blaze of his youth Mark was hardly a thing of sinew and cells, soft down and skin. Only his spirit was animal, and the very atmosphere was responsive to his presence, as if the air breathed him and not him the air. He lifted the empty cider bottle and threw it into the wheels of the train.

We emerged from the place under the bridge and walked the short distance to a line of shops that nestled in blue light under the high flats. Outside the pizza shop, the telephone boxes had been shattered, the nuggets of glass lying frosted and pretty on the ground. 'Who cares about phone boxes?' said Mark when I pointed down. 'Everybody's got mobiles.' He took me around the back of the shops and shimmied over the wall, where he opened the wooden gates and told me to keep my voice down.

'Steady on,' I said. 'What are you doing?'

'It's an empty pub,' he said. He slurred a little but was still lucid given how late it was and what he might already have taken. His eyes were shining. 'Used to be the Ardeer Arms. The windaes are boarded up but there's a padlock on the back door.' He took off one of his shoes and lifted out a key. There was a strange smell inside the place, a smell of rotten beer mats and some kind of emptiness. Wires sprang from a box in the corridor and he hit a switch and a dim light flickered on in the pub's interior, a panel of yellow above a gantry of dusty bottles. A bicycle was mounted haphazardly in one of the booths, and there was a traffic cone on an old snooker table, the pockets burst and the edges of the table stacked with cigarette butts.

Again and again, I wonder why I didn't talk to myself. Why did I not stop at the door and listen to my own counsel? It was as if my enjoyment of the situation and my fear of losing favour with Mark engulfed me, and I couldn't stop going forward, ignoring whatever scraps of wisdom were left to me in the twilight world of that strange year. Sometimes stopping to think is itself a way of stopping harm, and I can only say that I didn't have it in me to stop or to remember who I was at that moment.

'Why did the pub close?' I asked.

'Dealers,' he said. 'It used to be a busy pub. They had cabaret acts and stuff like that. Quiz nights. But the neds moved in, selling, like, not just drugs but hard drugs, then the brewery gave up.'

Mark lit a candle that was stuck in an empty bottle of Budweiser and we watched it throw shadows on the ceiling, which moved up there like the ghosts of past laughter. I sat down as he went from place to place in the long room, lifting things, clearing space on the tables. He behaved as if the abandoned pub was a starter flat and he was proud of his possessions, wishing the place to appear at its best. He said he came to the den quite a lot, a few of them did. Sometimes they came when they bunked off school. 'At night, though,' he said, 'it's usually just me on my own, and that's when I like it the best.' He lifted some darts from the bar and started throwing them at a lopsided board. 'My mum and dad used to come down here,' he said. 'Everybody on the estate came down.'

There was a small stage up the back, a fringe of sequins. A bottle of Martini Bianco stood inside a glass bingo cabinet.

'So it was busy?'

'Packed Friday and Saturday nights. It was, like, couples,' Mark said. 'Mainly married couples and all that shite. There's better pubs up the town. There were a few good stramashes in here. That guy who is married to your housekeeper, what's his name – Jack Poole. He once threw a full pint of Guinness into the fruit machine.'

'Right.'

Mark seemed thoughtful. 'I bought this myself,' he said, lifting up a Glade air freshener from the bar. Then he went over to the wall and switched on a two-bar fire.

'Do you like pubs?'

'I used to,' I said. 'When I was a student.'

126

'Were you clever at being a student?'

'Not especially.'

'Did you always get top marks?'

'I think I was more interested in pubs,' I said. As I said this I thought of St Giles and the glowing windows on cold nights when I'd walk back from the chapel at Blackfriars. 'One loses sight of pubs,' I said.

'Does one?' he said, and he smiled.

He cleaned the butts off the snooker table and found a half-bottle of vodka and washed it under the tap. He went off to find two clean glasses and I looked at his shoulders, his hair that curved sleekly into the nape of his neck, and I considered how nice a husband he might be for somebody some day, if that were possible, if the world were kind.

We walked into the estate and he showed me the window of his bedroom, the short distance from the window to the roof of the bin cupboard, which he scaled down – 'dreeped,' he said – on the nights he wanted to escape the boredom of his bed-clothes. 'I just wake up,' he said, 'and I think, I want to get out of here. I want to go down the railway or up the Cash & Carry.' He said he knew how to get into the front part of a storehouse up there, where they kept packs of Lucozade and things like that. And he said that recently he stole a whole box of lip balms, cherry-flavoured, his favourite kind, he said, and that even when he was in his bed sometimes and half asleep he would see the coloured bottles of Lucozade like a gold light in his head. 'That's why I like working at the petrol station,' he said. 'Open all night. You don't have to lie in bed just wasting your life.'

Mark's house, like all the houses, was clad with thousands of tiny white stones: he said the stones were grey now because of the rain but in the summer he used to pick them off, collect them in a football sock and use the sock as a weapon in pitched battles with young people from rival squares. He seemed happy describing these seasonal events, this world of his; it was hard for him to believe we sat in a place that was once a marshy field, so filled now with names and little stories and all the business of life. We sat in the middle of the square, under the umbrella, looking up at the strange blue darkness of his house.

'Keep your voice down,' he said.

'Is your father still not working?'

'Retired,' he said. 'He's a fat bastard.'

'Be kind, Mark. He gets depressed, doesn't he?'

'How do you know?'

'It's quite a small parish,' I said.

'He thought he had a job recently,' said Mark. 'He was para.'

'Paralytic?'

'No, stupid. Paranoid.'

'Right.'

'He thought he had a job. The people in the next square used to call him The Man Who Thought It Was Time for Work. He would come down early, like, every morning for ages and put on a pair of working boots and then go out in the front garden there. He was completely out of it. He would bring a shovel sometimes and start digging up the garden, saying, "The boys are picking me up in the van this morning. I'm getting a lift in."'

'He thought he had a job to go to?'

'Aye. He was The Man Who Thought It Was Time for Work. He was off his face half the time, and depressed, that's right. This was only like a year ago or something. The fucker would stand in his boxers and that – those big tackety boots – talking shite about tea breaks and overtime and the van coming to pick him up.'

'That's very sad,' I said.

'I know,' said Mark. 'He's a sad fuck. He's been on the government cheese for years but still thinks he's a worker.'

'The dole?'

'Aye.'

'It's very upsetting, the idea of a man wanting to go to work.'

'You're a peach,' said Mark. 'He didnae really want to go to any work. You kiddin'? He wouldnae go to work if you paid him. Well, maybe if you paid him a lot. But he was jeest para. He's always been like that. Completely sparkled. At least he's got cable.'

'That's very sad.'

'He goes mental sometimes. The other week he buried the ironing board oot the back. My ma didnae know what was happening. He was oot there wi' that spade diggin' a hole in the garden for hours and he buried the ironing board and the drainin' thing off the sink and then filled the hole in wi' soil and sat on the back step rolling cigarettes. He's no' right in the head. I bet he wishes he'd never met my mother or me.'

The door of the rectory creaked as we came in and the night's journey paused for a second just beyond the porch. I put the umbrella against the wall. 'Any beer?' Mark said, walking across the sitting room.

'Just a second,' I said.

He pointed to a framed print of a caged blue parrot that hung above the bookcase. 'Cool bird,' he said. 'Green.'

'It's blue,' I said. 'Very old. Copied from a mosaic in the Basilica di San Clemente in Rome.'

'That's definitely green,' he said. 'I'm one person you don't have to explain green to. I know my green.'

'But it's blue, Mark. Very clearly blue. Cobalt, as a matter of fact. These old prints often have colours you just don't see any more. That's the glory of the print. You hardly ever see that blue anywhere.'

His pupils were black and glossy. 'You know I'm right,' he said. 'The bird is green.' Mark had a young person's disregard for the breakability of beautiful things. I could see it in the way he lifted and laid down the room's objects, the unsparing touch, and within minutes of coming in he almost tipped a vase in a bid to reach the stereo system. 'There's no beer, I'm afraid. It might have to be wine.'

'Any Cola?' he said. 'If you've got Cola we could mix it with the wine and get some Jesus Juice goin' in the house.'

'No,' I said. 'Just wine.'

'That'll do, then.'

I closed the curtains on the front windows. The morning was close and I didn't want to think about Mass just a few hours ahead with nothing prepared and my mind dull with drink. Yet I felt serene and unthreatened by events as I took a mouthful of wine and imagined the warmth of the sun through the soil of some Burgundy vineyard.

'This is all total crap,' he said. 'Have you no' got any music at all? Just these things by auld geezers wi' specs?'

'There's some geniuses in there,' I said.

'Some total loofahs, you mean.'

'You haven't heard them,' I said. 'Don't be a moron.'

Mark smiled over his shoulder as if humoured by a child's sudden audacity. He then twisted the radio dial through crackling worlds of inanity until he lit on a 'dance' station. 'Respect,' he said, then he drank the glass of wine in one go before lifting the bottle itself and glugging from it as he wandered to the kitchen. After drinking some more and opening another bottle, a better bottle, the rectory seemed pleasingly out of order. When I came through to the kitchen Mark had turned his vandal's fingers to the delicate pressing and sticking of cigarette papers.

'Any roach material?' he said.

I shrugged and he leaned over and lifted a business card from the top of the microwave and tore off a strip. 'That's a good one,' he said, looking at the card. 'The Social Work Department.'

'Good Lord,' I said, and he held it up.

'That's wicked. Don't worry. You can still see her number.'

He took something from the small pocket of his jeans and bent over it with a knife from the worktop. 'I got the Scooby snacks,' he said. 'There you go.' He appeared to have chopped a pill in half and I saw him lift half from the table with a wet finger and put it on his tongue.

'Amen,' he said.

'Please don't.'

'Well, just gub it down,' he said.

I came back later to fetch water and looked at the hob. Mrs Poole's pan of black rhubarb was sitting there from the day before. A morning had never seemed lighter or more accessible through the kitchen window; I wanted to walk through the garden touching the goodness of wood and leaves, sipping the atmosphere. Not in a long time had a day proved so becoming to the night before, and I drank the water and felt loose in my limbs, secure in my thoughts, in tune with the rhythm of certainty that poured from the garden light and swelled with the perfect-sounding music from the next room. I felt I could drink all the water in the tap. I rubbed rhubarb dust on a finger and touched my tongue, tasting the burntness. My head was racing and the taste seemed to flood me with adrenaline and memory.

'I'm fucked up,' said Mark.

He was dancing between the armchairs with a smile on his face and with his large eyes all inclusive. The sound from the radio had come to seem quite sensible. I'm not a dancer, but I felt it would be okay to dance just then, the loud repeating music seeming to involve everything it reached. I swayed a little in front of the mirror and Mark danced up to me and patted my chest softly in time to the music. I don't know how long we stayed like that, but my legs got tired eventually and Mark asked me to put out my tongue and placed another pill there. After a while I drank more water and thrived with interest for the pattern in the carpet. He seemed a little less jagged in the morning light. With his nodding head he seemed for the first time vaguely compassionate.

'It's my turn to choose the music,' I said.

'Nuttin crappy,' he said. 'You've got the Beatles. I'm cool with that.'

'Hold on.'

I went deep into the CD drawer and found Delius. Mark groaned but then said it was fine, and we sat down on the couch and the horns seemed incredible to both of us. We just sat on the sofa drinking from the tumblers of water and the bell sounded in the piece and the room was lathered with strangeness. 'This music would do your nut in,' said Mark, and he laughed into the glass.

'He was born in Yorkshire,' I said. 'Delius.'

'Good for him,' said Mark. He was smoking a joint and tapping his knees out of time, still tapping to the other music most probably. He flicked his ash onto the carpet. 'What does it matter where anybody's from?' he said. He said this rather compliantly, as if he were offering a concession, so I didn't ask him to square it with his views about foreign countries or the progress of his football team. The thought entered my head and left it the same vacant way.

'It matters,' I said.

'Top skunk,' he said. 'Want a puff?'

We closed our eyes and *Brigg Fair* turned into something more courageous before melting into the *Florida Suite*. I could see the long passage of my old school, boys in blazers rushing outside wearing bicycle clips, their fresh smiles, their sandwiches in an old leather bag, and I saw dozens of bicycle wheels, their silver spokes turning at speed and catching the sun on the way to the Gormire Bank.

I put my head on his shoulder and asked him if he minded terribly, and he said no, it was no bother. 'Knock yourself out,' he said. So I leaned over and kissed him. I drew my lips along his cold, smooth cheek, feeling on my tongue the pulse of his jaw and detecting a faint scent of medicated soap. I went further and kissed his mouth.

'Cut it out,' he said.

'By all means,' I said.

Delius played across the sitting room and unwelcome daylight began to burn at the edges of the curtains. I took his hand. 'This is mental,' he said, and I said yes, you are right, that is what it is, and the music swept through me with confidence as I registered the fact that Sunday Mass was looming.

'Mental,' I said. He turned his reclining head and we lay there laughing like innocent boyfriends, each drawing colour from the other's eyes. I don't know how long we lasted like that. Everything else seemed a mile away. Even the front door and the shadow passing through the glass, the key scratching at the lock, the soft click as the door closed and Mrs Poole walked across the hall to begin her Sunday shift. When she opened the sitting-room door she saw us on the sofa and sighed into the worn air of the room before dropping her plastic bags and leaving the house.

7

THE ECONOMY OF GRACE

By the second Saturday in August, some of the roses were into their second flowering and the back of the garden appeared like a red contagion of the eye, while inside the rectory I had grown accustomed to keeping house. I suppose the place had become rather dustier since Mrs Poole gave up the job, but I spent the better part of that morning clearing the surfaces and polishing the cutlery until it seemed new. It was warm outside, Scottish warm, which meant there was no rain, and Dalgarnock's beer gardens began to fill up with people enjoying the weather. I saw them when I drove out past the edge of town, familiar faces, young mothers hooting with laughter at the garden tables, each table crowded with bottles of fluorescent alcohol, their sugary rims kissed with lipstick.

Mrs Poole had a private room in Crosshouse Hospital. It was up on the top floor, the private ward, with a dinner menu, a telephone by the bed and a window that looked towards the Isle of Arran. At first she said she wouldn't take the room; she thought it wasn't my concern and her husband Jack said she wasn't a charity case. But she relented when I said my mother was paying. I told her she had put some money aside from the foreign sales of her books to help women, and with that, and a whole lot of objection from Jack, she finally said all right. 'I'm saying yes,' she said, 'but only because I don't want to offend your mother's kindness.'

'Look at you,' I said. 'You're the Queen of Sheba.'

'A normal ward would be good enough for me. It was good enough for everybody else I've ever met, before you came along with your obnoxious politics. Now look at me.'

'It's not about politics,' I said. 'It's a nice view. And the National Health Service won't crumble just because you have the option of ordering a sandwich when you want one.'

'It is crumbling,' said Mrs Poole, 'in case you haven't noticed. It's crumbling all right, thanks to people like me sitting here with my big bowls of grapes.'

She was on the phone when I arrived that day, and I tried to ignore the fact that her hair was gone as I placed the newspaper on the bed. 'I have to go,' she said into the receiver. 'It's him.'

Illness had made great and small modifications to Mrs Poole's face during those months. There was a certain shine in her cheeks, just where the bones pressed at the skin, and her lips were chapped. 'Have you no music?' I said.

'I'm just scunnered,' she said. 'Fed up with music.'

'That's a pity.'

'I've got this,' she said, pointing to a small unit shaped like an egg. The words 'Sound & Nature' were printed on the front. She twisted a grey knob and pressed a button: the sound of waves came surging into the room, water trickling onto sand, surf lapping over itself and gulls yelling above the waves. It suddenly felt absurd to hear these things amid the medical smells and signals of hospital efficiency. 'Sometimes you want to cut to the chase,' she said. 'These are natural sounds. I've been playing them through the day. At night too, sometimes, when I wake up and can't sleep. It's a very handy object. It makes me think of outside.'

The machine offered choices. The one we were listening to – the sea surf with urgent gulls – was called 'Ocean Beach', but one could also have 'Mountain Sunrise', a cacophony of singing birds and forest scrapings, or 'Gentle Stream', a noise to encourage the notion that one was idling beside a babbling brook. Mrs Poole leaned over and pressed the fourth button, 'Soothing Heartbeat', which seemed to suck all the action of the outside world into a single cell. 'This one is good at night,' she said. 'It just keeps going. It helps me think.'

I continued hearing the sound after she had turned it off. It played in my head like a stunning essay on the real and the imaginary. 'It's been a busy time in the parish,' I said.

'How's that?'

'Weddings,' I said. 'The parents seem to spend more and more money on outfits and dance bands. You should see the length of the limousines they hire. I was up at some of the houses, and all they ever talk about are the photographs and the cars.'

'Typical,' said Mrs Poole. 'You should put your foot down on that. You should tell them holy sacraments aren't about big cars. Plus they're wasting good resources and using up petrol. They all live within walking distance of the chapel. Why put out emissions for no reason?'

'Mass attendance is down, though.'

'That's right,' she said. 'They'll hire yer fancy photographers but they won't take their children to Mass. That's because the people round here are more interested in their mantelpieces than they are in their souls.'

'They have their moments,' I said. 'There was a great concert up at the Arranview Hospice. I led the prayers and some of them are very responsive. A very old lady – not in the best of health – wanted me to bless her room with holy water and say a decade of the rosary with her.'

'To improve her health?'

'No. She said it was in aid of her granddaughters, who are working the season in Jersey. She's worried about them. After the prayers and a cup of tea, the lady asked me to explain a word in her prayer book. "Manifestation".'

Mrs Poole looked at me with a second twinge of impatience. 'You've been doing some work in your parish, then,' she said. 'Well, at least that's something. I hope you didn't baffle the old woman with science.'

The quiet in the room was very different in texture from the quiet we used to enjoy in the rectory. Also different in meaning.

'I brought you a book,' I said.

'What is it?'

'An old one of my mother's. *A Parliament of Crows*.'

'What's it about?'

'Oh, the usual. Everything and nothing. It's about the lengths people will go to in order to remain unhappy.'

'Stop it. Your mother's good at what she does.' She turned the book in her hands and examined its cover.

'Indeed,' I said. 'It's a novel about the last years of Fanny Osbourne, the woman who married Robert Louis Stevenson. He was the one with the famous stories, of course, but Fanny had her stories too, secret ones. Her life was in some ways more interesting than his, according to my mother.'

Mrs Poole looked at me and licked her lips, as if to lubricate them out of her practised silence. Her face was pale. I poured some barley water into a glass and swigged it as she inspected the front page of the newspaper. 'It's a horrible world we're living in,' she said. 'I'll be glad to read the book rather than all this stuff.'

'The paper,' I said. 'No, it's not cheering.'

'Bloody shambles,' she said. 'Why don't we just leave people in peace?'

'Because some people don't know what peace is.'

'And you a good socialist as well.'

'Oh, that old chestnut,' I said. 'I'm just praying that things turn out well for everyone.'

'That'll be useful,' she said.

'Don't be sarcastic.'

'Well, don't be shallow. I'll tell you, Father David, I think you are getting more like those warmongers by the second.'

'No,' I said. 'Just by the decade.'

She tossed the paper further down the bed and I felt a slight tremor in the atmosphere as her mood changed. The more ill she got, the more eager she became to run me down on moral grounds. There was no longer an imagined life we could easily sustain together. 'You have more faces than the town clock,' she said.

I walked to the window and back and felt the sudden burden of her feelings towards me, her rising dislike, as if she imagined that I myself were master of all the world's wrongdoings. 'I think you expect too much of me, Mrs Poole,' I said. My words appeared to extinguish a light in her eyes, as if a person with bad breath had just blown out a candle.

'You are repulsive,' she said.

'I beg your pardon?'

'You are a coward. A hypocrite.'

'Mrs Poole, please . . .'

'What do you know of the world? Where have you been? Had you any life at all, ever?'

'I've had some.'

'You had none! None. I am nothing to you. We are all nothing to you. What do you care now for people? Oh, you had your five minutes of being the big man of action. Where was that? At Oxford University? Don't make me laugh. You told me about it yourself. You were the sort of person who had a chandelier when you were a student.'

'I've never spoken to anybody about my life.'

'And no wonder,' she said. 'There is no life. Nothing. It's all invisible with your kind. You had a good way of thinking once. Just once. How long did it last? A month? A year? And now you're like those warmongers, believing whatever it suits you to believe.'

'Mrs Poole,' I said, 'you're not well.'

'Aye,' she said. 'But I know what my illness is. What is yours?'

'Mrs Poole.'

'You talk about morality. What morality? I tried to do the right thing and Jack knows that. But everything is just lies. People just lie about who they are and you are just . . . you are just part of it.'

I said it was just the way she was feeling. I was a priest and that was what priests were here for, times of crisis. 'Oh, please,' she said. 'Don't make a hero of yourself every time.'

'The house misses you,' I said.

'No,' she said. 'You. It misses you. At least I'm there in my head.'

'Mrs Poole, let me help you.'

'I saw you with him. You *desecrated* that house. And I loved it there.'

'Yes,' I said. 'I loved it too.'

'The garden,' she said.

'It will always be there,' I said, and she turned her eyes to me, her eyes filled with tears and full of pity.

'You are a fool, Father,' she said. 'And I feel sorry for you. I really do. You don't know what you've done.'

I rubbed my hands with the alcohol cleanser by the sink, and it dried very cold on them. 'You know so much,' she said from the bed. 'Except loyalty. You know nothing about loyalty, Father.'

'Listen to the way you talk,' I said. 'You didn't learn that from your husband.'

'I know,' she said, quite sadly. 'I learnt it from you.'

There's a way of feeling homesick, not for any house, not for any particular place, but just feeling homesick as a manner of being alive, every day a sense of existing in exile from a place where you might belong. The Germans have a word for it: *Heimweh*. I sat in the chair and the chair was a momentary prison: Mrs Poole had her view of me now, and there was no way back to our jokes and our music. At last she put down my mother's book and smiled oddly.

'His name is Toby,' she said. 'My own son.'

She looked at the window, seeing something through the glass, I imagine, that none of us will ever see precisely the same way, not mere clouds and streaks of blue next to Arran but a vast and personal ether of possible rights and wrongs. She seemed to draw all confusion down from the sky and through the windows and into her lungs as she sat upright in the bed with her eyes shining.

'That's a fine name,' I said. 'Different.'

'I suppose you think it's very wrong,' she said, 'for a mother to give her child away to someone else. But Irene's a special person. I knew she would give him the life he deserves.'

'Everyone has their reasons,' I said.

'Yes,' she said. 'We do, don't we? I didn't save Jack or myself any unhappiness by it, but I think I saved the boy some.'

'Perhaps that's true.'

She looked at me. 'I had a great-aunt who did the same,' she said. 'She had a handicapped son. And she let my granny bring the boy up because she had a better husband. It worked out, but the boy never really knew his mother again, and that's how it goes.'

We sat for half an hour with our own thoughts, a nurse coming at one point to take a menu away. I washed my hands again with the alcohol cleanser and sat back down with things to say but no way to say them. 'Families,' said Mrs Poole after a while. 'More than anything, I didn't want to have the same disease as Jack's mother died of. I really didn't want that. I wanted to show him I was better.'

'You are better,' I said.

She smiled. 'See how easy it comes to you, Father? You didn't even know the woman.' She patted the sound machine on the bedside cabinet. 'You're just like this,' she said. 'You sound perfectly natural but you are not natural at all.'

I bought the fish at a little shop in Troon. It all lay there in the window on hillocks of crushed ice – the clear-eyed perch, the pike, eels and carp, the shellfish heaped all orange and black – everything framed not like a haul from that morning's boats, not like a piece of reality standing at the centre of an actual day but like a picture of freshness invented and frozen behind glass: a still life with haggis. I took the credit card from my pocket. 'David,' my mother had said years before when she handed me the card and told me to sign the back. 'Spend whatever you have to in order to be yourself. I don't care about money.'

In the kitchen, I took out a small knife. I sliced the fish into slivers and cooked them in the pan with a dozen small onions. I crushed six cloves of garlic and noticed the clock. The voices in the next room were rising together in soft agreement, giving way to one another, allowing the room's atmosphere to expand into the music coming from the corner speakers, an attempt by Schumann at something blithe. The book was balanced on a perspex stand: *Les meilleures recettes de ma pauvre mère* by M. Huguenin, a first edition from 1936. I did as I was told and added the butter little by little, after the wine, and I shook the pan and watched the flame and thought of my father's meanness at games. He had that horrible habit of thinking card games were a wonderful test of human character: those evenings in Heysham, he laid the cards out like a man exposing his best instincts. I used to get nervous playing games with him. So did my mother. 'You don't keep your cards in good order,' he said. 'Tidy your cards. Then see.'

The supper was for Bishop Gerard. He sat at the table, using his hands, as usual, to weigh the words he spoke, fondling the air in front of him, shaping their rhyme and reason. He appeared to think all said things were over-said, and no sooner had he come out with something than his hands would knead the words down from their clear, high summit of expression. He would grab the words back, to leaven them, to limit their potential for damage. One imagines the little he spoke was measured well enough before he opened his mouth, but that was never the end of it: he continued to inflect those phrases with his fingers, as if it were part of the body's function, or a bishop's function, to protect the world from the motions of the mind. This was a delicate, parsimonious business, one made odd by the look of the hands themselves: in their ruddy plumpness they showed evidence of some gouging work on the part of his ancestors.

'Now, David,' he said, 'what is this you're giving us?'

'Burgundian fish stew,' I said. 'A favourite recipe. I'm afraid I'll have to insist on you all drinking the wine in the prescribed order. No mixing the wine in your glasses, either. I'm feeling very bossy tonight.'

I put His Lordship at the head of the table, and, on either side of him, two priests from the nearby parishes of Dalry and Irvine. I have to confess it was Gerard who preferred that I ask Father Damian, a young, untutored, patriotic fool, encumbered with a giant chip and a very broad sense of class merit, the latter facet owing everything to the impeccable miserableness of his origins. He was thought to put all this resentment to very good use in the former mining town of Dalry.

The other guests were charming. Father Michael was fifty-something, bookish, perfectly capable, and I noticed, while giving out the stew, that his eyebrows had been trimmed with scissors. Michael knew how to enjoy himself and I always found him generous. That evening, he spoke little and ate a lot, just as Father Damian ate nothing and spoke incessantly. At the other end of the table I put Mr McCallum, the headmaster of St Andrew's, wearing a blue pinstripe suit and a thin smile of alcoholic amity. I was very glad of him, though everybody else found him troublesome, and perhaps – with hindsight's unsparing clarity – I can see that it was unfair of me to expose him to the rigours of such a supper, where ambition and obligation tinkled with such menace among the bottles.

I imagined McCallum might do well next to Angela Path. She was one of those rather likeable, big-laughing women, red-headed and plastic-bangled and impatiently lipsticked, cynical by experience and intrepid by temperament, one would have thought. At any rate, she was quite high up in the Dalgarnock social-work department. I saw her often as I went about my business, and I knew she liked dinners and liked saying all her monstrous things about men and oppression and so on. She made me laugh. She had a frightful tendency to use the word 'dichotomies'. She was into astrology and something in her manner suggested she mightn't believe anything she said, which is rather exciting in its own way.

She handed me a bottle of Beaujolais Nouveau. 'Right, listen,' she said. 'I've been keeping it since last November. Is that a mistake?'

'*Il est arrivé!*' I said and kissed her on both cheeks. I remember taking her rather theatrical coat and putting the bottle in the fridge. I came back to the sitting room with a sparkling Burgundy, by which time Angela was already laughing gutsily with the Bishop.

After serving the fish stew, I opened an Aligoté from Meursault, a very nice Clos Vougeot and a Musigny. 'These two are from vineyards right next to each other,' I said.

'I'm not really a wine man,' said Father Damian. 'You couldn't manage a wee whisky?'

'Ice?'

'You're joking, man,' said Damian. 'We don't have ice in our whisky up here. This is Scotland.'

'Oh.'

'Talk about sacrilegious.'

Damian looked to the Bishop for confirmation and received it with a careful ghost of a smile. Then the young priest made a cradle of his fork and scooped up some peas, while Gerard, I noticed, set about spearing each pea with his fork.

'A lovely glass of wine, that,' said Mr McCallum. 'Not too dry.'

'Each is from the same region as the recipe for the stew,' I said.

'Very nice,' said Mr McCallum. Then he blushed. 'You certainly know your way around a menu, Father David.'

'It was ever thus,' said the Bishop.

'It must have cost you,' said Father Damian.

'Oh,' I said, 'we don't discuss that.'

'It was ever thus,' said the Bishop, but again good-naturedly. I went to the cupboard and brought back a bottle of Laphroaig and sat it down in front of Damian. He sniffed as some people do when they feel they are required to make a polite response.

'That'll do,' he said.

'What a totally divine concoction,' said Angela, speaking of the fish stew. 'You can taste the sea. Is that not what they say, Bishop?'

'You'll know better than me, I'm sure,' he said. 'But it's interesting, you know, when it comes to the sea.' The Bishop put down his fork and began moving his hands. 'I've always been quite nervous of it. I don't like the sea one bit. Of course, the gospels have a great deal to say about the sea, and where would the human family be without it? I think of Galilee and the Apostles out there with Christ. I get the message of all that, of course, but I never liked the actual water myself. That's my own opinion. And I stick to it. I think the ocean is a very overrated thing.'

'Well, perhaps if you walked on it, Bishop,' said Angela. 'I don't know if you've quite got to that yet. Ha! But they say it's a nice stroll once you get used to it.'

A moment of cordial laughter curled around the table.

'I'm willing to see it as a family thing,' said the Bishop. 'My people came from County Monaghan. That's a landlocked county. We don't have a strong sense of the sea.'

'That's a pity, Gerard,' I said. 'The sea is a great fund of miracles. And we have crossed a great many seas to be where we are now.'

'That's true,' said Father Michael.

'And we are fisher priests,' I said.

'You need to beware what you catch,' said Father Damian. He laughed loudly at his own remark and Angela joined him, though there was something rather different in the tone of each person's mirth. I cast a look in the direction of the Bishop.

'Untoward, Father Damian,' he said.

'Sorry, My Lord,' said Damian. 'Just one of my wee jokes. You can't get far in this world without a wee joke, sure you can't.'

'Well, I grew up by the sea,' I said.

'In England,' said Damian, but I ignored him, addressing my remarks to the ruby-coloured cheeks of Mr McCallum.

'It enters your daily business,' I said, 'whether you work the waters or not.' I paused. 'I think perhaps people who grew up by the sea have a different feeling about nationhood. You have this country at your back, one's own country, and one is standing on it, but facing out to sea you tend to think of other countries. The world beyond.'

'And you like other nations, do you, David?' asked the Bishop.

I poured some wine for the others and myself. There happened to be a small element of criticism in Gerard's voice, and I would, in normal circumstances, have found it a natural part of the joshing that had existed between us for many years. But we call for extra loyalty from old friends when we have a new adversary in our midst. At that supper, with Father Damian smirking into his tumbler, the Bishop's words seemed mocking. I don't know if he was aware of it, but his hard words were made harder by the soft gesticulations of his fingers: behind the guard of seasoned camaraderie, he was giving licence to his neighbour, the young priest, who only took strength from the Bishop's prosecuting tone.

'Other nations?' I said. 'Well, I have cared for them a great deal in the past, Gerard, as you know. But one gets older. Perhaps one looks more inwardly as time goes on. In any event, I am sure I care much less about other nations than I once did.'

'Ha! That's a bit of a danger,' said Angela. 'You don't want to become complacent. We're in a strange place right now, with every country feeling their sovereignty matters above all others. I mean, we live in a time when an American life is taken to be a far more valuable thing than any other sort of life, especially a Muslim one.'

'Surely not,' said Mr McCallum.

'Every time,' said Angela. 'Now, you men like to talk about the sanctity of life . . .'

'Oh, heavens,' said the Bishop. 'Let's not get into that this evening.'

'Forgive me, sir,' she said, 'but you all talk about the sanctity of life. And so does the Christian Right in America. You want everything that can be born to be born, am I right? But when you're talking about actual lives – people already living – the Americans have a rather different notion. What notion of the sanctity of life informs the carpet-bombing in Iraq?'

The Bishop raised a finger to stall other contributions. 'The Church agrees with you,' he said. 'The Holy Father agrees. We are not always in a position to direct national feelings, but the substance of your comment is not offensive to a Catholic ear.'

Father Michael put down his fork. 'Things have changed,' he said. 'I'm sure it comforts a great many intelligent people to see America as the great enemy. But what progressive country didn't have an eye for its own interests? The country we are sitting in, Scotland, has been looking after its own interests since the beginning, as anyone who has looked into the colonial experience in India or Africa or Canada will tell you. Yes, our countries wish to be rich and they wish to be powerful.'

'Bravo, Michael,' I said. 'And when I was young . . .'

'When you were young,' said Bishop Gerard.

'Yes,' I said. 'When I was young, we were moved sometimes to oppose capitalism or whatever you want to call it. We hated Wilson.'

'You had a stomach for the game, then,' said Father Damian.

'You were a baby,' I said. 'And it wasn't a game.'

'It wasn't a game,' said Father Michael.

'Students,' said Angela. 'You're talking about being a student, when you all had your five minutes of thinking it was possible for people to live in peace and harmony.'

'It wasn't five minutes, it was another world,' said Father Michael. 'Different from this one.'

'It was just the same,' said Angela. 'The same powers in the west trying to dominate everybody else. Making war for their own profit.'

'Exactly,' said Father Damian. 'You may have changed sides but the same agenda informs what's happening.'

'That's right,' said Angela. 'It's definitely a political agenda.'

'Look,' I said. 'We wanted America to leave the people of Vietnam to build their own society. But now? There are leaders in the Middle East harming their own people. A nest of caliphs. They want nuclear weapons. People who are not merely sentimental in their politics will see that we must gather our forces to prevent them. It is a dirty job.'

'It's immoral!' said Father Damian. 'We have no right.'

'People will die,' I said. 'And people in the likes of Texas will be allowed to feel their lives are more important. But many of those Middle Eastern leaders are fascists. Those terrorists are fascists. They have no sense of the value of life, and if we are civilised people then we will help the people of Iraq or Iran or the Sudan out of the dark. It is our moral duty.'

'Man alive,' said Angela. 'Moral duty? I didn't realise I had been invited to the Republican National Convention.'

She put down her glass as if the wine suddenly appalled her.

'Nobody agrees with him,' said Father Damian. 'Nobody here.'

'I agree with him,' said Father Michael. 'You are not thinking about the issue. You are only thinking about the consistency of your own positions, and that is totally narrow. We know Saddam fears democracy. We know he hurts his own people.'

'On whose evidence?' said Angela. 'We were selling him arms only a couple of years ago. It's a terrible dichotomy.'

'We should be ashamed of having armed them or having appeased them,' said Father Michael. 'But we are where we are. And we have been here before. These dictators want to hurt people and now they want nuclear weapons and they have to be stopped or else we are cowards and not worthy of our resolutions.'

'What are you two *thinking*?' she said, and you could tell from the look on her charming face that she simply didn't believe it was possible for anybody to say what Michael had just said. 'America at the moment is only about self-interest. The children on the streets could tell you that.'

'And we should listen to them,' said Father Damian.

'You're promoting a religious war,' said Angela. 'It's not about the poor people of the Middle East. It's about oil.'

'Do you mind?' said Mr McCallum, and he reached his arm over for the Musigny.

'By all means,' I said.

'It's about protecting Israel,' said Father Damian.

'Israel is a rather unfortunate nation,' I said, 'with rather unfortunate leaders. But I think you are wrong. It is about protecting people from being gassed by their own leaders. It is about protecting women from being executed in public places. And it is about stopping terrorists and unstable governments from getting their hands on these weapons, weapons that Iraq and Iran would certainly seek to use, if they had them. We are not being mature if we imagine what these governments seek is a nuclear deterrent.'

'There are no weapons!' said Angela and Father Damian, almost in unison.

'They have these weapons in their minds,' said Father Michael. 'And that is enough for me and should be enough for anybody.'

'Excuse me, pal,' said Father Damian.

'Yes,' said the social worker, growing flushed. 'There's an irony here, in that the only country ever to use one of your weapons is America.'

'History is imperfect,' I said. 'And so is America. But the world is too dangerous now. We may, each of us, have to trade in a little of our old idealism for the sake of new realities.'

'This is disgusting,' said Father Damian. 'You are blind. We have joined the Americans, trying to capitalise on a situation, trying to get a foothold in the Middle East, trying to protect their own interests. America used the thing in New York as an excuse for an invasion. You're blind if you don't see that. We had Iraq in our sights for years. The Americans scared everybody into thinking the Iraqis had chemical weapons ready to explode in every city in the west. You're *blind*.'

'There are good reasons . . .' said Father Michael.

'No, there are not!' said Father Damian. 'They're all despicable.'

His plate was almost untouched and he seemed to include it and everything around it in his denunciation. He raised his voice again.

'Our government has lost the plot. You have lost the plot. We nurtured these nutcases over there, and now that it's no longer in our interests we want to bomb them. There are no weapons.'

'There may be,' I said.

'There are none! We have been lied to. There are no suitcases exploding in Washington. It's all a fantasy, a shocking fantasy. And people like you are propping it up. Let us say the Iraqi government is no good. Well, it's the business of the people of Iraq to mobilise against it. Not us, forcing our views on cultures we barely understand. I'll tell you something, Father. It's arrogance. Nothing but arrogance. And we'll pay for it, a thousand-fold. We are currently tramping over ancient religious places. Not my religion. Not yours, either. But you talk about people living in darkness. This will unleash the darkness. It already has. Just you wait.'

'David,' said the Bishop, joining his hands, 'we must not ignore what our vocation tells us. It tells us to understand the hate in the eyes of our enemies. We have not done that, in this case. We have not sought to understand ourselves or them. America has simply closed its eyes and pulled the trigger, and we have followed them in that. We have flattered ourselves into thinking there is nothing to understand, but that is no way to defend ourselves. That is an offensive action. Everything we have done speaks of some smallness of vision. That is where we are. And in the process we have not lessened hatred – not at all. We have increased hatred and made it noble in the eyes of millions.'

'It was always noble in their eyes.'

'You believe that?'

'We have arrived at different places, Gerard,' I said. 'Out of the past, we have come to different places. My view has not changed, or not much. The vista has changed, and what we are looking at is not the same as Vietnam.'

'You are blind,' said Angela. 'This is serious. We're in a really problematic situation here.'

'It does the Church no favours,' said Father Damian, 'that we should be harbouring people who think such things, support such hatred.'

'Harbour?' said Father Michael. He leaned his elbows among the bottles and looked straight at his colleague. 'Forgive me, but people like you will do anything before you'll renovate your views. You'll *say* anything before you'll ask yourself a difficult question.'

Father Damian looked at me as if I was responsible for a possible rift with the older gentleman.

'The difference between now and the past,' he said, 'the past that you have turned your backs on, is that America has now forced the world into being a place that is dominated by some fairly primitive notions of good and evil. You're either with them or against them. You're either part of their good or an ally of evil forces.'

'You're a Catholic priest,' I said. 'Isn't that what we always believed ourselves? Isn't that our creed?'

'Rubbish!'

'Really? I don't think so. We spend our days being rather certain about where goodness lies and where evil prevails.'

'Good and evil,' said the Bishop. 'Too much for one supper.'

'No basis for foreign policy,' said Angela.

'Well, it's our policy in everything else,' I said.

Bishop Gerard looked down and ran a fingernail along the edge of his napkin, before looking up, not quite at me, and smiling broadly.

'Scotland has always been a socialist country,' he said. 'And some forms of wisdom are hard to import. Perhaps the English, perhaps the Americans have lost some sense of subtlety when it comes to the handling of good and evil. We see it differently here in Scotland.'

'Don't be patronising, Gerard,' I said. 'Perhaps the people of Scotland are above their own nationalist fixations. Young Scottish men have died over there.'

'Yes,' he said. 'We continue to pray for them.'

'Indeed,' I said.

'Don't fret about it, David,' he said. 'You have many people on your side. You even have some Scots on your side: the cabinet is filled with them. Scotsmen of some description.'

The table was nodding in agreement, except Father Michael, and I had the feeling that anything I might say could only serve to make my guests more satisfied with themselves and their certainties.

'I hate your assumptions,' said Angela. 'From where I'm sitting, the Americans seem like the biggest terrorists of all.'

'Aye,' said Father Damian. 'You don't *get* it, our way of thinking. We can judge for ourselves what is good and what is evil.'

'In a town like this,' I said, 'with the history of bigotry and Orangeism and everything else, you're going to give me a lecture about the fair-mindedness of the Scottish people? About their working-class camaraderie and feeling for the international poor? Their native opposition to economic self-interest? Their inclusiveness?'

'Ha!' said Mr McCallum.

'In the name of Jesus, Gerard,' I said. 'A girl in Glasgow had her throat cut in broad daylight the other month for wearing a Celtic scarf. Two asylum seekers were thrown off the top of a block of flats not ten miles from here. You know why? Because they were not from around here. Please spare me your homily about the glory of the tribe.'

'Oh, the tribe,' said Mr McCallum, drunkenly. 'That's a good one.'

Events often move more slowly in the memory than they do in life. As I remember it, the dinner, which had started in my mind as a showcase of personal delights, moved achingly towards discord, but really we covered many topics that night and there was laughter at the table. Ms Path had a wonderful manner of chivvying the men's religious certainties with counter-dogmas of the feminist kind. As I collected the plates and made my way to the kitchen to get pudding, she rolled a cigarette and lobbed one of her infelicities in the direction of Father Damian. 'It's ironic,' she said, 'that your Pope has so much time for the Virgin Mary. You'd have thought her being of the female persuasion might have bothered him.'

'What you saying?' asked Father Damian. 'The Church doesn't approve of women?'

'You prefer saints,' she said. 'Bless the Pope. But he's much more understanding of celestial bodies than he is of women's.'

'That's polytechnic speak,' he said, at which point, not unfunnily, her side of the table became a hubbub of statistics and dichotomies. Bishop Gerard spoke of a visit he had recently made to Rome and of a meeting with Pope John Paul at which the old man had sat on a chair lower than the bishops. 'That's the sort of man he is,' said Gerard.

In the kitchen, I looked down at the board and decided the cheese was too *recherché* for its waiting audience, so I took the stranger things away, meaning the French and English cheeses, leaving among the muscat grapes a clump of cheddars that reeked of the Western Isles. Next to the kettle my mobile was beeping to show a text had arrived. I hadn't seen the young people for a week, but they were the only ones who sent me texts. The beeping phone felt like a gift. It turned out the message came from Lisa's phone and I remember being disappointed at how short it was:

It's Mark. Watch out 4 cops. I'm sorry.

And I wrote back:

How come?

As I organised the bowls and opened a Beaumes de Venise, there was silence from the phone. Mark had never again mentioned the night we ended up in the rectory, the night of the dancing and the kiss. I thought it was just like the text: he had my attention for a second or two before dropping me for something more instant and vivid. 'Oh, Mark,' I thought, 'what on earth have you got to be sorry about?' And I glanced at the window and thought of them out there in the dark.

'David,' said the Bishop, 'do you ever hear anything from your old monks, the ones from Ampleforth?'

'I don't,' I said. 'I never hear of them. There were one or two very good ones. To be honest, one never thinks of school now.'

'David went to a very good school.'

'It was a long time ago,' I said.

'A famous one,' he said. 'Down in Yorkshire.'

'It's all in the past,' I said.

'I don't think so,' said Father Damian, pressing his bowl forward and putting a balled-up napkin in the middle. He winked horribly. 'You still have a touch of the lobster salad about you,

Father.' He laughed at this and solicited grim chuckles from his neighbours, and I knew my lips had grown so thin as to form a line under the possibility of any future interaction with that boring little man.

'Well, that is to our benefit this evening,' said Bishop Gerard.

I wasn't wise and I knew it. A less disaffected person than myself, a more reliable person, would have known easily how to placate the priest from Dalry, how to flatter his small notions and deliver him somewhat from his native aggression. He wasn't a tall order. A few simple manoeuvres would have calmed him down. But I know too much about how life-smothering people like that are, how seedy in their negative requirements, and so I gave him the full force of the snob he craved. 'In this house,' I said to him over the cheeseboard, 'we pass the port clockwise.'

'In this country,' he said, 'we don't drink port.'

Father Damian stared at me with pity, and I knew in that second that he and I had not the merest understanding of one another, and that in itself was a kind of understanding.

The Bishop dropped his napkin onto the table and clasped his hands together. 'We have circumnavigated the globe this evening,' he said, 'and here we are back in Scotland once more. Thank you for such an ample supper, David. We are a generous people ourselves and we mark generosity in others.'

Father Damian was staring into space.

'A frank exchange of views is an invigorating thing,' the Bishop added.

'Indeed,' said Father Michael.

'Then let an old Glasgow hand have the final word,' said the Bishop. 'It is the modern world: we do not have all the answers, but in Scotland I believe it is our oldest habit to Live and Let Live.'

'That's right,' said Father Damian. 'We are too busy with practical things to harp on about good and evil.'

Bishop Gerard dipped his eyes at him. 'The last word,' he said.

Once they had gone, I tied the last of the black bags and started up the dishwasher. Mrs Poole would certainly have objected to my putting the bottles into the rubbish bags, but I did so all the same and put the bags by the side of the house. It wasn't especially cold, but I felt the chill somehow. Up in my bedroom I built a fire and sat for hours with the purr of the flames and the thought of absent friends.

I woke in the chair when I heard a noise.

Tish, tish, at the window.

The town glowed yellow beyond the parted curtains. On the chapel roof the starlings were sleeping in their black corners, a soft web of Ayrshire rain shining the slates and covering the statue of Our Lady at the doors with a sheen of cold perspiration. Somewhere, I could hear pigeons cooing, and somewhere further, deeper than that, the sound of a police siren waking the mind and binding the night.

Tish, tish.

I heard anticipation in my own breathing as I stood half concealed, but there was no surprise: I knew it would be one or other of the young people. Through the dark I could see it was Lisa standing on the path with wet hair. She was underdressed, as usual, and overdressed at the same time, her arms folded against the chill and her eyes glistening with tears.

'It's awright, Father,' she whispered. 'I don't want tae come in. Just open the windae and talk tae me.'

Freshness came into the room, and I heard a sudden rush from the trees at the end of the lane, the breeze like an ambush of voices among the leaves. Beneath the open window, Lisa was looking up, saying, 'Father, Father.'

'What's the matter?'

'He stole ma phone. He's off his face, Father. I'm like: what did you do that for? And he's like: you don't have a clue what's goin' on. His da made him go to the police station and somethin's happening.'

'Don't worry, Lisa,' I said.

'You need to know,' she said. 'It's gonnae be bad news.'

'Don't pay any attention,' I said. 'Go home and go to sleep. You'll get your phone back, I'm sure.'

Her eyes were filled with fear and soap opera. The moment was both terrible for her and exhilarating, and I tried to say nothing.

'But you need tae watch what you're doin', Father. You don't know what they're like. They want to get somebody and I'm not joking.'

'Don't worry, Lisa. Go on home.'

'I was always your friend,' she said.

'I know. You're a nice girl. Go on home.'

Walking across the room, I began then to remember what Cardinal Manning said of Cardinal Wiseman, writing of the latter's slow and ponderous death. 'It was like the hours of a still afternoon,' he wrote, 'when the work of the day begins to linger, and the silence of evening is near.' We were beyond that now. The evening had given way to the night's cold equation of sadness and desire, and I felt the comfort of knowing it as I stared into the fire and felt the heat on my face. On the rug at the side of the armchair I found a dead butterfly covered in dust.

Red Cardinal, I said. But I saw my mistake: *Red Admiral*.

I can still see those creatures fluttering in pairs over the Fellows' Garden at Balliol. I recall them too as caterpillars, black with orange stripes, those languid bugs feeding at night on violets. His name was Conor, the man whom I loved in those days, and my mind flooded with thoughts of him as I placed the dry butterfly in the fire and saw it consumed into nothingness, the energy going out from that tiny body now glowing white hot in a cradle of burning coals.

8

BALLIOL

Memory is a kind of friendship, a friendship with the more necessary parts of oneself. How often do we reach for the past's genial knowledge to meet the unknowables of the present, asking once again that the anterior world might blossom into life and colour the current day? In this at least I cannot be alone. Oxford both made and unmade me, the temper of my affections as much as the idle drone of conscience, the loyalty to youth as much as the persistent hope of some better conversation with the dead.

It was all Oxford. It was all the work of those grey, damp buildings between the Broad and the High, and it comes to me yet by daily instalments, some fresh footfall on the college gravel, some wafting smell of soup and furniture polish from the inner sanctum. Each of life's non-trivial events brings me again to those years. Every other day I am back in the grasp of that marvellous time, sitting in the evening by the lake at Worcester, listening to music, waving midges from around my head, watching people across the grass.

'I was a modest, good-humoured boy,' said Max Beerbohm. 'It was Oxford that made me insufferable.' When I left Ample-forth and those serious, faithful, unfinished men, I now see that I must have been quite filled with the epic action of other people's belief. Plainsong had lodged itself, you might say, in my inner ear, and I suppose even then I knew the monks had begun something that couldn't be unbegun. I came up to Balliol for Michaelmas Term, 1965.

A bottle of malt whisky supplied by my mother. A bag of novels and history texts bought at Blackwell's. A sack containing a chandelier courtesy of my mother's sister, Aunt Jean. And a pristine copy of *Rubber Soul*. These are the things I had in my Lancashire suitcase that first term, along with some old-fashioned clothes I soon replaced. I bought some drinking glasses and a raffia mat, arranged everything just so, put up the chandelier with the help of a borrowed stepladder and stood in the middle of the room feeling proud and independent as I stared at a window patterned with early ice. It was the coldest October on record.

As a young man I didn't believe anything was true unless I'd read about it first. I was addicted to guidebooks and miniature histories, always seeking to augment the work of my eyes and ears, wanting history and precedence to upbraid my inexperience and temper every intuition. None of my initial contemporaries knew anything about Balliol except that it had Trinity over the wall and was brainier than some, but I thought I knew everything worth knowing, including the names and great deeds of its former Masters: John Wyclif, whose religious teachings gave rise to the Lollards, and Benjamin Jowett, who wanted to 'inoculate England with Balliol'. I must have liked the notion of being among the ghosts of great men, for I'd lapped up their stories before I knew my tutors or had settled properly in my rooms. I read Hopkins and Swinburne and Arnold before I came up, and they turned me into someone, I suppose; at least, they got me ready – not Swinburne, he hated the place – for what I imagined would be a beautiful escape into 'mystic eloquence'.

The spirit of Oxford, at least among the people I took up with in those lazy, leather-jacketed days before change became the only anthem, was slightly in thrall to the dead boys of the Great War. It was those benighted undergraduates – wraiths, every one, and clichés, passing through the quadrangles with their gowns and golden hair – who fed one's notion of what it meant to be a son of Oxford and a servant of the world. Their absence came to mind with the toll of the bells; for me, and such as me, an image of courage and folly and blighted hope hovered somewhere above the spires and cupolas, though I can't be sure they survived the 1960s in the form we knew them.

Great snowfalls filled November. My early days were spent next to an electric heater, rubbing a spyhole on the frosted pane of my window and looking down into the Garden Quad from Staircase XI to see the trees shagged with snow. From the bed, it looked as if exotic birds had brushed the windows with their great feathers, and I lay back and thought of Ampleforth. Occasionally I ventured out to a lecture. But the window soon cleared and voices began to enlarge themselves at Balliol; winter changed to spring and I never went home, finding my feet in the library and in persevering visits to the Dominican church and study house of Blackfriars. Later, when wisteria had grown unchecked over the buildings on my side of the college, I took a room for the summer in a guesthouse in Jericho run by a spying matriarch with varicose veins. She had me down for a misfit. 'I don't mind the occasional cigarette,' she said. 'I'm a brandy woman, myself. If you meet some friends you can ask them into the sitting room for a glass in front of the fire, if you like. Long as they take off their shoes. I hate loud talkers and manky shoes on the carpet.'

Friends emerged over the following year. I was reading History and got in with a wonderful host of wine-bibbing undergraduates, some from Balliol but others from Christ Church and a Welsh guy from Jesus – or, as they would have said, Beggars, the House and Jeggers – who were reading French or English and were delinquent in the old style while professing to be very high-minded. Edward Hippisley-Cox was an ugly former Etonian with a valiant attitude towards the smoking of cigars. He was a good painter too: he did a portrait of me sitting in my college rooms, which I took from place to place in the years that followed and which finished up in the rectory at Dalgarnock. He was very funny, Edward, inordinately fond of names and literary trivia. When I first met him, he was especially keen on names for people's wives and mothers. He liked it, for example, that Rimbaud called his mother 'Shadowmouth', and liked it no less that Zola called Cezanne's mistress 'La Boule'.

Curtis Wenderoth was the son of a New York dentist. He later became a leading light in psychiatry at Harvard and wrote a number of camp plays and musicals. There were half a dozen more in the group, but Edward and Curtis led the procession. This involved some rather staged champagne parties in their rooms, hours of backgammon, interminable lunches at the Gridiron Club, afternoon pranks that usually relied on an attempt by Curtis and his acolytes to intoxicate the deer in Magdalen Grove, or else evenings spent sitting on deckchairs under the mulberry tree next to the Fellows' Garden at Balliol, some of us lolling on the grass and competing to see who could remember the most stuff from Proust.

'The sun's fading,' Edward said. 'In this light you look very American, old sausage. I believe you are making a great effort to be handsomely American. Is that so?'

'Reason not the effort,' said Curtis.

'You look rather angelic.'

'I've been in the Park Avenue sun.'

Edward sniggered into a paper cup. 'Who had a horror of sunsets?' he said.

'Mme de Cambremer,' said Curtis instantly.

'And why?' said Edward, biting the cup.

'She found them so operatic,' said Curtis, with a flash of his good Yankee teeth.

'Damn your eyes,' said Edward. 'You're wickedly good.' I was lying on the grass beside them, taking in the sky and the sound of some minor bell when the thought struck.

'He's more generous than good,' I said. 'Aren't you, Curtis? This wine is ridiculous. Sweeter than chocolate mice. How much of your daddy's tooth money went on this?'

'Who cares?' he said.

'Reason not the care,' I said. 'Eddie, how much do you reckon for the goodly bottle of weggers?'

'An insurmountable number of cruel-faced dollars,' said Edward. 'And I raise my glass to it, every cent. I raise my cup to Curtis Sr's heavenly skill with the back molars.'

'Generosity's my middle name,' said Curtis, drinking back the last of his cup and lightly burping.

'Now!' I said. 'Of whom, in the big book, is it conjectured that he understood that generosity is often no more than the inner aspect which our egotistical feelings assume when we have not yet named them?'

'Swann, naturally,' said Curtis. 'And it's not just named them but "named and classified them".'

'Bugger!' I said.

'Not comprehensively,' Edward said.

'Altruism that is without egoism is sterile,' Curtis said.

'Curtis, you are amazing,' I said. 'Even thinking about self-esteem adds to your self-esteem.'

'You sound like the Brasenose radicals,' he said. 'Of course, radicals do the same thing. They grow fat on caring about other people's thinness. But they don't call it self-esteem. They call it selflessness.'

'Bravo!' said Edward.

'I'm afraid we are the best endowed of men,' said Curtis. 'And the radicals would say that of themselves, and indeed, the men the radicals pity would say it too of their men. "The optics of our social perspective makes every grade of society seem the best to him who occupies it." Eddie: which volume? There's a good Beaumes de Venise in it and I want page numbers.'

'Volume Four,' said Edward. 'I can't say which page. Early.'

'How early?' said Curtis.

'Within the first hundred paggers.'

'Just,' said Curtis. 'But I choose to accept your half-knowledge and the pleading expression on your English kisser.'

'You have a wonderfully bad character,' I said to Curtis.

He didn't deny it. He opened another bottle under the secrecy of his carefully torn winter coat. 'You remember Mme Verdurin's party, where she confesses to not feeling bad about her friend's illness?'

'Yes,' I said. 'Mme Verdurin kept dwelling on her want of grief, not without a certain proud satisfaction.'

'Ten points,' said Edward. 'Yes, she thought it was stylish not to care.'

'Not caring added to her self-esteem,' said Curtis.

'Precisely,' said Edward. He leaned up on his elbow. 'Anderton. For extra points. And a decent swig of Wenderoth's bottle. What did she smell of at her party – Mme Verdurin?'

A cloud moved gently overhead. 'Easy,' I said. 'She smelled of the far-from-pleasant odour of rhino-gomenol.'

'Blessings!' shouted Edward.

'Because she gets colds after she weeps,' I added. 'And a student rubs her lip with the stuff before the music begins.'

'Not quite,' said Curtis, topping up the mug that stood on the grass next to my arm. 'Not her lip, Davvers. He "greases her nose" with the rhino-gomenol.'

'I dispute it,' I said.

'Don't be boring.'

'No, I'm disputing it. The stuff is on her lip.'

'Son of a gun,' Curtis said, before sloping off to his rooms to consult his well-worn Scott Moncrieff.

'He's right, my dear,' said Edward, after he'd gone.

'I know,' I said. 'But he didn't take the bottle.'

That is how it was with us: fifty years out of date. People at Oxford during my time didn't pride themselves on being original. Being wisely unoriginal was more in the style of the time. It felt so new for people to pick and choose the possibilities for themselves, and where they didn't choose to join their personal hungers to a movement – though many did, giving the 1960s its famous reputation – they became like Edward Hippisley-Cox, a very self-conscious, lurid amalgam of borrowings from the beautiful past. 'One is an A to B sort of person, darling,' said Edward. 'From Aubrey Beardsley to Anthony Blanche.'

'Oh, heavens,' I said. 'Proust is one thing, but *Brideshead*?'

'Don't be difficult,' he said. 'One discovers oneself to be nostalgic for nothing so much as nostalgia.'

In my day, groups at Oxford never gave themselves names but were given them by other people, often their opponents. One of the student radicals called us the Marcellists, owing to our irritating addiction to Proust's big book, and, exactly one day later, Edward arrived in the Junior Common Room to announce that the radicals and associated worshippers of Mao and haters of Lyndon Johnson were to be known forthwith as the Bombastics. To me it was an amusing Swiftian extravaganza, the Marcellists and the Bombastics. 'More like *West Side Story*,' said Curtis. 'They've taken over the goddamn Union with their gruesome red book. Best place for them. They simply adore the Vietcong. *Quelle horreur*.'

As befitted his Eton background, Edward liked to drink only in the dingiest, most hangdog of Oxford bars. He liked places stained yellow with nicotine and full of darkened brass, as if to conform to some Baudelairean stereotype. That's why he favoured the Grapes, just off the Cornmarket. 'Hark,' he said one afternoon when a workman stopped at the bar. 'It's the People. Godders in heaven. Ask him if he's one of zem undergradders sponsored till the end of time by the National Union of Mineworkers.'

'Stop it, Eddie,' I said.

'Comely, comely, Anders, my delicious,' he said – that's how he spoke all the time, even to his mother – 'we've got to get the laughers going before the old death cracks in. Mightens we scoff a glass of the old Pope's Chartreuse before you shove off to your boring concertina?'

One of Edward's great attractions lay in his mysterious, rather mature acquaintanceship with London. He was forever going up on the train with a fiver in his pocket. He came back speaking of Muriel's and dirty bars in Soho, and speaking about them, too, in the half-cocked Polari he must have picked up in those places. It was the sort of queer world I'd never considered. But Eddie kept us all informed, sneaking back to Oxford on Monday afternoons like a drowned ferret, his lips rather blue and his eyes empty of wonder.

'Your portraits are good, Eddie,' I said. 'You should do more of them. Make a bit of money. Get some of those London bods to have a look at them. You've got a touch.'

'Oh, darling,' he said. 'You're rotten sweet to say that, but it isn't true. I'll be painting my face from here to eternity, but that's about it.'

The Bombastics were up in the corner of the Grapes one night. Edward was swathed in fifteen miles of scarf, smoking Sweet Aftons one after the other like he was taking some vile medicine. He gazed semi-lovingly at the People as the smoke and the scarf unfurled. The Bombastics always had papers spread out among the beer jugs. They leaned over them, their faces burning with some great intensity or other. Some of that crowd later became known among the *Enragés* of 1968, but then, before Paris, before Berkeley, before Prague, they just ran action groups and committees and won their debates with enormous ease. It was obvious even to the terminally pretentious that these ruddy youths had the times on their side.

'Capture the horror,' said Edward. 'Over in the black corner there, the Ban the Bombastics.'

'Yes,' I said. 'Jolly serious.'

'Dreaming the good dream, my dear,' said Edward. 'Flying stolen helicopters for the Vietcong. Handing over the keys of the kingdom to dem dat's as black as the Ace. Oh, stoppers. Sinking a few punts in a tough stand against the Toggers.'

'The whatters?'

'The Torpids Boat Race, my dear,' said Edward. 'You really must keep up, Anderton. Life is rotten slow.'

Oxford invented gunpowder, bottled ale, the Church of England and gilded youth. It also invented the MG car. But its greatest addition to the glory of nations, in my view, was Geoffrey Nashe, my favourite tutor at Balliol and the greatest Frenchman England ever produced.

Nashe kept a set of oak-panelled rooms filled with first editions and daft French postcards. Outside of religion (which he laughed at, thinking it 'all poppycock and painted idols'), he was to become my captain in all issues relating to the mind and how to capitalise on a little devoted reading. When I first came to him, he had just published his monumental work on the strategies and manners of the mob during the French Revolution. It made him famous, the first sign of which was a sharp increase in the amount of sherry he doled out during our weekly tutorials. He was small in stature, about sixty-two I'd have said, with silver hair that seemed slick and moulded like a helmet over his head. Everything about Nashe was the opposite of hostile: he wore round tortoise-shell glasses, a succession of green cardigans, he liked booze and was forever shaking his watch at his ear, waiting for time to move on and jokes to improve.

Nashe took what you might call the anti-Carlyle view of history: it wasn't the bigwigs that concerned him so much as the ones wearing aprons stained with blood and sweat. This was clear from his interest in the flower-sellers and butchers of the French Revolution, but, even more so, from the way he spoke about himself and his own background. Those years with Nashe left me with a full picture of the great historian's personal England, a place which, in his animated telling, could seem to outline all the parameters of English life, a view which included, I'm afraid, the notion that the better part of civilised experience began with the boat to France.

He grew up in the riverless town of Tunbridge Wells, and he used every square inch of it – the blackberry thickets, the efforts of the Luftwaffe to bomb the town, the speech of his mother's friends, their sensible shoes, their gins and tonics at five o'clock, their watercolours of Scottish glens – to describe a notion of middle-class contentment that he made seem a matter of history to me, my childhood's holy details having temporarily faded in a blur of ambition, the prevailing upward draught of the scholarship boy. 'I am attempting to illustrate a society both immensely self-confident and largely immune from class conflict and social tension,' he would say, before going on to give a short history of the manufacture of Romary's Water Biscuits in Tunbridge Wells. That was how he did it – 'they were the very cream of middle-class biscuits' – and more than any single thing in my life it was Nashe's method that revealed to me the raw material of history and the inconspicuous material of oneself.

Nashe spoke about Sussex as if it were Babylon, which I suppose it was from the perspective of Tunbridge Wells. He had strange cousins, the Pemberton-Aulds, who did nothing all day and who had ignored the war playing cards in Lewes, and he expressed their decadence as a matter relating to the downfall of the English counties. Not that he was at all socialistic. He adored privilege, counting it among those traditions that enlarged the life of good taste, but he was one of those, unlike me, who held his public school (Shrewsbury, in his case) personally responsible for what he called 'the British tendency to ridicule passion'. He sometimes mentioned the host of satirical young men – 'the *Private Eye* crowd' – who came through Shrewsbury and Oxford in the years just before me. But more often he told the story of Daniel Plunkett, an Irish friend from school who had murdered his mother and tried to put her dead body over the cliffs of Howth in a faulty car. Just as Nashe wasn't a socialist, he wasn't a Freudian either. 'Too programmatic,' he'd say, before outlining, in his anecdotal way, the general faults of mothers and the shocks of the Irish legal system.

'Aha!' he said one morning in his Balliol rooms. 'The mind of the college was expressing itself the other evening.'

'How so?' I asked.

'I brought my friend to dine in college. You may have heard me speak of him, a gentleman by the name of Plunkett. He killed his mother over a quantity of money. She was a terrible wretch and an hysteric, poor woman. Yet he was a joy at high table. I might say the other fellows were mightily alarmed in the first instance, yet by the end, when a discussion of Harold Wilson's penal policy took hold, my friend rather distinguished himself and I can report that everyone was frightfully keen on more brandy.'

'Good heavens,' I said. 'A murderer in the SCR.'

'Yes,' said Nashe. 'Quite distinctive.'

'I hope he has learned his lesson,' I said.

'Naturally,' said Nashe. 'And I hope we have learned ours. It is not the first time the murder-minded have scaled the college walls. Only a few yards to the west of here there was once an inn called the Catherine Wheel. It was there that the Gunpowder plotter Robert Catesby told of his intentions to Robert Wyntour. And these things still go on. A couple of your clever accomplices are said to have cut up some new turf from the gardens over the wall' – he meant Trinity – 'and they carpeted the JCR with it. Caused a terrible fuss with the janitorially-minded.'

The intermingling of history and autobiography was essential to Nashe, and yet one always felt it was the personal part that struck him as carrying the larger portion of educated wisdom. 'I hear you are still thriving as a social phenomenon, young Anderton,' Nashe said at the end of my second year, when I sat in his easy chair to read out my essay. 'Let's dispense with the essay for now,' he added. 'What have you been doing? Still stealing cigars?'

'Sorry?'

'Come now,' he said. 'From the Master's Mondays. The whole point of them is to steal the old leaf, is it not?' With this he opened a drawer of his desk and smilingly passed me a cigar and some matches.

'Heavens,' I said, 'this is festive,' as he poured a couple of sherries.

'Indeed,' he said. 'And those young friends of yours, the Rhodes Scholar and the other one from out of college – are they well? I hear you have now completely conquered Proust.'

'Just a wheeze . . .'

'Not at all. A jolly pursuit. Good young men, I gather. It's bracing to see young men of that sort still pounding the quads, their faces shining with . . . what might one say . . . with polished ungodliness.'

'Yes.'

'But not you, Anderton. You're still for God, aren't you? You're still with the old team?'

'Yes,' I said. 'It would appear to be the case.'

'It would appear, yes.' I remember feeling exposed in some way. There was nothing sinister in Nashe's words. He was just being a historian. But I felt uncertain.

'Shall I read my essay?' I said.

'By all means,' said Nashe. 'You are a free man, Mr Anderton – *l'homme disponible*. Ever ready to fill the gap, what, what?

I blushed, I'm sure, and lowered my head. But my answer was in the essay before me, which started with an account of my Lancashire ancestors and the trials of English faith. By then Nashe's method had turned me into a new version of myself, or was it Proust, or the rhythmic bleating of Hippisley-Cox and Curtis? It's really impossible to tell. Oxford had me. The room filled with smoke and the sherry was perfectly sweet.

And then, a season of pain. In that parish house in Scotland, I often sat in the bedroom at night staring at the bright window, thinking of those young people and their easy, terrible laughter. And sitting up, hearing the trees at the end of the lane performing their dark susurrations, my mind would go beyond them to the places of my own youth, Oxford in those long-ago dreamed-up summers and the words I could still see carved into the bricks on the outside wall of Staircase XI:

Verbum Non Amplivs

'A word and no more.'
Conor.
I first saw him at the back of the Grapes, lifting a pint jug to his fresh smile amid a group of leather jackets. He was a beautiful listener, an almond-eyed person with a head of chestnut hair. Edward was with me that night. I'm afraid my friend was railing against the grammar of the Civil Rights leaders, flicking his white hand in the direction of the Bombastics, and when I looked up I saw Conor sitting among them. What can I say? I ordered more drinks and watched him over Edward's shoulder, the way he picked up papers and smiled his self-possessed smile in the amber light. And then, not for a second stepping out of his world, he looked at me. The look was both casual and piercing. I imagined a world of opportunity in that look. The pub bustled with its smaller concerns, while Conor, the man at the end of the room, his arms enfolding himself in

mirth, looked at me again, inhabiting every quiet hope I had.

Hippisley-Cox continued his banter at my side, but I didn't hear a word he said and he faded out, like a distant piano. I could feel the glorious young man at the ends of my fingers and in the gin scorching my throat. I looked at him again.

He turned to rub his shoulder, and seeing his hand on his jacket, I suddenly wanted to be his jacket or be the cotton of his shirt. For nearly forty years I have thought about the amber light and the smile on him that evening. For I loved him the second before I saw him, just as one does with love: we know whom we love before we find them, or think we do. We feel we have waited for such a person, and when we see him, he is perfectly familiar.

Love me back, I whispered into the short glass.

I found out the next day that he was at Worcester. I heard he came from Liverpool – 'how impossibly thrilling', said Edward – and eventually I found my way to one of those political meetings. I went to other meetings after that, and Conor was always there with his timidly devouring eyes. When I first walked up to him I stared at the badges on his jacket. 'You're one of them Balliol aesthetes,' he said.

His accent was intimidatingly friendly.

'Not exclusively,' I said. 'I like the Beatles.'

'Oh, them four.'

'Sorry,' I said. 'That's a bit pathetic.'

'You have nice skin,' he said.

'I'm sorry?'

'Good skin. Where you from?'

'Lancashire.'

'Thought as much,' he said. 'Lancashire or Yorkshire. I knew I could hear something in there.'

'I don't know what to say to you,' I said.

'Let's go for coffee and think of something,' he said. 'Don't you think Wilson is a war-loving hypocrite?'

We took a short trip to Florence that August and at the end of the summer he took me to see his parents in Liverpool. There wasn't much of them to see, though Conor brought me into their company as if they were a special room at the British Museum. We had two rounds of drinks in a large Victorian hotel next to a bingo hall in King Street. His father owned a clockmakers and was a keen gardener. He spent most of the time talking about rose bushes and his battles with the weather, while his wife, Conor's mother, made it clear that she ran her life (and everybody else's) according to principles rigorously upheld in Holy Catholic Ireland. Conor, by then, wasn't Catholic at all, but he went to Mass whenever his mother was around and said it was sensible to see her piety as an apt expression of all that her people had suffered at the hands of the English. I smiled when he told me that. 'Just play up the Scottish bit,' he said.

'Does she care that much?' I asked. I remember he struck a match off the sole of his shoe and lit a cigarette, whispering the smoke into the space between us.

'Just give the Voice what she needs,' he said. 'She doesn't need a great deal. She's not hard to manage.'

It was my friend Edward, when I told him about Conor's mother in advance of meeting her, who had christened her the Voice – short for the Voice of Doom – and even Conor took it up. In the hotel bar she proved that the name was not ill-suited. 'These Oxford ones,' she said, 'the best of them would sit down on the pavement and weep before they'd accept a day's work or a sign from God. Is that not right, Conor? And the best of it is, their gowns and their degrees and their mortar boards won't keep them safe during the nuclear war. Is that not right, Conor Docherty? Their eyes will melt away from their heads in the nuclear war – soon enough, mark my words – before they can so much as reach out to pick up their books. Where will your Willie Shakespeare be to lend you a hand then, Conor Docherty?'

For me, Conor was the better part of the 1960s. He expressed the times better than anyone I ever met. Looking back on those years now, people speak as if they were little more than a pantomime of alternative ideas, but Conor taught me how glorious it might be to live in colour for the first time. That night in Liverpool he spoke about the matter with a personal urgency. 'People forget what it was like in the 1950s,' he said, 'how grim Britain was. I used to worry that the world would never have a place for our way of thinking.'

'What way of thinking?' I asked.

'I don't know,' he said. 'Being who you want to be as opposed to who you were born to be.'

'Heaven forfend,' I said. I was never a 1960s person in the way that Conor was, partly, I suspect, because my father was dead and my mother was a 1960s person before her time.

'I thought I might never be allowed to say anything,' said Conor, 'or be anything that mattered to me. It was all cloth caps up here. Or petit bourgeois rubbish about refrigerators and savings. When I got to Oxford I thought somebody had turned the lights on.'

We were alone. I put my hand into the pocket of his coat.

'And it's political,' he said.

I could never share that feeling very precisely, but I had my share of the freedoms he spoke about, my share of the decade's hopes too. Conor looked up with his Bob Dylan eyes: 'These are our changes. Yours as much as anybody's.'

'Hell knows,' I said, walking down the pavement in a Liverpool of tin chapels and sleeping docks, the set of an old movie. 'I fear some of us are even more subjective than that.'

He smiled.

'Spoken like a true Marcellist,' he said.

Back in his beloved second-hand Triumph Herald, Conor meshed his hands in his hair as he leaned over the steering wheel. It was dark in those streets and Liverpool's own popular songs seemed to animate the living air and render the old buildings closed and lonely. We didn't see it as a decade then but just as now, now, now. He turned round to face me in the passenger seat, laughing and biting his bottom lip, then he leaned over and kissed me. 'It was a masterstroke,' he said. 'Did you see the way the Voice's tone just changed when you mentioned the ancestors?'

'But they're real,' I said.

'I don't care if they're real. It was perfect. The Voice likes a martyr more than anything in the world.'

'I like a martyr myself,' I said.

'Must be a Balliol thing.'

A ferryboat sounded on the Mersey. 'This is good, Conor,' I said. 'A wonderful night.' We got lost driving in the city and at one point he pulled up in Scotland Road next to a shop that said Cookson's Diamonds. His eyes were so alive and only the audible burn of his cigarette hung between us as we discussed our plans in a pool of yellow light falling from the shop window.

'These dead recusants of yours can't be far away from here,' he said. 'Let's drive to Lancs and visit them.'

'No,' I said. 'Let's go south. I don't know how to find them.'

He turned the ignition and we moved at speed through the grey roads of northern England, the car filling with pot smoke and sudden laughter, the towns blurring past in the dark.

'De Gaulle betrayed the workers,' he said.

That was what he did all the time, tried to improve my politics. I can picture the exact greyness of that journey, Conor's beautiful face, a downpour outside Birmingham, the oily rain on the windscreen, a tunnel of trees sucking us into Oxford and the sound of John Lennon's voice suspending all other voices as it emerged from the new car radio.

Men had a sense of danger about these things. You had to have: homosexuality was not yet legal for people our age. It is not often said, but the need for discretion suited some of us perfectly. It certainly suited Conor and me, the idea that privacy was not just a survival requirement but something quite central to what we had. I've seen men holding hands in the years since and wondered if something wasn't lost by what they gained. Maybe not. We found it easy to outwit the law because our own law called for caution.

I remember Hippisley-Cox stopping at the gate to the Fellows' Garden to tell me, under his breath and with his London face on, that I must dread the outcome of such a passion. 'Your admiration of that young political rogue has become exclusive,' he said.

'He's interesting.'

'Don't be ridiculous,' said Edward. 'You're interesting. Your curiosity about him is just another way for you to be curious about yourself. That's how love works.'

'That's hideous, Edward,' I said. 'And not at all the case.'

'You're becoming more like him,' he said.

'Is that an illness?'

'Not quite,' said Edward, 'but a form of suffering, yes. Just look after your pride, dear heart.'

'It seems so necessary,' I said. It took a lot for me to say that: I've never been good at saying what I wanted to say.

Edward looked at the base of the gate and pointed down. It was the Fellows' Garden tortoise, Hector, who had crawled out of the bushes covered in purple juice, having gorged, as usual, on the mulberries. We stared for a moment at the pawing reptile in its dark shell.

'Nothing about fondness is necessary,' said Edward.

'Is that from the Big Book?' I asked.

'No,' said Edward. 'It's just from me to you.'

I felt a flush in my cheeks and a rush of feeling. I wanted to tell Edward once and for all what it was like. I wanted to say to him: 'I am finally myself with this man and he is interesting and good and makes everything else seem cold.' But it didn't feel possible for me to say those things, and I realised that my undergraduate friends and I had never really wanted to know each other.

'He is a reality,' I said.

Edward took a breath and released it from his mouth both slowly and sadly, as if a tyre was being let down on purpose, along with his hopes for me and his hopes for himself. 'Love is a striking example of how little reality means to us,' he said. 'And that is from the book. Volume Two. Page 207. Good evening, Anderton.'

I saw less of the Marcellists after that. At Oxford I seemed constantly to be moving between realms of belief. I had an authoritarian tutor who hated the authorities and loved the people in their ideal state. Nashe somehow continued, via anecdotes about Tunbridge Wells, to feed me wisdom in regard to the libertarian and fraternal instincts of the revolutionary French. But, when it came down to it, Nashe was no fan of the new student politics. He found those students to be false, spoiled, unfunny and lacking in proper social zeal. He favoured the Marcellists as examples of the good old-fashioned college sort.

'So, Anderton,' he said, 'I gather you are venturing towards the environs of Worcester College. A rather conservative place, but I hear one may find radicals among the twisted boughs over there. You must beware of ill humour.'

'Not to worry,' I said. 'We are seldom about the college.'

'Oh,' he said. 'And have we arrived already at "we"? I must refer you to the latter chapters of my imperfect book, *The Way of the People*, referring to the tyrannical though not uncolourful assumptions that may underlie the potency of this "we". And we are marching in aid of the workers now, I gather?'

'The Cowley men, yes,' I said, sheepishly. 'For better wages.'

'Ahh,' said Nashe. 'Better wages. That is a project almost certainly enhanced by the kindness of good men. Now, dear Anderton, mind how these new friends of yours will make mincemeat of your God. Those excessively in favour of the people are always unforgiving of the Man Upstairs. That is a principle of the modern age.'

'You seem to be rather well informed about my doings,' I said.

'Oh, heavens,' he said. 'You needn't vex on that point. You are one of those fine gentlemen like Maurice Bowra, a man much more dined against than dining.'

The Oxford of the First World War was a dead place to the likes of Conor. The past didn't interest him in that way. There used to be a sign at Oxford railway station that said: 'Welcome to Oxford, The Home of Pressed Steel.' My early friends and I used to find that hilariously funny, but Conor didn't. The Oxford of pressed steel was the only one he really cared about, and that great belt of manufacturers and printers to the east was his spiritual glade. Conor never allowed anyone to forget that the Cowley car plant was only three miles from the Sheldonian.

In my final year, 1968, Conor was everything, and his friends, the Bombastics, were all about us in their leafleting, polo-necked way. They knew all the student leaders at Berkeley, at Columbia, in Paris and in Germany. Whole evenings would be spent raising petitions for the people of Prague or the Deep South, and I can still see Conor smoking between sentences and creasing his forehead with concentration or shyness. And I can see him standing in his denim jacket among the wild tulips in Christ Church Meadow, listening to a clever young woman demanding a solution to Mexico's economic problems. Turning to see me at the edge of the trees, he would wink over and make me feel that love between men was part of the easy new world he wished to argue into being. It wasn't difficult, his smile seemed to say. It was our world to make right.

'Hello, old sausage.' It was Hippisley-Cox. He was standing with some of his new friends one night, outside the Eagle and Child in St Giles. I remember my scarf was wound halfway up my face against the cold. 'Off to a meeting are you, old sauce?' asked Edward.

'Just back.'

'Good, good,' he said. 'Fancy a glass of the old peculiar?'

'No thanks, Eddie. Have one for me.'

'We shall,' he said. 'We shall drink wine. Something made from grapes trampled by a thousand Sunderland peasants.' The young men around him laughed. Several were recent undergraduates.

'Excellent,' I said.

'True, isn't it?' said Edward. 'Please confirm the matter for my *confrères*. The Bombastics like nothing more than heading up north for a bit of unpaid graft in the company of some sooty-faced Britter. Was it not yourself and the Son of Voice who recently darkened the plains of Wales to help miners out with their allotments?'

'Not me,' I said. 'But I hear they are very nice. You can advise your *confrères* where to find their names in Debrett's.'

I looked up at the pub sign.

'The Bird and Babe,' I said. 'A rather elevated venue for you, Edward?'

He drank me in with his inebriated eyes.

'But of course,' he said, bowing from the waist. His head seemed so old at the time, though actually he was painfully young. 'We must each seek elevation in our own way.'

I came to feel those people had vitality but no values. They were just decadents; worse than that, the shadows of decadents, actors really, living up to a half-formed picture of some mythical Oxford past. They used daring old novels for the better parts of their scripts and slivers of Wildean dogma to freshen their afternoons. In fact, I see now that I probably underestimated them, that they had more grasp of the world than they seemed to have at the time of my abandoning them. In the scramble for Conor and his world of commitment and change, I came to see Edward's world as a road not taken. Later on I would take it, but by then I was walking on my own. I said goodbye to Hippisley-Cox for the last time as if I were saying goodbye to some terrible possibility for myself. A few months later, he was arrested in London for soliciting in a public toilet.

I was going to Blackfriars every evening, sometimes morning Mass too, or afternoon office, but more often vespers, and I was glad to be among the Dominicans and out of reach of the Ampleforth monks at St Benet's Hall. Ampleforth was part of some great innocence, and I wanted to leave it behind, much as one wants to leave one's family behind at the first sight of romance. Conor's rebellion meant staying up late and questioning all authority; mine meant choosing to take up with the Dominican friars, the rival bunch, who represented the natural reach of my rebellious instincts. In any event, I found new, important holy hours in that place, in which to praise God and contemplate my duty.

He never tried to talk me out of it. Conor was too gracious in his handsome bones for that. He joked about religion, but he must have understood the impulse somewhere, for salvation was his great theme too: we each yearned for peace and unity, like the peace and unity we had made for ourselves out of our mad differences. I loved Conor: that is the central matter in all this. In a sense, my story ends at the point where it may appear to begin, for when he put his hand through my hair and held the back of my head and kissed me, I knew I had found an answer to the question of how to live and what to do.

There was music one evening by the lake at Worcester. I remember walking down the stone steps of the quad – there were thirteen steps – and Conor was tipsy with beer and ambition. 'David, I tell you now, pubs are the only parliaments.'

'Please don't get sentimental about pubs now. Most of them are hellholes filled with con artists.'

'And so are most parliaments.'

'For the sake of the evening,' I said, 'let's agree to abandon the analogy.'

He pushed me playfully in the chest.

'You're so particular!' he said. 'You must look to the general if you want to see anything worth seeing. Otherwise, you're just one man on his own.' I stopped on the gravel path next to the lake and two geese came pecking at my shoes.

'But ultimately,' I said, 'that's what everybody is, a person on their own.'

'No,' he said. 'That's all over now.'

I don't know if he meant the old us or the old society: I suppose it must have been both, given him, given the times.

'Okay,' I said.

His eyes glittered when he spoke, and I saw the trees' branches were bent over the lake and dipping into the green water. That evening at Worcester we listened to Borodin's Nocturne played by an orchestra of Welsh nationalists. We sat on the grass in the old college gardens, amid the wisdom that honours itself, and Conor made one of his bad but winningly delivered arguments. I think he ventured that the superior state of mind produced by music is an illusion. 'And what is wrong with an illusion?' I asked him.

'Society has enjoyed too many of them,' he said.

The dusk seemed to appear not from the sky but from the water, from the music, from the sycamore trees that crowded the lake. And Borodin's melody seemed to exert a loving grip across the grass. We listened together and I know the sound may flare in my ears in the last moments of life. In the dark, with the last notes swithering in the distance, Conor reached out and wiped loose earth from the palms of my hands.

We had a nightcap in the Grapes. He walked me back to Balliol and we bribed the porter with a packet of cigarettes to let us into the college for a nightcap in my rooms. We walked into the chapel passage that night and struck matches to look at the memorial wall. Conor wasn't so cautious when it came to smoking pot: he lit a joint from one of the matches, and at first I was nervous, looking out for the porter. I took a few drags from it and we stood close against the wall, taking in the names of the dead. 'Five of the names are German,' he said. 'See how they've separated them off from the English boys.'

'At least they're on the memorial,' I said.

'Only just,' said Conor. 'They're dropping off the bottom.

Typical England, typical Oxford: patriotic to the end. They all died, those guys, no matter where they were from.' He blew smoke on the memorial, and the sweet smell rebounded as he touched my hair and pressed me back against the wall of the passage. His tongue was warm in my mouth. I felt his cheek grazing mine and he breathed into my hair a word or two before we stole away to my rooms.

Geoffrey Nashe came to hate the *Enragés* of 1968. 'They are spoiled reprobates,' he said in one of our last tutorials. He packed his pipe with Jean Bart tobacco and sat in his usual chair, spinning a handsome globe with the stem of his pipe and taking a puff every other time he passed North America. 'What a disgusting carnival,' he said. 'These so-called demonstrators are spoiling France. They are manhandling French philosophy with their idiotic graffiti and their *enfantillages*. Totally disreputable. You ought to mind how you go with that crowd. I can't tell you what mischief they would seek to enact on one of your monks if they were given the chance.'

'I wouldn't be so sure,' I said. 'The Church is changing too.'

Nashe smiled into his beautiful oak bookcase, a smile that travelled through the glass panels to reach his first editions. I had sometimes wondered what it must be like to be there in the college, year after year, while the young people came and went. Many of us left his rooms very different from the people we had been when we entered them. And we learned to upset him, for that was one of the things he taught us to do. When I said those words about the Catholic Church, I saw him register a change between us. It was the growth of some foreign commitment, perhaps, something beyond his hopes for the college. Balliol had always been leftist, but there was something new in our reading of the world, and, seeing it, he inaugurated a moment of perfect silence before lifting me out of his affections.

'The Vatican Council and its aftermath,' he said. 'I see. And are they now part of your personal plan for the making of a new society?' He knocked his pipe on the wooden arm of his chair and smiled. His cheeks were as round as two Kent apples. 'I wish you well, Mr Anderton. I sincerely hope your world can marry up these separate beatitudes, graffiti and Our Lady.'

'I am happy, Geoffrey.'

The words came out as a whisper, but only because it made me embarrassed to say them in his company. And for a moment a pulse appeared in his pink cheek. I had never seen him so angry as he appeared to be at that meeting. The notion of my happiness, it seems, disgusted him about as much as our efforts to oppose the war in Vietnam.

'"True happiness is found only in the comforting of the unhappy,"' he said, citing Saint-Just.

'So now you are quoting a Jacobin at me,' I replied with all the venom I could muster.

'Oh, they have their uses,' said Nashe.

'Vietnam is a ridiculous imbroglio,' I said, my face growing hot with sudden passion. 'The students in Paris have every reason to protest. I find I admire them and I stand by them.' I remember stabbing the tip of my finger with a fountain pen as I said this.

'That is rather a pity, David,' said Nashe. 'If you pay attention to the world for long enough, you may find better things to admire than the bored, pseudo-revolutionary antics of middle-class children from the VIIIème and XVIème arrondissements. I am not against your ideals: I wish you the use of both hands. But I happen to know those ideals are not well served, or served at all, by shutting professors out of their offices or kicking in their doors as happened to my friend at the University of Rouen. He is a man of singular intelligence and liberal sentiments, and his office was wrecked and his face slapped by the student action committee. You want to know about totalitarianism? This is it. An old man being slapped for the crime of being old. I should not expect you, in your current state of fascination, to see the point of my defence of my colleague Vidalenc.'

'The people are restless,' I said. 'They have had enough. They want change.'

'Please, Anderton,' he said. 'Don't speak to me of the people. I am considered an authority on the people in some quarters, and the one thing I can be sure of is their capacity to turn tyrannical in each other's company and in the face of elements they neither see nor comprehend. I'm sure you have good reasons for joining the throng, but please accept a word of advice from me, your old friend. Learn above all to read the political unconscious.'

'I thought you didn't believe in Freud? Too programmatic, you said.'

He sniffed. 'I believe in the political unconscious,' he said. 'And I advise you to know about it too, for without such knowledge one is apt to find oneself among the victims of its blunt determinations.'

'We are young,' I said.

'And what is the merit of simply being young?' Nashe said.

It was a good question. It remains a good question. Yet I was not old enough to provide a decent answer then and I am still not the person one would call upon to solve the matter. But people are sometimes grateful for the strange power of the young. Aren't they? When I first went to Blackpool, I was a young priest and I could see how pleased and hopeful it made the parishioners to be led by someone young.

'It's good to have a person half alive,' said a woman in the Blackpool parish who always wore a hearing aid. 'Someone with a head of hair.'

'I was doubly alive as a student,' I said.

'What's that, Father?'

'I loved somebody then.'

'What? You have to speak up.'

'We were very wise in my college!'

'Oh good,' she said. 'Good. There's nothing wrong with a bit of wise.'

Central London in March 1968. The sun was glinting off the Bloomsbury windows and the grass was warm in Russell Square. I sat there in the morning with a flask of tea, the buses coming from Euston and sandwich bags heaped in the litter bins. I spread a book of Victorian poetry on top of my duffel bag and read while absorbing the morning – the terrific shine on the square's black railings, a ladybird's journey across the page – until it was time to make my way to meet Conor in Holborn.

He had been up all night at the Union painting banners, and by noon he was tossing slogans into the air. Conor gave directions and handed out leaflets by the Conway Hall, his face full of sunlight and everyone around him tuned to some bold new frequency, as if life could never be boring again or grey with complacent ideas. I was given the end of a banner to hold and we marched past the shops and along the streets of a beautiful London, each of us shouting out for the Vietnam Solidarity Campaign.

That will remain my image of him. My image of life. Conor saying yes to the prospect of change and some new condition of society. When we got to Grosvenor Square, and when

189

Conor and the other leaders said the word, we pressed across the square in the direction of the American Embassy. The guards looked nervous of the future; they looked uncomprehending. Twenty thousand people and a chorus of moral sense; Conor down there throwing firecrackers under the police horses.

'Ho, Ho, Ho Chi Minh! NLF is gonna win!'

The press of people down South Audley Street. The linking of arms. The middle of Grosvenor Square. The sunshine. The sunshine sparking through the trees. High windows. It looked for a moment as if the Tower of Babel might fall to a group of flowery innocents. The comic songs. Policemen scampering after their helmets or pressing the faces of curly-haired youths to the pavement. The whistles and shouts. The armbands and the shoving and the sense of outrage. The new world appeared and departed over a blossoming two hours, my life as a radical, and then the day dissolved into an afternoon of pubs and forty years of chatter.

Love's cruel paternity. We were hardly born. We were hardly named. I often see the ways real life would have made us banal. Victims of forgotten hope, we would have lived too closely, perhaps, and learned to hate the smallness of each other's habits, the unlovable, tense hostility of needs and doubts and supposed obligations. Conor had the bad grace to lose his life at a moment of unimpeachable promise. But we might have come to hate one another, to see only faults and bad faith. It comforts me to think so. He lost his life before his love of life or of me was tested, so becoming one of the golden boys of Oxford after all, not falling down in a hail of foreign fire at Ypres, not dying of consumption on a wormy bench, but growing drowsy, it seems, in the foothills of the Chilterns and crashing his car on the main road outside High Wycombe. I had gone back to Oxford on the train and must have been asleep when he died, the scent of him still on the pillows and daylight coming in at the window.

I see Conor reaching into the crowd with a smile as large as the decade that made him. I see the great hope on his face and his readiness to invent the air one might breathe. At night, I sometimes see him driving down to the place where the River Wye runs through a valley in Buckinghamshire. I hear his sacred heart and see his eyes closing as he falls asleep. And I say: be near me. The world is rowdy and nothing is certain. Do not stray. None of us was meant to face the day and the night alone, though that is what we do and memory now is a place of fading togetherness. Be near me. True love is what God intends.

I never saw Conor's body. I never spoke to his mother or father in Liverpool and I didn't attend the funeral. I never took my degree and the years I think have only enlarged the space filled by his absence. That is all I know. I went once to find the spot where they say he died. There was a stone bridge and some beech trees there; just a dimple in the land. I kept a taxi waiting and the driver said that most of the trees in that area had been cut down by the furniture industry. He told me that furniture was a way of life down there. Even the football team kept the fact in mind, he said, calling themselves the Chair Boys. There wasn't a cloud in the sky. No markings to ponder on. It was the year everybody got shot. Martin Luther King. Rudi Dutschke. Andy Warhol. Bobby Kennedy. Conor would perhaps have grown to like the world of professional politics. So many of his comrades did. He hadn't time to see, as we have done, how the spark of rebellion might one day become the glow of opportunism, the burn of compromise, the hail of fire in new foreign lands. We know that death has its fearsome prerogatives: to freeze ethics in their prime, to make a ghost of a beautiful face, and all who survive the Conors of the world must live with the accident of their high example. He will not change. He cannot change. It is we who change and make our way, the prices of the real world becoming more tolerable with time. Yes indeed. We look around and they have gone and we are left to betray their world.

I couldn't face my exams but I could face Blackfriars. It gave my long afternoons of grief an acceptable pattern, and so, by and by, with the help of those gentlemen of God, I came to see that all the answers were old ones. People often say to me: 'Father, how long will the grief last?' I want to say to them that it will last as long as life. When I came to the English College in Rome, that first summer of the new decade, I remember sitting by the small pool in the garden at the back of the college. I saw other young seminarians up at the windows and I wondered, sitting there with my legs dangling in the turquoise water, whether they too might gain from duty and discipline what freedom could only deny them. I went into the pool and looked up at the savage sun. The bones of the English martyrs were kept in the chapel, and my own bones, filled with air, it seemed, like a bird's, were under a covering of memorial flesh now cleansed by the Roman water.

It takes for ever to forget the past. And then longer again to see that forgetting the past is a vivid illusion. A time came in Rome during those seven years when I could walk across the Campo dei Fiori without thinking of Grosvenor Square. One afternoon, I travelled to the Capitoline Hill. There was an orange grove there, a place on the hill where one could pick the fruit from the trees. A mulch of citrus lay among the ruins, loading the cracks of antiquity with sweet scent. I sat on the shaded grass, the great world at some long distance and my lips moving in prayer. It was like an afternoon eclipse on the ridges of the old city, one kind of belief passing slowly over another to silence the birds.

That was the day of my ordination.

In my mind, I said: 'Conor is gone, but the Lord is here. My life will pass and I will never taste a kiss on my mouth again.'

A decision had been made while the sky turned from emerald to lilac. The slow moon had passed. It was over now. One becomes such a master of departures, such an opponent of doubt. Making my way down the hill I saw a party of goldfinches flying overhead, and the heavens seemed more familiar than the green earth as I fastened my coat and walked in search of the road.

9

THE PEOPLE

The police came to the rectory at noon on the last Sunday in August. I had said the first Mass and was looking over some builders' estimates when the knock came. My father always said a policeman's knock is unmistakable, and so it is, the rap on the paintwork a very public command, feasting on the hearer's capacity for guilt. 'There it is,' I said. 'The immoderate summons.'

Stepping into the house, one of the young officers took off his hat. His friend said: 'Are you David Anderton?'

'That's right.'

One hears of the good cop and the bad cop. This was the handsome one and the ugly one. Scanning the room with his hat under his arm, the handsome one lowered his eyes and let me dwell for a second on his toffee-coloured hair. 'Mr Anderton,' said the ugly one, seeming too rounded in his tunic, as if all his potentialities were localised in his puffed-out chest. 'I'm afraid we have to ask you some questions.'

'By all means.'

'Not here. You must come to the station.'

He coughed rather too delicately into his tiny fist.

'I'm afraid you are under arrest.'

The face of the other policeman graduated quickly through a palette of exquisite pinks. It was difficult to imagine such a man thriving in the world as it is today, never mind rolling in the street with the criminal classes. 'Sorry, Father,' he said. 'Do you by any chance have a glass of water you could give me?'

'Of course,' I said.

In the kitchen, I waited for the tap to run cold. Taking the cloth, I wiped the table, seeing my shadow in the wood and catching the smell of oranges that rose from the detergent spray favoured by Mrs Poole. I had used the last of the spray the week before, when clearing up after the supper for Bishop Gerard, but the smell lingered and felt oppressive. I lifted a glass to fill it with water and saw that my hands were shaking.

At the police station, they took me to an interview room. There was stewed tea in styrofoam cups, pencil shavings on the sergeant's desk, and for hours – six to be precise – they told me in magnificent detail the story of who I was and what I had done. The handsome officer sat with me during one of the middle hours, explaining that his colleagues were only doing their job and that everything was a shame. He told me he had recently got married, and I imagined him raking leaves in the yard behind a brand-new bungalow. I saw him carrying boxes to the loft and fixing plugs on a series of paper lamps. He would do these things in a loose shirt and khaki shorts, wearing training shoes, the fuses held between his teeth as he bent down with the screwdriver, flecks of emulsion showing in his hair as he looked over at his wife. I'd say the officer knew nothing of his own slow mind or the dimple on his chin.

'I am going to charge you,' said the sergeant. 'But before I do so I must caution you that you do not need to say anything in answer to the charge, but anything you do say will be noted and may be used in evidence. Do you understand?'

I said that I did understand.

'The charge against you is that in the early hours of 11 July this year you did sexually assault a minor, Mark McNulty, in the chapel-house of the Church of St John Ogilvie in the town of Dalgarnock. Do you understand? Do you have anything you would like to say?'

'Yes,' I said. 'The charge is false.'

'We'll see about that soon enough, sir,' he said. 'Please follow me.'

They took photographs and fingerprints, the dark smudge indwelling as I lifted up my hand. Then they rubbed the inside of my cheek with a cotton swab: a DNA sample. I remember looking at the damp cotton and thinking that old family habits must be traceable there, the many Andertons with their devout notions and closed mouths. Could the DNA tell a story of the way my people have refined themselves for victimhood over the centuries? What did it say, this swab? That I'd inherited my ancestors' propensity for Catholic belief and its attendant disasters? Perhaps that my own blood was poorer than theirs, a dilution of the old stuff resulting in this sorrowful Sunday? The cotton swab lay in a plastic dish, radiating portents. Surely the information captured there could explain this frightful mistake.

'Let's book you in,' the sergeant said.

'You mean I'm staying here?'

'Just tonight,' he said. 'You'll be detained in custody until you appear in court tomorrow morning.'

'What happens then?' I asked. He put a pencil behind his ear and looked at me through dipped eyes.

'Most likely,' he said, 'you'll be bailed to appear for trial at some point in the future. What's your date of birth?'

'24 March 1947.'

'Could you empty your pockets, please?'

I took out my keys, a case of rosary beads, my mobile phone. There was an envelope symbol on the phone indicating a text. I pushed the button and saw the message:

They made me.

'You'll get all these back tomorrow,' said the sergeant.

'It doesn't *matter*,' I whispered.

'Sorry, sir?'

'Oh, nothing,' I said.

There were voices in the night. They came from the disquieted environment of my own mind. I lay on a foam bed and saw the weakest of lights out there in the corridor, not a light really – not a bulb or a filament – but a cold gathering of shadows. The darkest hour had arrived, and I listened carefully to the words that arrived across the empty room, ignoring the smell of urine as I followed the goodness and friendliness of those voices back to the places where they lived.

My father and I would spend nights in the garden with tea and ginger biscuits. He would try to make sense of the sky. Forever pointing, he'd divine a great cluster of stars some-where about Neptune, saying to me: 'There you have one of the oldest formations. We're talking hundreds of millions of years old, and that's just for starters.' The night sky was not a dead and cold thing in my father's company but a living show – bears and bulls pawing through the grand universe, or ploughs turning over the sizeable detritus of space. He made it sound like the heavens were an action painting of the Earth's best objects, stretching across the untold dark, these images looking down on us with a godly sense of themselves and their own meaning for the likes of us, watching below.

'That's Mars,' he would say, indicating some ruby-shaded pinprick out there, and I'd feel giggly in my pyjamas, thinking the vision was only ours. But sometimes he'd point to things I couldn't see.

'Oh, yes,' I'd say. 'It's very bright.'

The smell of chimneys filled the garden; the taste of ginger snaps numbed my tongue. Our kitchen was yellow behind us. As my father looked up at the sky, my oohs and aahs, I now see, like my sudden questions, were an actor's disclosures of deference. I didn't really know what he was looking at or what he was saying, but I liked the garden, the moonlight making pulsars round the rim of his silver glasses.

Kilmarnock Sheriff Court was quick the next morning. They took me up in handcuffs to the pinewood court and the charge was read out, the sheriff looking down from his perch, biting the arm of his spectacles.

'This will be difficult,' the canon lawyer said later. We were standing in a private corner of the corridor. 'We must have faith.'

'We shall need more than that.'

He looked me up and down as if the remark was my second contribution to a life of crime. 'God will suffice,' he said.

'And Bishop Gerard,' I said, 'have you spoken to him?'

'Of course,' he said. 'He is very upset, as you can imagine.'

'Yes.'

'You are free to go,' he said. 'For the time being.'

'And so are you, Father,' I said. He turned to face me.

'What's that you're saying?'

'Thank you for your work this morning,' I said. 'I won't be requiring any further assistance.'

'You have only just been bailed,' he said. 'You have a trial to face. We must begin to prepare for your defence.'

'My defence will be my own concern.'

'Are you mad?'

'Very possibly,' I said. 'But I have spoken to my mother. We will be engaging an advocate in due course. Thank you for your trouble.'

'But, David,' he said, his voice low and seasoned with panic, 'this is unprecedented. You must follow procedure. You will be crucified for hiring an expensive advocate in a case such as this. As you know, the Church has some experience. We will handle things.'

'I don't want things *handled*.'

The face of the canon lawyer grew red. He gathered up his papers and nodded towards the dull, scuffed tiles of the corridor, while young people in anoraks passed sleepily by and lawyers made their way in a whirl of gowns and ring binders.

'Heaven help you, Father,' he said. 'You know, the Bishop sponsored you. He made a special case for you in this diocese. He will take a lot of flak for this. It is not right.'

'Let other authorities be the judge of what is right.'

'You are lost,' he said. 'Do you know what is out there?'

He pointed to the entrance of the court.

'I know what is in here,' I said, and I tapped a finger to my chest and took a step back from the canon lawyer.

'It is vanity that will bring you down,' he said. 'We have known it since first you came to this diocese. You have spent more time with books than you have with parishioners. I'm afraid you are a hedonist, Father David, and your indulgences are well known, even to those who would wish to help you. Forgive me if I have spoken too frankly.'

'Your bond is not with me,' I said.

I felt strangely resolved leaving the Sheriff Court that first time, but I lacked whatever is required to realise how easily such resolution can be mistaken for arrogance. My stupidities were obvious, even to me, but I felt the matter required honesty and patience, quite forgetting that the world has a name for people like me and ways of bringing us down. I saw there were some photographers in St Marnock Street but thought little of it until the following morning when my picture appeared in the *Daily Record*. 'The Face of Evil,' it said. 'English Priest in Ayrshire Kiddie Abuse Scandal.'

There were no cars. No dogs or children. The landing window showed a blazing sun that seemed part of a life elsewhere, as the sun always is. But that August afternoon the sun was African yellow and brought the life of elsewhere burning into Dalgarnock, the coast for an hour or two bending in the heat of an equatorial illusion.

Mrs Poole would have spoken of the hole in the sky's protective layer, and the strange, spineless warmth argued her case. One felt unprotected. It was the day of Marymass, the annual summer fair, and I drove across the town to buy eggs and orange juice from a farm near the moor. It seemed as if the whole population had evacuated to the site of enjoyment, the streets deserted, the houses emptied, the roads cordoned off for the parade and bordered with flags and bunting. I drove past the Blue Star garage and pulled over to inspect something spray-painted on the wall. It said:

Celebrate and Dance for Free. Celtic FC.

I took coins from the glove compartment. I drove up and put them in the car wash and went through, the blue brushes closing in, the soap and water covering the car and making a secure world of swirling brushes, total privacy and strange motion. For a moment I felt like Jonah, sloshing in the mouth of a great whale, a mouth of saliva, until the rinsing water came from every direction and the windscreen cleared and the sea glittered before me, the sea that went over to Ireland.

The farm shop was closed. I could hear the sound of a loud-speaker from the moor and faint eddies of applause. I drove closer and parked next to the generators that fed the fair-ground attractions and the gypsy caravans. You could see it then, the moor crowded with Marymass revellers, the town's inhabitants. Stalls, barbecues, waltzers, shooting galleries and burger vans crowded down to the river, with children running amok, decorated horses being led here and there by the bridle. There was a stage in the middle of the moor and it was sur-rounded by the time I arrived. The town bailie, in red frock coat and gold chain, was placing a crown on the head of the Marymass Queen, a teenage girl with a professional smile for the local paper.

Marymass has been going since medieval times. My tutors at Balliol would have found it eternally interesting: the Carters' Association with its horses and banners and heralds; the papingo, of which there are etchings from the sixteenth cen-tury, a game in which archers shoot arrows at partridges set on the ramparts of the old abbey. I could see that the partridges were now made of cardboard and the arrows had rubber tips. The ancient pageant had become a beer festival. The crowd wore football colours and they jostled on the moor with their foaming plastic cups. There was a hideous drum. It pounded on the hazy side of the moor and the sun was pulsing too, like a rotary blade that churned the atmosphere.

I was wearing civvies, a shirt open at the neck, and I found a baseball cap on the back seat of the car. I pulled the visor down and walked into the crowd that cross-hatched the grass, everywhere smelling of suntan lotion and chips. Children ran holding sticks of candy floss and took pictures of one another with their phones. Disco music shrieked from the fairground. I shouldn't have gone there. I should have been back in the rectory making calls and taking counsel. But something of the Marymass buzz drew me onto the moor, and I walked among the excited bodies wishing I could join them, 'the people', as Nashe used to call them from his armchair.

A black pole rose some thirty feet into the air. It stood on a hill at the edge of the moor and the people gathered round, the girls with their coloured alcopops and the babies holding ice creams. The pole was smeared with black tar all the way to the top, where a side of beef, its upper side browning in the morning sun, was impaled on a large butcher's hook. The beef was a prize for the worthiest climbers. I went up close to the fence surrounding the pole. The men played in teams, climbing up on each other's shoulders and driving up through the grease, squeezing tins of lager into their mouths before and during the effort. 'Let's fucken go!' said a particularly broken-nosed one. 'Let's fucken *do them*!'

Oh, that high-flying flamingo, that sweet Geoffrey Nashe. He thought, along with my father, that the working class consisted of young, moderate, hard-working men, scented with soap and certificates. They never saw that violent face or the gold ring on every finger. 'It's not actually about class,' Nashe would have said. 'It's about *character*.'

The winning team were the most sunburnt. They drank the greatest number of lagers and they had the flattest faces. They didn't mind stepping on each other's heads in the attempt to reach the top or crushing one another's fingers into the black goo of the pole. The last man, a fierce, aggressive, hollering, self-conscious brute, reached the beef at the top of the greasy pole and gripped it with his giant hands, and then, with a final push, raised himself up and sank his teeth into the stewed rump, shouting with laughter and flashing his gold fillings to the heavens.

I had seen Mrs Poole's husband at the start of the contest. He was with one of the junior teams, one of the sports clubs, I imagine, and was drinking from a small bottle of whisky. He hadn't noticed me. His face was ashen and his cheeks were drawn. His team was knocked out early, after failing to scale even halfway up the pole, but they were jeering from the side during the other attempts. I should have left then, but the short sad truth is that I didn't want to leave.

My pleasure came to a sudden halt. The cap was knocked from my head and a bare-chested man stood in front of me. He had an Indian-ink tattoo on his neck. It was a broken blue line and the words said: 'Cut Here in Case of Emergency.' Like men of that sort, he seemed excessively aware of the crowd's presence and he played to it. 'You're that paedophile cunt of a priest! Ya dirty bastard.'

'Steady on,' I said.

'Dirty Fenian scumbag,' he said. There was a brief moment of hesitation and the man swayed before me; it seemed he was weighing the exact measure of violence to deploy, and he flexed his terrible fingers, as if beckoning the crowd's assent.

One never buys a house or pays school fees. One sleeps in a single bed. One lives like an orphan in a beautiful paternalistic dream. As a priest one may never grow up. In a sense, one lives as an infant before the practical trials of reality, and I never in my life felt old before standing in that field and facing that young man, the sun uncommonly warm. But the young man was grinding his teeth like an expert, his crimson face and his shocking vitality bare before his neighbours, making me old, making me unsteady on my legs and far from reason. I had

203

travelled a long way to this field and the terror of his unholy face. His mouth was moving. I imagined he was another species from me. His eyes were like a bird's, and so were those of the crowd: in that instant they were like ospreys, their spiked hair tearing away from their skulls full of gel and motion, their eyes sharp with murderous intelligence as I put out my hands to stop him.

I heard a moan in the crowd and I found myself numb on the grass. I think I closed my eyes, then eruptions of panic and weakness and embarrassment filled the moment. I could feel a trickle of blood running down my cheek and it entered my mouth, salt and metal stopping my tongue as the man reached down to slap me. I could feel him tearing at my shirt and poking an iron finger into my chest. 'Fucken no-use peedo bastard. I'm gonnae waste you for what you've done.'

'Get off me,' I said.

'Dirty English cunt.'

'That's bang out of order,' a voice said at the young man's side. 'Come on, Sammy, son. You're gonnae get into bother here.'

'Jeest leave him,' said a girl.

'Ah, Sammy. That's enough. He's an old guy.'

I got to my feet and saw the young man was surrounded by a group of people clutching drinks.

'Thank you,' I said to them.

'Thank *fuck all!*' said the man. 'I hope you burn in hell, ya dirty fucken beast. I hope you swing for this, tamperin' wi' weans.'

A man had me by the arm. I could smell drink on him and I dusted grass off myself before turning. It was Mr Poole. 'Come on,' he said. 'You better get away frae here.' One of the girls handed him a baby's bib, and he used it to wipe the blood.

'Just keep it,' said the girl. I could see through my good eye that she curled her lip as she said the words, backing away.

Mr Poole drove the car back to the rectory. He was any number of times over the limit, having trouble at first with the automatic gearbox, but I was too upset to question him. 'It's all right,' he said, over and over. He kept shaking his head as he drove and he drummed his nicotine-stained fingers on the steering wheel. 'Everything's all right.' When he pulled to a stop on the gravel outside the chapel I felt a twinge in my eye.

'Jesus Christ,' he said. The glass on the rectory door was cracked and someone had sprayed 'PEEDAPHILE' on the path.

'Good Lord,' I said.

Mr Poole handed me the car keys. His hands were shaking but he wouldn't come into the house.

'No, you're awright,' he said. 'You'll be okay from here.'

'You've been very kind, Mr Poole,' I said. 'Are you sure you won't come inside? I could make some tea.'

He looked sadly at the broken door.

'Not at all,' he said. 'That's . . .' He paused. 'That's where Anne goes to work. It wouldnae be right. I've never been where she works. She wouldnae like it.'

'Well, thank you ever so much.'

The situation seemed to make him shy. He wanted no part of it. He shook his head outside the car and wiped his mouth, as if to still himself and still what others might say. Eventually, he nodded goodbye. 'It's a rough business,' he said. Then he walked down the side of the chapel and vanished at the corner where a rose bush hung in ruins over the garden wall. There was only the sound of birds twittering in the lane. From there I stepped into the house and locked the storm doors behind me.

Here again: the fortifying thrill of solitude. The house was silent. The most refreshing shade could be found in the bathroom, where I swabbed my eye with antiseptic and cleaned my face. Then I brushed my teeth and turned on the radio, the sound travelling through the house like a cool and edifying breeze, Radio 4, an announcer with humour in his voice and a regulating tone of seriousness. 'The American Army Surgeon General announced an investigation,' he said, 'into the deaths of two soldiers in Iraq. This comes on the heels of news that a further hundred in the region were hospitalised with severe pneumonia. It has been argued that the soldiers' exposure to the US military's anthrax vaccine may be the cause of the fatalities.'

Downstairs, when I poured boiling water into the cup, the teabag flopped and released its flavours in a dark effusion. The radio played upstairs but the voices were muffled by carpets and doors. Everything seemed to be passing to another place, the professional voices on the radio retaining their tone but none of their meaning as they travelled into the woodwork and fibres of a desecrated house.

The garden. It was a mercy the flowers had gone. The months had marched on and only a few roses were left, but these had been ripped and kicked apart, the remaining white petals gone dark with stomping. I lifted the teacup and walked out among the broken bushes, and, sitting on the bench against the wall, I absorbed for a while the ruin of peace and the rising scent of lunacy. I caught again the sound of the radio upstairs. My great failures were not diminished by the terrible climate in which the people enjoyed them, by the way they could say I had met their worst fears and prejudices. It was a trap which time had set for me, not them. They knew of the scandals involving Catholic priests, and now they had one too, their very own, and forgive me for feeling the riot of execration in that place was tinged with a sense of wonderful achieve-ment, for the crowd now had its bogeyman and its spot on the news. There is no pleasure in seeing how the badness of one's nature may give rise to a tribal fulfilment no prettier than its cause. But I would be stupid to ignore it, just as I had been stu-pid to ignore those parts of myself which brought the young people to my door in the first place.

My tea was cold when the telephone rang.

'It's Gerard,' he said, with an undertow of the River Clyde.

'Good afternoon, Bishop.'

'How are you?'

'Quite chipper,' I said. 'For someone who was charged yes-terday.'

'But you're all right?'

'Not a hundred per cent. But don't worry, Gerard. I won't be inflicting any further wounds.'

'Don't be daft, David. This is a serious matter. Father Bren-dan tells me you're refusing counsel.'

'I'm not guilty. I didn't assault anybody. I'm not apologising to the families and hanging my head before the tabloids.'

'David,' he said, more in anger, 'the boy was in the rectory at seven o'clock in the morning. There were bottles on the table. Drugs were involved. He's given a statement. So have others.'

'It wasn't assault. Not to my mind.'

'And what is your mind?' he said, his anger now charging down the line with a mitre of authority. 'I took a chance bring-ing you to this diocese. I went against advice to bring you from England. You know what, David: the Bishop of Lancaster gave you a questionable reference. He said you'd spent twenty years being an excellent administrator and a poor pastor. He said you'd organised a cabal – that was his word – of classical-music lovers and wine tasters. Wine tasters! That's what your ministry at Blackpool consisted of in the mind of your Bishop.'

'So why didn't he fire me?'

'For the same reasons I didn't,' he said. 'Because he thought you were intelligent and because we're short of priests.'

'I'm grateful.'

'No,' he said. 'God strengthen us. I don't think you are. All those years ago in Rome, when I met you, David, you were full of zeal for the Church. Things were changing. It was our time, and you had the character to meet all the challenges. Is that not right? And what happened to you? You end up frittering away your vocation, reading paperbacks and cooking fish?'

'I never had the character, Gerard,' I said. 'I was just a lonely young man. I think you knew that.'

'Don't tell me what I knew! You had a calling. You had faith in God. And I had faith in you. How dare you deny that now?'

'Nevertheless,' I said, 'my faith was built on the wrong foundation. It was built on . . . the wrong things.'

'There are no wrong things to build faith on.'

'I'm sorry, but there are.'

'What are you saying?'

'I'm saying I think I used the Church. It was a beautiful hiding place. I'm sure it has been for others.'

'You're having a crisis,' said Bishop Gerard. 'I've seen it before. You need to retreat and examine your faith. I've seen it before in my life, with other priests. You need a holiday.'

'My life has been a holiday,' I said. He coughed down the phone and the anger lengthened through his voice.

'And you bring this to *my door*?'

'I'm sorry for that. I truly am. Please believe that, Gerard. And I am sorry to the parishioners and to God.'

He sighed. 'I remember you coming to see me at Santa

Maria sopra Minerva. The Dominicans worshipped you. You were full of ideas in Rome and you were holy, David. I won't hear any different now. I was thinking about it this morning: maybe you always had a touch of the victim. I remember showing you around the chapel and the room where Galileo was interrogated. The house next to the church. You wanted to stand there for ever, you said. You were full of all your Oxford University questions. Book questions. Faith questions. I remember that.'

'I've always been interested in the telescope,' I said.

'No, David. I remember your actions. You were playing the part of Galileo. One of the old friars was telling us about the Dominicans' suspicion of Galileo and their interrogation of him, and you were transfixed, mouthing the words along with him. You've always been an actor, David. An actor will always want to play the part.'

'My confusions were genuine.'

'But why now?' he said. 'Why has it all come back now? Our troubles are behind us, and we've all had troubles.' He sounded personally defeated, and I hated to think of that.

'Our lives are liable to catch up with us, Gerard.'

He was silent for a moment. I felt there was great intimacy in the silence, as there used to be those years ago at sopra Minerva when he heard my heartfelt and selective confession. 'This is only egotism,' he said. 'The great destroyer.'

I didn't mention the Bishop's own doubts, the walks we used to take along the Appian Way, the feeling once expressed by my proud Glaswegian friend that the Church might offer a refuge against temptation, somewhere to exist as a noble animal in the struggle against the nights, to bed down on ancient stone like the cats in the Coliseum. Gerard was silent about most things – silence being oxygen to men like us – but I knew there hadn't been six months together in his adult life when he wasn't in love and when he didn't go to sleep wanting to be loved.

'We can fix this,' he said.

'How?'

'Inside the Church. We have experience and we can solve the problem in our own way. That is our strength.'

'It is a criminal matter,' I said. 'That is how it will be fixed.'

'Don't misunderstand me,' he said, protecting himself. 'I have already asked the police if it was okay for me to speak with you. I am not interested in covering anything up.'

'Heaven forfend.'

He ignored me. His voice softened, and I recalled how vivid and consoling a pastor he used to be. 'You are not considering your parishioners. Their faith is in your hands and we cannot suffer this to happen. David, think again. Cleave to the love of the faithful. You have never loved them. You took your role seriously, but only as a role.'

'I didn't set out to possess their hearts.'

'That is a wicked statement. Is that one of your *aesthetic* defences? Because art will not defend you now.'

'Sadly not,' I said. 'But I had a beautiful garden. We managed to destroy it together, them and me. I will face it now.'

'Don't do this,' he said. 'You're not thinking straight. No matter what you say, the public will crucify you.'

'I appreciate all the efforts you have made for me, Gerard. But I am my own Judas. My own Pontius Pilate. I kissed the boy and will fight the matter in my own way.'

'It will all be politics and newspapers,' he said. 'And you're bad at politics. You know nothing about the papers up here. You don't understand what people will try to make of this.'

'I must take my chances.'

'I will cut you adrift,' he said.

'As you must.'

'You don't know where you are heading.'

'Then I quote Seneca,' I said. '"If one does not know to which port one is sailing, no wind is favourable."'

He coughed again into the phone. 'That is the kind of remark that will destroy you,' he said.

Someone had been thumping again and again on the front door. I stared at the sideboard as Gerard spoke – Ampleforth in watercolours, a bottle of Haut-Bailly 1999 – and slowly the caring flavour departed from my old friend's voice as he turned bureaucratic.

'What happens now?' I said.

'I must place you on administrative leave,' he said. 'You will leave the rectory by midday tomorrow. We could arrange a place for you at the Dirrans Monastery.'

'That won't be necessary.'

'Look, David,' he said, 'think about what I'm saying. He that yields to reproof shows understanding. A little humility would help you now.'

'It's a little late in the day for that, is it not?'

I rang off and placed the phone back in its cradle. Thirty years of friendship liquidated just like that, in a lather of busted proprieties and self-defences. I wondered what habit had said of us; what Church conventions had revealed of Gerard, what they had hidden. It seemed to me his anger was inseparable from a threatened sense of himself, and I could not blame him for that or for anything worse.

A voice purred at the letterbox. 'We only want to get the facts right,' said the person. 'Listen. Yer gonnae have the chance to put your ane side of the story. Hello. Father Anderton. It's jeest to get the facts. It's in yer ane interests to speak to me.'

They sounded like cattle. I could hear them and smell their pleasure. Who could be sure if the photographers were there for the people or the people there for the photographers, but the noise they made was a lustful and carnival sound and it grew closer, madder, like the sound of drums approaching from the distance to deafen the sinful. I turned off the radio on my way past the upstairs loo and positioned myself in the bedroom, the edge of the curtain between my fingers.

'Come oot, ya child molestin' bastard!'

'Paedophile!'

'Beastie!'

'Come on, ya English bastard!'

Dead flies lay on the windowsill, crisp in the sun. Some of the people down there held placards daubed with hideous words, and they laughed into each other's faces, women holding onto themselves with mirth and a younger one jigging on the spot. I saw a young girl cup her hands around her mouth for increased volume. 'Scumbag!' she shouted.

A man held up a rope, and another one was smoking and digging the air with his finger as he spoke to a reporter. A photographer climbed onto a gravestone to get a better picture of the crowd. Every face was white, and I knew a number of them. The people weren't churchgoers, but they had been to weddings and funerals, and I knew them by their haircuts and their piercings. I'm sure several children were eating ice cream and taking pictures with their phones. It was that kind of day. It was that kind of atmosphere. It was Marymass, after all. And in the middle of the crowd stood the father of Mark McNulty.

He had a certain sleepy menace. A depressed look. I kept hold of the net curtain but tried not to let it move. Mark's father was the dead centre of the crowd and I could see people stroking and patting his arms. The women kissed his cheeks, soothing some terrible feeling. One of them, very plump, wore a turquoise tracksuit and had crimson hair, and she fluttered around the main man like a green-winged macaw. They gave Mark's father the role of chief mourner at a funeral, except they looked towards him for an heroic action.

I could see him taking breaths, each deeper than the last, each denser with the feeling of the crowd, until he heaved in his chest one last time and charged towards the storm doors. I'll always remember it, the look of confusion and hatred on his face and the inward rush, his sudden vanishing from my field of vision and then the thunder at the door.

'Fucken beastie!'

'Paedophile!'

The people. Watching them from the window, I noticed, for all their ferocity, how easy a communion existed between them. A sense of loyalty to one another – the idea of one another – was powerful down there in the lane among the colours and the fizzy drinks. Some of them were Protestants, and a generality of historical dislike and dark heresies must have informed their anger, but I feel most of them were decent in themselves and wanted some sort of improved life, a life in which religious leaders could be trusted and children could be safe. Even to my eyes, there was something objective about the warriors outside the door. I didn't really know them; I didn't know what it might be like to live so certain of togetherness. We each have our rights to idealism, and theirs was theirs, thwarted again by a man in a collar who stood behind the curtains that day, protecting himself from all they could be and all their supposed decencies.

Leave a man to his fate. Let the moments of his life speak either for or against the goodness of his heart. The pillow was cool like nothing on earth. I put my head there, summer, autumn, winter and spring, and was sure as I lay down and felt a twinge of pain in my eye that all might be well and that some old friend might come to my aid. It was not my father, and not yet the distant and distancing music of Chopin. It was not Conor. He passed for a moment through my thoughts, only to tell me he could never help me. None of this world was the world we shared.

The door banged again and I heard it split. None of my teachers came into the room. No mother. No saving grace. The only person in those moments was my oldest acquaintance – myself – waiting as usual for a creak on the stairs, the feel of the cotton against my ear drawing me back to the sound of my own blood turning. I watched the bright window for another moment and then closed my eyes and drowned in a perfect solitude of prayer.

10

THE ECHO OF SOMETHING REAL

Mr McNulty failed to reach the landing before the police came in and dragged him out of the house. I opened my eyes to find the familiar young officer standing in polished shoes. 'Father, I think you should let us take you out of here,' he said. 'There's a mob outside and I don't think you want to hang about any longer.' He bit his lip and seemed to scan the room for superior advice. 'Have you a bag you can pack?'

'I don't want to leave all my things,' I said.

'You'll have to,' he said. 'Between you and me; there are total bampots out there. You're not safe here. Idiots, you know. Have you somewhere else to go?'

I could hear a drum. 'Has the Orange band arrived?'

'One of their drummers,' said the officer. I stood up from the bed and walked to the window. 'I really think you should leave.'

'How absurd,' I said. 'I don't believe this is happening.'

'It's happening all right,' he said. 'There's dozens of press people out there, so everything's by the book. I suggest you pack some clothes.' I asked him if I could drive away in my own car.

'I'm sorry, Father,' he said. 'They've totalled it.'

Coming down the stairs, I ran my hand over the wallpaper. I think I knew I would never see the house again. The banister was warm. It brought to mind the old house in Heysham. The hall carpet was covered in splinters from the broken door, and, seeing them, I wanted again to know the person I had been when I lived in the house unwatched. Who was the person who ascended the stairs each night, the priest in the house alone with a book and a candle by the bed? The noise out there, the shouts: it seemed to come from a place much deeper than I could ever know. The policemen pushed me into the van, a sheet over my head.

'Child molester! I hope ye burn in hell!'

I sat in the van with the darkened windows flashing silver with cameras, my head down, and then a man shouted again. 'I hope you burn in hell for what you did.' The van moved away from the chapel and the crowd opened up, and I dwelled on the man's voice and wondered again if I knew it from the confessional.

My mother and I played cards each night and drank the best part of a 1962 Armagnac, the sound of her low black heels across the floor an echo of Morningside habits, the routines of comfort and sense. She has always been a great advocate of the hot bath and the stiff drink. Especially in a crisis, my mother knows how to behave like a good analyst, someone who feels your desertion was always part of the deal. She never tried to promote her own version of who I ought to be and she was careful never to mechanise the impulses of childhood. She had no smallness in that way.

Some people understand the need to be more than one person. That is one of her strengths and one of the things that shows my mother to be rather superior. She has been many people herself – the wife, the adventurous mother, the romance-seeker, the lady novelist – and during those days in Edinburgh she began by seeking no explanations. She introduced me to several new creams intended for the relief of stressed skin. She made a salade Niçoise with things from Valvona & Crolla. Every day in life she would go to her desk and work like a person expecting a cessation of talent or the final demise of her opportunity. She favours the notion that work defines one's moral worth. She said she was writing a rather windswept tale about the Viking invasion of Largs. And so, each evening, without a care for the modern world and its horrors, she'd return from her desk with colour in her cheeks, ready for olives and a glass of the old Marcel Trépout.

I'd go to the bathroom to be upset. It was a very moving room, her Guerlain perfumes lined up on the shelf, their perfect labels, their beautiful bottles with rounded shoulders, together telling a story about my mother's ventures in the years since my father died. Above the towels she kept a photograph of me on the Indian elephant, and there, against the window surrounded by strings of sparkling beads, one of Conor and me on Magdalen Bridge with sunglasses and ice creams. The room was a delicate mausoleum. The room was a shrine to self-sufficiency and it made me long for my own dear things and the Ayrshire garden of knots.

Four weeks before the trial, it felt like the horizon was clearing. I knew it couldn't be – the worst was yet to come – but I decided to honour the feeling. I put on a new shirt fresh from a Jenners box and combed my hair and walked into my mother's study. The communal gardens looked busy with children and bees, the city just visible through an old sash window. 'I want to talk about it, Mother.'

'By all means,' she said. 'Take this armchair.'

'How's the book?' I said.

'Oh, rather coarse,' she said. 'It involves a quantity of devastating emotion on the headland. You know the sort of thing. My readers wouldn't have it any other way.'

'The books are great. Heaps of life.'

'You're very sweet,' she said, putting a pencil into a pot. 'I'm trying to create an innocent girl in a plaid wrap. She may or may not be carried off on a longship by a horny-helmeted gentleman.'

'Excellent,' I said.

'They'll love it in France,' she said.

'Is there sex?'

'Oh, buckets, my dear. It all happens by torchlight. The usual idea, I'm afraid. One seeks to make all the sexual encounters obscurely invigorating of the national cause.'

'Perfect.'

She said what she said with a smile on her lips, bringing her hands together in a pleased and accomplished way. My mother has long since come to be at home with her nature and the manner of her talent. In conversation, she takes it for granted that many people are better than her, which, to my mind, almost guarantees that few are. She actually works very hard at her books. Spread on the desk in front of her, I could see pictures of gold ingots and reams of notes in her best handwriting. Her room had the wealthy atmosphere of a place where imagination has lived and where tidy thoughts accumulated over the years.

'They are entertainments,' she said.

'That is the best we can hope for.'

'I don't believe it,' she said. She gestured towards a bookshelf lined with foreign editions of her own books. 'These little productions have worked very well for me, but I think you could do better. Something more searching, my dear. I'm afraid

I don't have a great deal of what your old friend Proust called "ascending power".'

'You give yourself too little credit,' I said. 'None of us could do what you have done. I'm afraid I have used up all my circumspection on old hymns and riotous living.'

'In that order?' she asked.

'I hope so.'

A wasp was failing to scale the height of the window. It just crawled up for a while and then lost stamina and dropped back down. 'I heard a fly buzz when I died,' my mother said to herself as she opened the window. From the rear I saw her grey hair was still flattened from bed, though her lips when she turned showed a stain of lipstick. Sitting there, I thought it possible that people lost parts of themselves with age: the back of the head was a place for young people, was it not? 'It's a bit of a performance, getting ready every morning,' she said.

'It's getting to sleep that's hard for me.'

'Perhaps one day you'll write something,' she said. 'Ever since you were young you have looked at things with feeling. Not oddly. Just that you see the shape of things very nicely. When you opted to become a priest, I remember thinking it was that quality that might serve you well. But we're talking about writing. It's customary for writers to be made by their parents, in one way or another. With us it was the other way round. I'm sure I became a novelist to keep up with you.'

'Not true,' I said. 'It's your own gift.'

'I see you're keen to avoid responsibility for these excited tracts,' she said. 'But I'm afraid you may be to blame. My parents didn't equip me for such a life: they made me happy, made me want to marry a happy and moral man. That's all. It was you who added the spice.'

'Oh, silly.'

'Well, I don't care what you say. I'm rather proud of the fact that my outer child gave my inner child a job.'

'You're off your head,' I said. She laughed and took a drink from a bottle of Highland Spring by her desk.

'I'm too old and too grand to care,' she said.

For a minute I thought it might be perfect never to leave that civilised room and the assurance of my mother and her pretty paperweights. She had pinned postcards of seascapes, stones and Rembrandts to the wall; for a minute I wanted to dwell within the compass of her neat capacities, the dailyness of artistic effort. Her face grew serene. She looked at me with a level and levelling gaze. 'What happened?'

'Well, I didn't tell you much on the phone.'

'Go on.'

'I let the past catch up with me.'

'How?'

'These young people. I got involved with them. One of their fathers was depressed and he told me stuff about himself and I guess he wanted to take it back.'

'Go on.'

'The boy's name is Mark. He's very young. I tried to kiss him one night. It was just my own stupidity. I don't think the boy cared that much, but his father has a score to settle and it's all quite sad.'

'You kissed the young man?'

'Yes. I got drunk with him. We took other stuff. I definitely kissed him and held his hand. He must have told his father. I don't know how it came out but the poor man hasn't worked for years. He's taking a stand. And the whole parish wants to kill me. They want some sport.'

'Don't be dismissive, David,' she said. 'You knew what kind of community it was down there, for a Catholic priest.'

'And they say I'm English.'

'Oh dear,' she said.

'And they think I'm posh.'

'And you're now up on some molesting charge?'

'It's not called that, but yes: sexual assault.'

'Oh dear,' she said. She looked into the wood of her desk as if to imagine the possible outcomes. 'You'll have spoken to that nice advocate, Hamilton? You intend to fight?'

'Yes,' I said.

'For your career?'

'No,' I said. 'That's gone. I know that now. And perhaps it should have been gone a long time ago. Or never begun.'

'But what about your friend – your God?'

'You're so mercilessly practical, Mother,' I said. I watched her eyes and hoped they wouldn't stop me. 'You won't like me for saying this, but I believe God is present in all this too.'

'I see,' she said. 'Well, that's the sort of thing you people say. He's never caused anything but trouble in the world before now.'

'Shush,' I said. She shook her small head in a private way and pulled out a drawer of her desk.

'Let's smoke,' she said, handing me a Consulate. 'Of course you are right to fight,' she said. 'These words are grotesque.'

The smoke appeared to make her room even cosier.

'And what does Hamilton say?' she asked.

'He said the boy is a thug. He says it was a kiss of affection, a way of saying goodnight.'

'And you can go with that?'

'I don't think so,' I said. 'I want to tell the truth.'

'Well,' she said, 'this is Scotland. That might seriously hamper your chances of getting a fair hearing.'

'Be serious,' I said.

'You want to tell the truth?'

'If I know it, yes. And if I can.'

'Well,' she said, 'let me ask you something. Would you have gone to bed with that boy if he'd said yes?'

'Almost certainly.'

'But you want to say that you didn't assault him?'

'Precisely,' I said. 'I don't mind saying I fell for him. I don't mind saying I would have slept with him. I admit to being the most stupid person on earth. But I am not a paedophile or anything of that sort and I won't agree to it being called assault.'

'In this area, the law is not built for subtleties,' she said. 'Or, at least, the public nowadays is not minded for subtlety. It may be difficult. But I'd hang onto Hamilton if I were you. He'll follow your instruction with more dedication than you could yourself.'

'Yes,' I said. 'I'm guilty of something – of many things, perhaps – but not of what they say.'

'The times are hysterical,' she said.

'Thank you for noticing.'

'It's my job to notice such things,' she said. 'I know it is within the habits of your cult to feel guilty, but you must be very clear about where any possible wrong existed. Don't feel guilty about feelings. Don't feel guilty about thoughts. Just look to what you actually did.'

'Thank you, Mother.'

'Just try to keep calm.'

'My actions were minimal,' I said. 'It's all the other stuff that matters. My vocation has run its course. I need a new life.'

'Or an old one.'

'Perhaps.'

'But the court won't bother with that. They will be dealing with the image of a lascivious priest.'

'I know,' I said. 'The very least of it.'

'Not in their eyes,' she said. 'Speak to Hamilton. The town will be baying for blood. They've watched a lot of television, one presumes?'

'Some very good people live there,' I said.

'I'm sure. But every small town loves a scapegoat.'

'They've been seeking scapegoats in that town for five hundred years,' I said.

'Well, they've got one now,' she said, stubbing out her cigarette and taking a sip from her glass. 'And he went to Oxford.'

They burned the ground floor of the rectory that night. Father Michael from Irvine called me the next morning with the news. The fire was apparently so fierce the smoke had blackened the walls of the church. My mother had gone to the National Library, and I sat against the bathtub all morning with my head on my knees and a cold silence around me. The police found a cider bottle on the garden path and said it was half filled with petrol, the fire most probably the work of more than one person. I thought of the flames bursting through Mrs Poole's well-ordered cupboards, consuming the dust on the jars of spices and boiling the pickled onions.

He said the sitting room was gutted. The fire must have spread over the carpet and up the sides of the piano. And did it make a sound as it burned? Was there any of the old music? I know the Chopin recordings must have melted into one another, as they do in the mind. They must have fizzed at last into non-existence on the shelf, and then, perhaps, the shelf itself collapsed and the Italian etchings burned along with the blue and white volumes of the Scott Moncrieff, the only books I had taken from Balliol after Conor died, when my calling began, when the start of life was over. I thought of Marcel in

his Paris bedroom as the fire in the grate drew over a pile of
twigs, the smell reminding him of being lost in books at Com-
bray and Doncières.

'What have you lost?' my mother asked.

'Everything and nothing,' I said.

My things were gone: the books, the wine. Only ideas were
left, the fire gone out on the west coast but the twigs still burning in Marcel's hearth. That evening, I wanted to spread into
the sky over Leith and join that body of imagined beings in the
heart of Midlothian. In the warm Edinburgh night I began to
survive my own losses, knowing the city out there was a glory
of invention, a glory defying the blunt reality of the rock it
stood on.

We went to the Usher Hall. My mother wanted to get my
mind off things, so she had bought two tickets for us to see the
BBC Scottish Symphony Orchestra, a programme of Messiaen.
I remember sitting down within the buzz of the dressy crowd.
I could smell my mother's perfume and could feel the weight of
everything behind me. God knows how conscious I was of
some old song now ended, and my heart was sore when I
thought of the rectory, but I stared at the stage and willed it to
produce something grand and new.

'It's like poetry,' my mother said. 'Like Wallace Stevens.'

'Yes,' I said.

'Celestial.'

Messiaen's *Oiseaux exotiques* became a wild aviary of
earthly things struggling to wing the imaginary sky.

'Birds were the first musicians,' I said.

My mother nodded and placed a mint in her mouth. I looked
through the crimson dusk to see the words in the programme.

'*Messiaen spoke of the sovereign liberty of birdsong. The
earth's birds never learned harmony and counterpoint.*'

The percussion exploded into a passion of discordant nature and I turned over the page. '*Messiaen was taking over from Debussy*,' it said. I felt the sound was more real than birds. My mother reached over and touched my hand as the music ended, and I set my eyes on the programme again. '"*What is left for me," said Messiaen, "but to seek out the true, lost face of music somewhere off in the forest, in the fields, in the mountains or on the seashore, among the birds."*'

We walked along Princes Street to the Café Royal. My mother took my arm and we spoke to each other in the pretty light of passing buses. She asked me the name of the second piece we had heard.

'*Trois petites liturgies de la Présence Divine.*'

'They were very young, weren't they, the singers?'

'They were lovely,' I said. She squeezed her arm further through mine and sniffed against the cold wind, making as if to close the gaps in her coat and take in the smell of the buses' diesel.

'I think I preferred the birds one.'

'Me too,' I said. 'It was more religious.'

She smiled. We stopped beside the Scott Monument and my mother went into her bag to find her gloves. 'This is like something by George Gilbert Scott,' I said. 'The man who built the Martyrs' Memorial outside Balliol.'

'Clever man,' she said. 'Your Roman friends certainly made mincemeat of those poor Oxford heretic buggers.'

'No need to look so amused,' I said. She took time to pause and enjoy our exchange.

'His grandson built Liverpool Cathedral,' I said.

'A beautiful thing.' Her lips moved as if she was going to say more about Liverpool, but she halted and looked up at me. 'Did you love that boy?' she said.

'Which one?'

'The one in Ayrshire.'

'I don't imagine so,' I said, then hesitated. 'Perhaps I've been lonely for a very long time.'

She stretched up and kissed my cheek.

'That business is never easy. Not for anyone,' she said.

We crossed the road and disappeared into the darkness of a cobbled street, ready to enter a warm room with napkins and wine glasses and a dozen oysters from the depths of Loch Fyne.

The lights in the tower blocks on the other side of Ayr harbour seemed to glimmer with unknowable life. A young man shaved at a bathroom mirror with a rose light over his head, and I saw him turn at the sink and shout through to a pair of children in yellow pyjamas who bounced on a bed in the next room. As it grew late, the harbour was dark and seagulls swooped down to an abandoned barge.

I had never been bored in my life. Not even during those long evening Masses in Rome or endless mornings of confessions, listening to old ladies dote on their sinful lives. None of it bored me, not the long liturgies nor the screed of petty crimes, but the afternoons in the harbour flat at Ayr were spent in a fanfare of ennui. Perhaps it was the waiting. Perhaps there is nothing more tedious than self-doubt. But that rented apartment had no discernible breath in its furnished rooms, except for the central heating, a warm drone that clicked all day and itched my conscience.

'Thank you, Mother,' I said on the phone.

'You don't have to be there,' she said. 'You were fine here. You might do better to keep your distance.'

'I won't,' I said. 'Too late now for that.'

Junk mail clattered on the mat. Free newspapers. Sometimes

I'd wander round the harbour, passing the public swimming baths that were situated behind my building. I didn't go in, much as I liked the coffee machine and the sound of voices echoing off the tiles. The staff were trained to stare at you oddly, so I walked past and occasionally stopped for a second to look through the huge window. Old ladies in the afternoon would be swimming in twos, as if grateful for the water, their painted nails gleaming as they smoothed back their hair. One could see children up on the diving boards, and I walked away, thinking their chlorine hours must appear to last for ever while they are happening.

My mobile rang in the bedroom. Her voice sounded nervous and her words were rather obscure, stranded for a moment or two in a haze of uncertain obligation. 'I've missed our times,' she said.

'Me too, Mrs Poole.'

I knew Mrs Poole must have spoken to the police. I knew she was the only real witness, but I myself was the greater witness, or so I thought, and it never occurred to me to blame her. On the phone, it was quickly a matter of resumed affection, Mrs Poole speaking as if our difficulty had not only faded out but had, like limbo, passed into the history of redundant moods. 'I couldn't get over it, about the house,' she said. 'Your beautiful things. They have no respect in this town and what a scunner to do a thing like that to the rectory.' Mrs Poole had never seemed more Scottish than she was just then, her good common sense measured against the infinite smallness of others. Her instinct to improve and overcome – even on the phone – came quickly to brighten the harbour flat and hoist my degraded spirits. 'Now,' she said, 'I won't have any more nonsense. Give me your address. I'll come with lunch.'

She turned up the next day in the grip of her old efficiency, shopping bags dangling at the end of each arm, her thin body balancing the scales of justice. She put down the bags and looked around the sitting room in a familiar way. 'This place isn't for you, Father.'

'Very spartan, isn't it?'

'Not for you at all. Is this what they call executive flats?'

'I think so,' I said.

She took out a cucumber, some butter, and walked briskly to the kitchen and brought down a pan. Her motions caused me to think she didn't want to be scrutinised. She spoke as she worked, but her eyes were turned down and there was something self-conscious, something vulnerable, even in her decisiveness. Our eyes met as she lifted two packets from one of the bags and held them up. 'Salmon steaks,' she said. 'Organic.'

'Still saving the planet?' I said.

'I think it's past saving,' she said, scrunching cellophane into the bin and wiping the bin with a cloth.

'Your hair is different,' I said.

She bit her cheek. 'It's a wig.'

She bowed for a moment, making it funny, then showed me the label on a bottle of wine. It was a dry Anjou.

'I'm sorry,' I said.

'Oh, never mind. It's okay. Let's have a glass.' She found the corkscrew and plopped a bag of small potatoes into water, before coming back. 'I'll wait to do the salmon,' she said. 'Salmon is very quick.'

'How delicious.'

She tilted her glass in my direction.

'*Saumon poêlé au vin blanc de la Loire*,' she said, haltingly.

I asked her how the treatment was going. She touched her stomach and lowered her glass. 'I'm having chemotherapy,' she said. 'I had an operation, but it won't work. I've always known that.'

I swallowed my words with a mouthful of wine, and she seemed quite pleased with that, her mood of acceptance being undisturbed by the grief and the panic of other people.

'My mother told me you were fighting it.'

'I'm trying,' she said. 'But that's just a thing you do. It won't work. Your mother's been very good to me.'

Over lunch, Mrs Poole told me she had visited the rectory after the fire. 'I thought I might be able to save some of the rose bushes,' she said, 'but they were wasted. I always knew those people were vandals, but to hurt innocent plants is just beyond the beyonds.'

'That happened before the fire,' I said.

She told me the Bishop had been down to address the parishioners. He said an investigation was under way. He said it was a criminal matter and that I was suspended until the matter was concluded. 'But he gave the impression you wouldn't be coming back,' she said. Apparently, Bishop Gerard reminded the people of their faith and advised the young ones to take confession. 'It went down like a lead balloon,' said Mrs Poole. 'That boy's father stood up in the middle of the church and shouted that the children had nothing to confess.'

I barely said anything as she spoke. Some of it was hard to listen to, but of course I was curious. Anyhow, I was glad to find the salmon was fresh. The main thing I noticed was the change in Mrs Poole's attitude. She spoke kindly, but I felt the kindness she expressed was a new and vital thing for her. In some way my reduction had redressed the balance in our relationship. She was the wiser one now; she was the more powerful. Like a spurned lover in a Russian story, she came back from the Grand Tour wearing silver buttons and with knowledge in her eyes. So I accepted my own part in that story without complaint: the fallen idol, no longer spurning but subtly spurned.

'I have to tell you something,' she said. 'I gave a statement to the police and I worry that it won't help you.'

'It's not your job to help me in that way,' I said. 'You're helping me now and that's all that matters.'

'They want me to appear at the trial.'

'You must do what is right,' I said.

'I suppose it's wrong being here. But I wanted to come.'

'No one will ever know.'

She nodded. She was free to act now like one of those people much busier than oneself. She spoke of her environmental pursuits and her struggle to find time for this and that, giving a sense of people chasing her and expecting more than is humanly possible. It was pleasant, though, our old phrases and teases coming back, over the hour, to energise her voice. 'One of my nurses is studying art at the Open University,' she said. 'I told her Matisse had no manners. Forget the red wallpaper. He was one of them who behaved as if he had no talent. Totally horrible to all the women in his life.'

'They probably deserved it.'

'Listen to you,' she said. 'Foreign dictator.'

'Part-time now,' I said.

I noticed she hadn't eaten much, but the wine was gold in the glasses. I looked out and saw a man coughing as he walked past the window. Mrs Poole was putting on her coat as seagulls scattered behind the man and soared over the harbour.

'That looked like Mr Poole,' I said.

'That's right,' she said. 'He's been sitting out in the car.'

'All this time?'

She just looked at me and pursed her lips. The answer was lost in some acreage of pain that Mrs Poole traversed alone.

'He probably went to the pub at the end of the street,' she said. I lifted the plates through to the kitchen and she followed me, tying a scarf round her head. She kissed my cheek next to the microwave oven. 'Good luck,' she said. I noticed a faint metallic smell. 'Tell you what. I'll bring you some CDs the next time I come. I have lots of music now.'

'Thank you,' I said. 'That would be kind.'

She paused next to the entryphone, lifting it off to wipe with the tails of her headscarf. There was evidence on Mrs Poole's face of the old quick-change artist. 'I've been thinking about it,' she said, 'and I think you probably are quite English.'

'Really?'

'Just like that,' she said. 'The way you can say "really?". It's English not to say things, to go on like you don't know things.'

'So, I'm English now. Was that the summit of my crimes?'

'No,' said Mrs Poole. 'It's not a crime not to know yourself. It's not a crime to send life away. It's just a shame.'

'Good Lord. A man in hiding from himself.'

'That's right,' she said. 'And very English to know how to put a name to a problem but not care how to solve it.'

'Mrs Poole, I believe in God.'

'That's right.'

(I recalled Geoffrey Nashe: *It's not the existence of God we're bothered about but the existence of you who say you believe in him.*)

She clutched her handbag close to her chest and smiled. 'I wish I could do more for you,' she said.

'You've done such a lot already.'

'All right,' she said. 'I'll be seeing you.' She went along the hall, the echo of her voice then lost in a rush of cold air.

The sands of Ayr were blue after midnight. The sea was silent and black. It seemed that the morning might never come, but the light on Ailsa Craig shone methodically over the sea, like a beckoning star that winked in defiance of dangers. The night seemed watchful of itself in those weeks before the trial. I walked along the esplanade each night, killing an hour or two, thinking of journeys made.

One Saturday night, I stopped to examine a plaque mounted on the sea railings. 'At Ayr the Scots Parliament met in 1315 after the victory at Bannockburn,' it said, 'to confirm Bruce and his family in possession of the Crown of Scotland.' The plaque was rusted with sea spray and scraps of chewing gum were lodged between its iron words. I would meet a great number of dogs on those nights along the esplanade. Some of them walked far in front of their owners, sniffing about the bases of the litter bins along the coastal path. 'Aye, aye,' said the owners, passing by with that likeable vulnerability that comes with sleepiness.

That night I heard the sound of the disco. The rave music. It was booming down from the Pavilion, a huge nightclub that stands above the beach. I passed a group of young people who were dancing on the esplanade. One of the boys had two neon sticks in his hands and was making fast coloured patterns against the dark water behind him. He stopped dancing. He put his hand on the back of another boy who was bent over the rail, puking on the sand. 'Yer awright, wee boy,' he said. Then he shouted over his shoulder: 'Geez that water ower, Chubb.' I looked over to the grass verge and saw that friend of Mark's. He was sitting on a bench smoking a reefer and sifting through a pile of CDs.

'Look,' he said. 'It's thingmi – the priest.'

Passing between them I noticed they were all sweating. Those without shaved heads had wet hair despite the cold night.

Lisa emerged from a blue, peeling shelter. A certain panic was evident in her eyes and I slowed down to a stop. 'Father,' she said, 'don't tell my dad you saw me. I'm supposed to be doing a sleepover at Julie's. You won't tell, sure you won't?' She had no notion of how powerless I had become since our friendship began, and listening to her, examining her worried face, I saw the depth of my Ayrshire folly. Lisa hadn't a clue. It had come too late to me as a piece of understanding: young people like her have no time for the weighing of priorities. I was facing some sort of ruin and Lisa faced being grounded and it all meant the same to her. Tears welled up in her eyes.

'I can't speak to you, Lisa,' I said.

'Whiddye mean?'

'I have to go. Please take care of yourself.'

We shared a bond of selfishness, perhaps of self-pity too. But Lisa was high on something, and she seized the moment to dramatise her needs. She wasn't a very tall girl but she stood in front of me and barred my way.

'I've been sticking up for you,' she said.

'I'm sure you have.'

'You're my friend,' she said. 'We had some right good laughs. That time we went over there tae the island.'

I tried to stare past her and see my way to the road.

'Julie!' she said. 'He's trying tae dizzy me. He willnae even talk. What have I ever done tae him?' She was shouting now and blubbing at the same time, as if the day's great occasion for hysteria had finally presented itself. I wanted to protect her but I didn't know how.

'Leave her alane,' said the other girl.

'I can't speak to either of you,' I said.

'Fucken homosexual,' said Julie.

Like a person in a soap opera, Lisa grabbed her friend's cigarette and took two quick puffs. 'I cannae handle this,' she said. I moved around them and began striding across the grass to get to the main road, and then Lisa came around and pushed me in the chest. 'You're jeest the same as everybody else,' she said. 'It was me that was yer friend. Nobody else gave a fuck about you.' She looked at her chum. 'Go and get McNuggets,' she said.

'Lisa. Please. Don't detain me here. I can't be seen talking to you. It's not my choice.'

'It is your choice! The good times we had before the summer. You said you'd take me tae London. The drives we went on. The wedding. The nights out with me and McNuggets. What about London? You said. Now everything's fucken spoiled because of you and him.'

'I didn't say that, Lisa, about London.'

'Just leave her alane!'

Lisa grabbed me by the arm. 'Whit is this new jack-shit attitude you're coming up with?' She plucked at her blouse and pointed her finger in my face. 'Know what this is?'

She nodded down at her blouse.

'Versace,' she said. It was painful to listen to her, more painful than I would have expected.

'I'm sorry, Lisa. About everything.'

'You're a fucken disappointment,' she said. 'And you know what? I'm finished with you.'

I saw her bright, tired eyes, the pupils engorged. I recalled how she had spoken that time on top of Ailsa Craig. How she wanted to be a make-up artist in films and own bundles of shoes. She let go of my arm and I wanted to say in that instant that I'd find another car and we'd drive to London and Oxford and maybe Rome, not stopping, not ending until we'd found all the things she wanted to possess.

'I'm sorry,' I said.

She gave me a steady look, a look, I think, that spoke of survival, the shrinking of dreams to fit the demands of everyday life.

'You will be sorry,' she said.

The squall of young people receded further behind me on the grass. I got to the road and walked into the pattern of streets that surround the Sandgate. I don't know how long I walked and how many useless thoughts disappeared into the shadows among the old kirks and causeways, but eventually I came to be standing in a lane next to an all-night kebab shop. The smell was of sweltering onions, and I slowly caught my breath, the dark of the lane beneficent. I tried to think of something clean, something fresh, and my mouth flooded with the taste of oranges, the ones, perhaps, that once glowed on the trees of Rome like orbs of infinite plenty. My heart beat quickly and I waited a while, fusing with the thought of these other places. Then I set off. Perhaps if I walked down the lane and across the kirkyard I'd emerge to see the closeness of the harbour lights.

11

KILMARNOCK

I suppose October will always remind me of school. No matter where I find myself in the world, autumn tastes of Ample-forth, and I see the mists over the fields and the leaves turning on the hill. As soon as the blackberries are glossy among the thorns, I feel Yorkshire rising out of my memory with its tangle of unbroken hopes, those of a religious people still waiting for God and willing the world to be orderly. For all the years that have passed, I still welcome autumn with a dream of divine wealth for the coming year, and I begin to hear the monks cloaking the evening with the sound of their devotions.

A clerk of Kilmarnock Sheriff Court rubbed her eyes and looked past the tables of Court Number One. The pine tables themselves were autumnal, stacked with auburn volumes on Scots law. 'Are you David Anderton?' she said. A person coughed behind me in the public gallery and I was seized by either a moment's fear or a lifetime's quantity of doubt. 'Is that correct?' she said.

'Yes. That's correct. I am David Anderton.'

Sheriff Wilson appeared to be a rather tight knot of a man. From his position on the bench he looked over the courtroom with disdain, preparing to find occasions both large and small for the display of his errant temper. People said he was an amateur expert in the writings of James Boswell: from the tilt of his wig, from the ruby flesh of his cheeks, to say nothing of the blue, meticulous eye with which he surveyed the shabby contents of the court, one could only assume that his amateur passions had come, over time, to weave themselves in with his professional concerns. One imagined him, indeed, coming into Kilmarnock each day from a house filled with the appurtenances of Boswellian admiration, the syllabubs, eighteenth-century drinking glasses and damp engravings that proved to such a man that there was once a more interesting time than the one he himself was condemned to inhabit. I'm afraid that's it. Sheriff Wilson had the pawky upper-class humour that makes very senior lawyers intolerable. He also had the claret-dimmed sense of his own grandness in a world of moral miniatures. I knew immediately he would have stuffed animals in his house and embossed invitations on his mantel for garden parties at Holyrood House. His hands were small and fidgety. His forehead was pallid. He took the trouble now to lower his half-moon spectacles and stare out at me, as if an entirely new manner of lowlife had appeared before him. 'I would ask you to speak with more volume,' he said. 'Your voice is of a tincture we don't often hear in this environment.'

'That will be fine,' I said.

'Sorry? Speak up.'

'That's fine.'

'Quite so,' he said. He hesitated over his notes. 'We gather you are a graduate of Oxford University?'

'Alas, not a graduate, Your Lordship. But, yes, I was a student there.'

'And which college?'

'Balliol, Your Lordship.'

'I see,' he said, before smiling, or showing a row of small dark teeth to the Procurator Fiscal. 'Never apologise, never explain,' he said. 'That's what Benjamin Jowett said, was it not?' He looked back at me like an over-rewarded schoolteacher. 'The head of Balliol.'

'Yes,' I said. 'The Master of Balliol.'

He took a handkerchief from a far corner of his gown, wiped his nose with it and waved it at the Fiscal. 'Proceed,' he said.

The clerk read out the indictment. 'It is alleged that in the early hours of 11 July 2003 you did sexually assault Mark McNulty in the chapel-house of the Church of St John Ogilvie in the town of Dalgarnock. How do you plead?'

'Not guilty,' I said.

Over the course of six hours, the Procurator Fiscal drew on the evidence of witnesses to point up my deceit, my cunning, my slow and cynical befriending of Mark and Lisa. It emerged it was well known in Dalgarnock that my attention was seldom on pastoral duties. His first witness was the music teacher from St Andrew's, Mr Dorran, who appeared in the witness box wearing a tie that looked as if it had been bought for the occasion. 'Mr Dorran,' said the Fiscal, 'how long have you been teaching at St Andrew's Academy?'

'Nearly twenty years.'

'And over that time, have you had much to do with the religious aspects of the children's education?'

'A great deal,' said Dorran. 'As a music teacher, I've always thought it important to help with hymns and that, to try and increase a child's faith if you like with the right use of music.'

'And so you would say you had the trust of the children and their parents when it came to religious education?'

'Oh, aye,' he said. 'I often work in partnership with the parents to improve the chances of the children getting a Catholic education.'

'And you have seen a number of priests in the parish, then?'

'Two or three, yes. Over the years.'

'And what did you think of David Anderton's contribution to your efforts in that regard?'

'Well, obviously, at first, he's well educated and that, so we were glad to have a parish priest who cared about teaching as a profession. He helped out very well at the school a couple of times. But Father David had what I'd call a character problem. Is it okay to say that?'

'Go on,' said the Sheriff.

'He had what I'd call a natural ability to wind people up.'

'A *what*?' said the Sheriff. 'He had what, did you say?'

'I said he wound people up, Your Honour.'

'I'm not Your Honour, I'm Mi Lord.'

'Sorry, sir. He wound all the staff up. He got snobby with them and made it difficult to get things done. Some of us thought he was having some sort of crisis during the year. He hardly wanted to talk about what you might call sacramental or pastoral issues. It was all food and wine with him or he'd be interested in talking about politics or whatever. We'd only ever had Irish priests in the parish before. They'd come in to take confessions.'

'And was that his worst crime, in your view?' said the Fiscal. 'Not bothering with Catholic care?'

'Not really,' said Dorran. 'That was just the icing. It was more noticeable the way he was with some of the pupils. My colleagues and I were aware of the fact that he saw some of them outside school hours. He seemed to cultivate the company of certain youngsters. They had a language. He was forever giving them CDs and presents. He took them on trips.'

'What sort of trips?'

'To places of interest. Castles and battlefields or whatever. Places that Father David decided were interesting. One time he took a group of them on a boat to Ailsa Craig. There was talk of drink being consumed.'

'The bird sanctuary?' said the Sheriff. 'Ailsa Craig, you say?'

'Yes, My Lord.'

'We will hear shortly from your colleague, Mr McCallum,' said the Fiscal. 'But in a statement to the police he said that he found it difficult to say no to Father David. Was that your experience also?'

'In a Catholic school,' said Dorran, 'it's always hard to say no to the chaplain. They have a kind of authority.'

The Fiscal walked in front of the bench and tapped his lips with a pencil.

'You say Mr Anderton had built some sort of relationship with these pupils. What sort of youngsters were these?'

'What you might call the more difficult element,' said Dorran. 'The ones in the funny farm. I mean the remedial group.'

'And would you say these pupils are especially vulnerable as young individuals?' said the Fiscal.

My advocate, Hamilton, stood up.

'Objection,' he said.

'Please, Mr Hamilton,' said the Sheriff. 'Do you really want to go this way? We have a lot to get through and the question is actually quite legitimate, wouldn't you say?'

'I have no interest in holding up the proceedings, Your Lordship,' said Hamilton, 'but the question contains an inference that it is beyond the power of this court to prove or disprove. Children's vulnerability is something we might take for granted without a special point being made of it in this case.'

The Sheriff sighed and wiped his nose.

'Overruled,' he said. 'Please answer the question.'

'Could it be repeated?' Dorran asked.

'Would you say the pupils who make up remedial classes at St Andrew's could be described as being especially vulnerable?'

'Yes,' he said. 'I would probably say that. More vulnerable and more tough as well.'

Other witnesses appeared. Most of them were more hurt than angry, and I wished I could reach over and right some of the wrongs, maybe just by being more of a friend than I had been. But during cross-examination my advocate swept them up like a whale consuming plankton. Everything he said made my situation better but my feelings worse, and I knew he had no sense in his dazzling Edinburgh cufflinks of the small ills that lead not only to crimes but the accusation of crimes. As always, the court officials, the lawyers, the Sheriff, though they seemed to power the move towards righteousness and good judgement, were actually just paid spectators to a very private set of personal disorders, about which they knew nothing and cared to know nothing.

'I call Mrs Anne Poole,' said the Fiscal.

I knew before God that I had a sin to answer to when I saw Mrs Poole make her way across the court. She had got worse in the weeks since I last saw her. She wasn't old but her face was changed by illness; you could see, as she walked, her struggle against the fraying of her personhood as the cancer moved to define her. When she reached the witness box she asked for a glass of water. I swallowed with her. Letting myself down had become a familiar way with me. I'd got so used to being equivocal and unsure and covering my life in caution. Yet as Mrs Poole looked up from the glass and caught my eye, I felt I was no good. She smiled. I am the servant of my own performance but she may have been one of its victims, and I wanted to say to the court that my innocence was academic next to hers. Our afternoons together had not been extra lessons for her – as she thought of them – but new lessons for me in how to bear the consequences of the past. Mrs Poole knew more about that than I might ever know. Her lips were trembling as the Fiscal looked up from his papers.

'Mrs Poole,' he said, 'thank you for coming to the court today. I gather you have not been in the best of health.'

She shook her head and gathered herself.

'Am I right in stating that you previously worked for David Anderton in the chapel-house at the Church of St John Ogilvie?'

'I worked there, yes,' she said. 'For Father David.'

'Right. And did you enjoy that work? I believe you cleaned the house and prepared meals and so on?'

'I enjoyed my work.'

'And are you a Catholic, Mrs Poole?'

'Yes,' she said.

'So you have the utmost respect for the clergy and believe they have a position of responsibility in their community? You would say that, would you not?'

'Yes,' she said.

'And you worked regular days, I believe?'

'Mondays and Fridays,' she said, before clearing her throat. 'And a half day on a Sunday.'

'A Sunday morning, yes?'

'That's right.'

'And would you be so kind, Mrs Poole, just in your own words, to tell the court what you saw when you arrived for work on Sunday 11 July?'

'I'd just like to say something first,' she said.

'Please answer the question, Mrs Poole.'

'Your Honour,' she said, looking up at Sheriff Wilson, 'I

want to say something before I answer the man's question.'

'We don't allow statements here, Mrs Poole.'

'I know,' she said, 'but I just want to say an important thing before answering the man's question.'

'Please be quick,' he said.

'Father David is not a bad man. I don't think he knows very much about people, and Dalgarnock was a strange place to him. He does not understand how they do things here and I just want to say that he is a good person underneath . . .'

'Mrs Poole,' said the Sheriff.

'He knows so much about other things,' she said.

'I must ask you to stop, Mrs Poole.'

'We didn't always agree about things,' she went on. 'I have always liked music and we disagreed about some topics. But Father David was good to me and I know he was to those kids, as well. They're no angels either.'

The Sheriff raised his voice.

'Mrs Poole! This is a court of law. I am sure you have very tender reminiscences of the accused, but we are here today to establish whether or not he committed a criminal offence. Do you understand what I am saying?'

'Yes,' she said.

'Well, please just confine yourself to answering this gentleman's questions.'

Mrs Poole's spirit rose with the severity of the Sheriff's counsel. She took a drink from her water glass and turned her shallow cheeks to face him, her voice like a smile inside a whisper. 'I'm not an uncultivated woman, Your Honour,' she said.

He fidgeted. 'I have no doubt . . .'

'No, sir. I was Father David's housekeeper. He paid for my work out of his own pocket. He paid for a great deal of things out of his own pocket, including the wine we would sometimes drink at lunch. He taught me something about how to choose it and how to taste it. I had been learning French for some time before I knew him and then he helped me improve it with a little conversation.'

'Mrs Poole,' he said.

'I will not be shushed by you or by anybody else!' she said, and a certain palpitation entered the atmosphere of the court. 'I am a cultured person. And so is he, the accused. And perhaps you are too, sir. Are you familiar with the works of Robert Burns?'

'Yes, I am, Mrs Poole. As a matter of fact, I'm Chairman of the North Ayrshire Association of Burns Clubs. Now, listen . . .'

'That's good,' she said very quietly. 'Then you'll know very well I'm sure his "Address to the Unco Guid".'

'*No, you don't!*' he said. 'This is a court of law.' And as she started to speak she smiled again and he raised his voice, saying, 'No.'

'About the Rigid Righteous and the Rigid Wise,' she said. 'The whole world is full of them now. These people running through the streets and outside this court today haven't a line of poetry between them and yet they would seek to destroy this man.'

'Mrs Poole,' the Sheriff shouted, 'I will have no hesitation . . .'

'*The cleanest corn that e'er was dight,*' she said. '*May hae some pyles o' caff in.*'

'. . . and I mean it, Mrs Poole.'

'There's yer Ayrshire wisdom,' she said.

Wilson brought his hand down on the wood and Mrs Poole went silent, and I never heard her speak like that again. '*Mrs Poole,*' he said, 'if there are any more outbursts of that sort I will have no hesitation whatever in removing you from this courtroom. You are showing contempt for these proceedings, and I will not tolerate that. Am I making myself clear?'

'Yes,' she said.

'Now, confine your remarks to what might be said in response to the questions put to you by this learned gentleman.'

'We hear you now speak in broad defence of your former employer, Mrs Poole,' said the Fiscal. 'But let us leap back. In a statement you gave to the police on the fifth of August this year you said, and I quote: "I don't think he took his vocation very seriously. I think it's all sentiment with Father David. He lives in the past or some other place. He was stupid to take up with those menaces and I told him as much." Are these your words, Mrs Poole?'

'I was upset at the time,' said Mrs Poole.

'Are these your words? Or are you now withdrawing these statements you made to the police?'

'I am not withdrawing anything,' she said. 'I was upset when I made these remarks. I have not been well.'

'So they reflect your views at the time?'

'Things are complicated sometimes,' she said.

'Complicated you say, Mrs Poole,' he said. 'And was there anything complicated about what you saw when you came to start work early on the morning of the eleventh of July?'

'I don't understand the question.'

'Let me refresh your memory. In your statement you said that David Anderton was "sitting in the living room surrounded by bottles of spirits and wine". You said he was holding Mark McNulty's hand when you entered. You said there was loud music playing and the young man looked inebriated. You said there was the smell of hashish or "something of that kind". You added: "Father David was stupid. He was hanging

245

over that boy McNulty like a cheap suit." Did you say these things, Mrs Poole?'

'Yes,' she said.

'And did the young man look comfortable?' he said.

'That young man always looks comfortable,' she said. 'It isn't in his nature not to be comfortable. He does what he pleases.'

'I put it to you, Mrs Poole, that you are in no position to judge that. Mark McNulty was fifteen years old at the time of the incident. You are in no position to judge what trauma he might have suffered at the hands of David Anderton. Or what situation of trust may have been exploited.'

'No,' she said. 'I suppose I'm not.'

He went around these topics for some time, and the fire slowly went out in Mrs Poole's eyes. She looked weary again, as if she had spent everything she had on that first outburst. Eventually the glare of the court lights made her seem very small and white. 'One last question,' said the Fiscal with a sweep of his gown. 'His Lordship referred at the beginning to your recent illness. We are very sorry to hear of it.'

She nodded into the middle distance.

'You recently underwent a series of operations at Crosshouse Hospital. Is that right?'

'Yes,' she said.

'And you were under the care of the private medical wing of that hospital, is that right?' She looked past him towards me and said nothing. 'It would appear to be the case,' continued the Fiscal. 'And may I ask you to tell the court who paid for that private treatment, Mrs Poole?'

'Objection!' said Hamilton. But Mrs Poole said nothing while the lawyers argued and the Sheriff took out his handkerchief and issued his views on the proprieties. She simply stared over the courtroom and held my eye very firmly, a long, far-seeing look which had about it nothing regretful and nothing beseeching, as if she were looking down the length of our former garden to see the sundial and the roses.

'That'll do for now,' said the Fiscal.

'It's okay,' I said to Mrs Poole's glittering eyes.

When they brought me from the cells the police had cuffed me in front so that I appeared to have praying hands. Before coming up, I had washed them in the metal basin by the bed, and I stopped there to read again the graffiti scratched into the walls. 'Young Tiny Cumbie,' said one. 'The Apache Rules the Nation,' said another. 'Big Shout Out to Sharon and Wee Santa from the Big Jello.'

Sitting on the bed, I remember wondering what the Bombastics would have said of all this: the building scored with the people's desires, the amount of personal history lodged in the names of gangs and girlfriends and babies evoked in solitude. When I came up the steps into the courtroom and heard the hissing, I felt my great appointment with the people's hatred had arrived. I looked up at the jury of men and women with their civic mouths and clean shirts and blouses. 'I have come some distance. Everything is personal. What I have done and what I have failed to do. What you will think and what you will fail to think. It is all personal. My journey towards you started a long time ago, and so did yours to me – a long time ago – and we must simply play our parts and move on.'

I would have said this, given half the chance. But I said nothing. I turned my head and saw my mother in the public gallery. There was no one from the Church and no one from England. The people of Dalgarnock were the world to me now, and they sat in rows in their puffy jackets, checking the style and the workings of each other's phones. Afternoons in court are like afternoons nowhere else: time and progress come to a stop, daylight falling from the glass panels like manna from a careless world.

Bishop Gerard had spoken about me in one of the papers. 'I knew him as a young man,' he said. 'In those days he was a person of very singular devotion. Father Anderton came from a good family. Before he arrived in our diocese, he spent many quiet years as a parish priest in Blackpool. We have looked into this time and found nothing untoward. I appointed him in the hope that he would bring a new vitality to our pastoral care. He is now on a different journey and we pray for him. The Dalgarnock parish is undergoing a period of healing and we must put the past behind us.' One of the policemen showed me the *Evening Times* as we left the court after the first day. There was a huddle round the car. It's hard to tell the difference between press people and ordinary people: they have a similar avarice for the drama of wasted lives, and as the car pulled out I could see them pressing forward with the same sort of pleasure.

The next morning, we heard evidence from the young people via a live television link, and, in this way, the Procurator Fiscal extracted their version of the damage done to them and the liberties taken. Lisa exhibited all the fear and excitement one might have expected: she seemed very pleased to be on television at last, and she told lies, though none that mattered a great deal by that stage. My advocate stood up to speak and my heart lurched, something in his method making him more objectionable than anyone.

'In the year prior to meeting Father David, would you say you were a good pupil, Miss Nolan?'

'No' bad.'

'Not bad,' he said. 'Yet not very good, either. It appears you had a truancy problem. It also appears you had been excluded from St Andrew's on two separate occasions for unacceptable behaviour. I put it to you, Miss Nolan, that you were in fact the very opposite of a good pupil, and that, far from Father David exploiting you and your friend, Father David was in fact very kind to you both. He took trouble with you that few other individuals would have taken, and you rewarded him by drawing him into circumstances you knew would be difficult for him. Is that not right?'

'Naw,' she said. 'It was him that wanted to go to places. It was him that rang us or texted us and wanted to go out. He never even acted like a priest. He acted like he wanted to be our pal or something.'

'You may say that, Miss Nolan, but the evidence suggests that you in fact turned up several times at the chapel-house uninvited. You pursued Father David at his place of work many times, did you not?'

'You're twisting everything.'

'On the contrary, Miss Nolan. I believe I am stating the facts as they occurred over the course of the spring and early summer of this year. Mark McNulty was your boyfriend, was he not? And you were having some difficulty with one another, were you not? And you in fact became jealous of the help that Father David was giving Mark and of the innocent friendship that had grown between them. Is that not right, Miss Nolan?'

'That's rubbish,' she said. 'He fancied Mark. Everybody knew that.'

'Did they, Miss Nolan? The record suggests that you could not maintain a relationship with any of your teachers. Your father was often unhappy with you. There is a suggestion here that you have been involved in several bouts of under-age drinking. But now, Miss Nolan, we are to accept you as an excellent judge of character?'

'You don't know him,' she said.

'Oh, but you do, Miss Nolan. You know him very well. This man who has been a devoted parish priest for nearly thirty years. This man who played a part in people's lives long before you were born. This civilised man whose reputation you now play with – you know him, do you?'

'I know he was wrong,' she said. 'He didnae behave right.'

'Thank you for your lessons in good behaviour, Miss Nolan. We shall be sure to bear them in mind. No more questions.'

I had asked Hamilton not to berate the witnesses. I wanted the evidence to say what it said and then for him to let me take the stand. He ignored these hopes, thinking me crazy and out of touch with the modes of legal reality, and the trial became a scrap between my world and theirs. I only wanted to answer for my sins, for the exhaustion of my wisdom, to say something true and then go. 'You'll lose if you go on like that,' Hamilton said. 'Think of your mother.'

'We have lost so much,' I said.

Mark appeared on the screen looking older. He was wearing a jacket and tie and his hair was combed with a side parting. I saw he had changed in small ways over the summer: he looked that day like a young man about to take on the world, using his hands to articulate the steps of his molestation as if explaining the rules of modern economics. Measures of pride and reason had embedded themselves in Mark's speech; he knew who he wanted to be and his charisma had quietened into a display of refreshing plausibility. In some rather even way, I was proud of him. That was my feeling. He didn't hate anybody and his evidence, if anything, was a show of love, a good and timely gift of loyalty to his broken father. I watched the screen without hearing many of his actual words: it was just his face, the face of the boy with brown eyes who shouted at passing trains. With every little thing he said I knew that my case was done for.

'Would you say you led this gentleman on?' said Hamilton.

'I wasn't in the best nick at the time,' said Mark.

'You *what*?' said the Sheriff.

'I'm sorry. I wasn't in the best of health at that time,' said Mark. 'I was drinking and . . . it was drugs. He took them with me.'

'Right,' said Hamilton. 'But, in your mind, there is no sense in which you took advantage of his generosity? You didn't abuse his weakness? It didn't occur to you that the accused might be lonely?'

'Aye,' said Mark. 'I felt sorry for him.'

'And you took him to one of your drinking dens, did you, because you felt sorry for him? You brought drugs into his house because you felt sorry for him? You danced in his sitting room for the same reason? And you lay down on the sofa with him that night because you felt sorry for him? Is that what you would like the court to believe, Mr McNulty?'

'He was my friend,' said Mark.

'And you were excited to have a friend like that, were you not? A priest with a powerful position in the parish?'

'It was just somewhere to go,' said Mark.

'And after your work at the service station, you thought it wise to go looking for your friend, to wake him up, and it never occurred to you that this would present a difficulty for my client?'

'He could have said no. He could have told me to go away. He was supposed to be the adult, wasn't he?'

There was a mumble from the gallery. Somebody raised

251

their voice. 'Ya dirty English bastard!' it said. 'Paedophile!'

Sheriff Wilson spoke loudly into the microphone and waved his hand at the court officers. 'Remove that man,' he said. 'I demand order in this court. Order!'

One could hear the shouts fade to nothing in the hall outside the courtroom. Mark was looking from right to left on the TV monitor. It must have been confusing not to know what was happening. At that point, with Hamilton walking forward with a flash of steel in his eyes, I decided the business had to end. The knot was so carefully folded in Mark's tie and his lips were red and his eyes open to the future as if the world of possibility was bright and new every day. His face was young and he could not see me as I got to my feet.

'Please stop,' I said, and Hamilton turned.

'What is it now?' said the Sheriff. 'This is your defence counsel, Mr Anderton. Do you wish to speak with him in private?'

'Will you just stop?' I said. 'It was my fault.'

'Please sit down,' said the Sheriff.

'It was my fault,' I said. 'Never mind about the words.'

'Silence! Would you please both approach the bench.'

Shaking his head, Hamilton joined the Fiscal and the Sheriff leaned down to speak with both of them. The Sheriff then said there would be an adjournment of fifteen minutes.

I waited downstairs with my eyes fixed on the concrete floor while Hamilton told me I was ruining my chances of acquittal. 'You mustn't lose your footing,' he said. 'We are in a stronger position than you think.'

'You might be,' I said. 'But I am not.'

'They will ask you to take the stand.'

'I'm ready for that,' I said. 'It is all I wanted.'

On the stand, I wasn't really listening to Hamilton's questions. I fear he didn't understand my position and was trying to wiggle me into blaming everybody other than myself. 'Father David,' he said, 'could this situation with the young people in Dalgarnock be described as having been a sort of culture clash?'

'Not really,' I said. 'Not in the terms you mean. When it comes down to it, I am more childish than they are. And, in relation to the things that matter to them, the young people were more pious than me.'

'I see.'

Hamilton hesitated, then he blushed, and he looked through me as if trying to find one final way of turning the proceedings to my advantage. He stroked his silk tie and waited for another moment, then he gathered up his gown and sat back at the table. 'No more questions.'

Sheriff Wilson probed under his wig with the blunt end of a pencil. The Fiscal had already cross-examined me, but the Sheriff seemed unhappy on a number of counts. He kept saying he wished to clarify things in order to assist the jury. He put down the pencil, propped his right elbow on the bench and cupped his face.

'David Anderton. Let me be sure of something. Have you shown contempt for this court?'

'No, Your Lordship,' I said, 'not for the court, only for me inside it.'

'Well, I'll take that on trust. This has been a most vexing few days. If I suspect you have been wasting my time I will come down very hard. Do you understand?'

'Yes, sir.'

'You came to this place and pled not guilty to a charge of assaulting this young man, Mark McNulty. Do you wish now to change your plea?'

'I hated the wording of the charge, sir. I cannot conceive of myself as having assaulted him or attacked him.'

'What precisely did you do?'

'I kissed him.'

'Well, Mr Anderton. He was a fifteen-year-old boy. I'm not at all sure what country you come from, but under the laws of Scotland, in the alleged circumstances, we may call that assault. We may choose to call it other things as well, but in this case you are accused of assault.'

'My crime, Your Lordship, if I may say so, was a crime of mis-recognition. For a short time, I allowed myself to be in thrall to an unsuitable person. But I did not assault him and could not go along with myself if I perceived that I did.'

'Then perhaps you might have to alter your perception, Mr Anderton. I am bound to tell you, sir, that your attitude in this court is annoying. Your remarks are obtuse. From your behaviour, sir, I dare say you imagine your case is soon to be taken down in the book of martyrs, but please allow me to tell you that it will not. You stand accused of assaulting a young man. A young man over whom you had influence and authority. Do you understand?'

'All too well, Your Lordship.'

'I take it you are not preparing for the role of Hamlet, Mr Anderton?'

'No, sir, I am not.'

'You might have destroyed that young man's innocence.' Something in his crimson-coloured face made me realise there was nothing to fight for and nothing to lose.

'I rather doubt it,' I said. 'The young man has no innocence. I say that not in my own defence but in his.'

'That is a horrible thing to say. And to hear it from a member of the clergy – the Catholic clergy – is shocking.'

'I don't mean to shock anyone,' I said, 'only to give a precise account of the circumstances.'

'I believe the chapel-house at Dalgarnock has been burned down,' he said. 'And you have left the parish, is that correct?'

'Yes, indeed, Your Lordship.'

'And you still have a job?'

'No, sir,' I said. 'My job is to tell the truth in this court.'

'I am glad to hear it. But you do not seem overly attached to your vocation, Mr Anderton. Is that right?'

'I could not have been more attached, Your Lordship. My job was to know God and to serve Him.'

'And you tried to do this in the parish of Dalgarnock?'

'My job was to help people to establish the kingdom of God in their own souls.'

'And you decided to go about this, did you, by staying up all night drinking with a difficult youth?'

I was silent at first. 'I made many mistakes,' I said.

'And perhaps none so costly,' said the Sheriff. 'Your selfish behaviour may have blighted this young man's youth, Mr Anderton. And you may have put a pall on the religious feelings of the people of that town.'

'I hope not,' I said. 'And may God forgive me if I did. But I believe the people will forget me before I forget them.'

'That is not for you to judge, sir,' he said. 'I must say, Mr Anderton, you are a stranger in this court, but one gets the impression from what you have said here today that you are as much a stranger to yourself. I share the young man's instinct to pity you.'

I turned to look at him and his eyes were rheumy.

'Perhaps your own parishioners,' I said, 'the ones you look over each day in these courts, will have more need of your pity than I do.'

Even I, a stranger, as he said, to the Scottish courts, knew that this conversation was irregular. My advocate stood to one side, smoothing the top of one hand with the other, too respectful by half, while the Fiscal, in a move that one could only imagine was bred of some great familiarity with His Lordship's methods, rolled his eyes and stacked his papers.

'I'm not particularly interested in your character, sir. Based on my experience of it in this court, it is not to my mind an especially admirable one. But it is not your vanity which is on trial. We will stick to the facts. After carousing on the housing estate with him, did you then invite this young man into your house?'

'Yes.'

'At what time?'

'It was rather late.'

'The middle of the night.'

'Yes, I'd say so.'

'And did you ply him with drink?'

'No, My Lord. He went in search of something to drink, and I allowed him to do that. I also allowed him to drink what he found. But I'd say he had fairly plied himself with drink before we met that night.'

'Yet you drank alongside him?'

'I did.'

'And you took drugs together?'

'Yes.'

'A quantity of Ecstasy tablets, we gather?'

'So I believe.'

'And you sat down with him on the sofa?'

'I did.'

'And you tried to kiss him there.'

'Yes.'

'And he refused.'

'That's right.'

'And at that point Mrs Poole entered the house?'

'Yes, indeed.'

'And let me ask you one more thing, Mr Anderton. If the young man had not refused, would you have gone further?'

I looked to the back of the court and saw the people. Their faces were almost brittle with hatred. They shook their heads in their winter jackets and swore to a communion with their own kind.

'Yes,' I said.

One or two jurors sighed into their folded arms. The day then floated into legalese, adjournments and delays. I thought the trial might afford my pride one last, intense hurrah, that some sense of dignity might contradict the filth of the accusation. But that did not happen in Court Number One, where larger, more traditional proprieties worked in their way to mock my idle romances. Due process murdered my conceit. Even my mother's face, when I saw it, was a mask of embarrassment.

'This man, for whatever reason, fooled a community into trusting him. He fooled them with his talk and with his faith. He fooled them with his background and the height of his ideals. We are not here to try his faith, yet the prosecution may have proved, as he himself may have proved by his own words, that his journey towards this young person was a journey of self-interest. But even that does not matter if he did not, in the event, assault this young man. The law in this case does not allow for equivocation when it comes to the naming of crimes: if he did what he says he did, then you are obliged to find him guilty of the charge.'

My mind wandered. There was a morning in the Borghese

Gardens, when I laughed at the freshness of the pines, sure as I walked that life was a long and beautiful and private matter. Inside the gallery the day was silent. I must have spent two hours in the company of Bernini's *David*. You never saw limbs so clean and strong in all the corners of eternity. His arms showed the strain of pulling back his sling to smite the enemy: his head was alive with curls and his neck appeared to have a pulse, Bernini's addition to God's excellence. Standing in the room with the light pouring through the window, I looked at the eyes and the chest and the broad, spread toes of the perfect man, knowing his beauty spelled out for me the grandeur of life and creation. The room was empty. I reached over and inhaled the old marble before leaning in further, kissing its cool surface with my own lips of flesh and blood.

'Mr Anderton,' said the Sheriff, 'you have been found guilty by the jury.'

There was another cheer from the rows of spectators.

Wilson looked down at them and paused. 'I have to tell you that the nature of this crime, coupled with your sinister justifications in this court, could persuade me that a custodial sentence might be imposed. However, I am mindful of the fact that this is a first offence. Let it be the last. I can assure you that any future appearances you might make will result in your going to prison. Do you understand?'

'Yes, My Lord.'

'This is a sad day for you, Father Anderton. You have come a long way down in the world to be answering a charge of this sort. However, the law is the law, and you now have a conviction against you. I order that you commit to 120 hours of community service.' He then explained what that would mean and asked for my consent.

The people came to their feet.

'No Pope of Rome!'

'You should've gone doon, ya English bastard!'

'Corruption.'

'Away tae fuck. Yous aw jeest stick thegither.'

'Paedophile!'

The police weren't obliged to escort me, but they did. My mother and I came down the steps of the courthouse to a waiting taxi. People were jeering around us and at one point a camera hit me on the head. 'Get back, yoose,' said the policeman. 'I mean it. Stay back.'

The taxi drove away and the shops of Kilmarnock seemed to blur into each other as we passed the lights and the streets grew empty of people. The driver kept looking into his mirror and the journey seemed unending. After a minute or two, my mother twined her fingers into mine on the seat between us and tears came down my face.

'Don't hate me,' I said.

'That's not possible,' she said. 'Unless you allow that carnival back there to make you stupid.'

'But I am stupid, Mother.'

'Nice people don't always get it right,' she said, and as she said this I could feel a certain resolve enter her frail hand.

'It's time you had your own car again,' she said.

THE SINGLE LIFE

Duty kept me in Ayrshire until the end of that year, or perhaps not duty so much as the struggle for dignity, the attraction of penance, the notion that fortune might startle the outcome and turn once more in my favour, allowing me to go from Scotland in a state of peace and with a heart reconciled to the terms of my disgrace. But two months passed and I worked my community service at Kennox Moss, peeling carrots with a supervisor at a home for handicapped pensioners. Many of the people who lived there had never left Ayrshire: they had stayed on the training farm, cleaning tools and haunting the greenhouses, and the years had passed in the company of rabbits and an annual show of strawberries.

Driving back from the farm one day, I stopped at the supermarket near Dalgarnock to buy some things for a stew. It happened like this: I stood with my basket and looked along the rows of red wine to the cold cabinets, and there in a pair of distressed sneakers was Mark McNulty. He clasped a skateboard with yellow wheels and he failed to see me at first, then he looked round, the boredom departing his face. He rolled along and didn't stop until his shin touched my basket.

'Hiya, Father,' he said.

'Mark,' I said. 'How are you?'

'I'm not trying to buy drink,' he said. 'I just came in to price a six-pack for my dad.'

'Good. But how are you doing?'

'Not bad,' he said. 'I've left school.'

'Why so soon? You're clever, Mark. You're too clever to give up on your education so early.'

'I'm going into the Army,' he said. 'Next week it is. I'm going to Plymouth for training. They give you a trade and everything.'

'Yes,' I said.

'The Army needs people,' he said. 'You know that. There's a war on. They say it's finished but nobody thinks it's finished.'

'I doubt it'll be finished for a long time,' I said.

'Good. Plenty of work, then. They might even send me out there eventually, to where it's all happening.'

'You wouldn't want that,' I said.

'Why not? We're making a difference out there. You know yourself it's the right thing. You've got to have your team, Father.'

'Yes,' I said. 'You told me that before.'

I wanted to shake him. I wanted to tell him it takes a whole lifetime to know anything about the right thing. 'Even so,' I said, 'just think carefully about what you're doing.'

'Have you ever known any soldiers?' he said.

'No, but I knew their names. They were carved into a wall at the old college I went to.'

'So you didn't know any, then?'

He spun one of the skateboard wheels and nipped nervously at the front of his jersey. The board's underside showed a drawing of a pirate and a torn sticker with the word 'Heroin' printed in black ink. Suddenly, he seemed just like a boy again,

a great and proud unawareness bleaching his face and empty-
ing the statements he made. 'What about your Irish Republican Army?' I said. 'I don't suppose they'd be very pleased with
your choice of career.'

I wondered if he was quick enough to catch the note of irri-
tation that came with the words. 'My dad says that's all over.
And it's not as if they're going to give me a trade, are they?'

We stood in silence for a moment and he flipped the end of
the board up into his hand. 'Lisa's pregnant,' he said.

People were beginning to pass us with their trolleys and I
began to experience a rather familiar edginess, the fear of hostile bystanders, the thought of comments or misunderstand-
ings. 'Oh dear,' I said.

'Don't be like that,' said Mark. 'She's happy enough.'

'Is the baby yours?'

'Nope,' he said. 'Nuttin to do with me.'

'God bless her,' I said.

'Ah, save it. Lisa's cool. She's keeping it. She'll be good at
being somebody's maw.'

'She's so young.'

Mark's ease and smiling made me dislike myself afresh. I
could feel my hand tightening its grip on the basket, and I
wanted to go. His eyes narrowed and his lips grew thin as a
serious look emerged on his face. 'It wasn't all bad, Father, was
it? We had a few laughs?'

He put out his hand.

I laid down the basket and swallowed hard. 'Wherever you
go, Mark,' I said, shaking his hand, 'be sure to look after yourself.'

The conversation was ended before it began. The events of
the year were already distant to him, one could tell, and his
mind was taken up with new ventures and the promise of other

people. There was a second when I thought I might say something more, but I simply nodded at him to vanquish the thought, and, like a cold benediction, I made to place some final acceptance before him and before myself. He didn't see it. He would never see it and his days will not be any the worse for that. As I prepared to take my leave from him, I knew that Mark had been many things to me, not least a vision of myself at a young age, a very different version of the person my life had allowed me to be. For a season or two, perhaps, I had wanted to be him, which wasn't really the same as wanting him, but none of it seemed important any more as I watched him spin the wheels of his skateboard. He was a fine-looking, reckless young man, who had answered the call of a moment and the sad old ghosts of self-love.

'Look out for me on the telly,' he said, smiling again and trapping the skateboard under his heel. He disappeared down the aisle and I know I will never see him again. The young man wasn't Conor, but I stood there with a burning in my throat all the same and wished him well, the back of his jacket vanishing past the juice cartons. I can only say it now. At the centre of himself, a man cannot choose whom to love. He can choose how to live and can honour the truth of himself where he may. But he cannot choose whom to love, any more than he can choose how tall he is or how good. One can take up platform shoes or fine deeds, but the heart will always have the last word, and when the word is love we can recognise, we can respond, we can submit and we can try to ignore, but we can never choose. Love is not a matter of choice but an obdurate fact of surrender.

Three weeks before Christmas, Mrs Poole called me on my mobile as I was walking over the Old Bridge at Ayr. I had some cards and things in a bag, and I put them down and looked at the harbour, listening to her words and hearing a weary slenderness in her voice. 'It's certainly me,' she said.

'But you sound so far away.'

'I've been practising that sound for years,' she said. 'That's the top and bottom of it, Father. I'm a sight for sore eyes. I don't have long.'

'Mrs Poole,' I said, 'you're going to get better.' There was a pause at the other end of the line, a pause much louder and clearer than her ailing voice.

'Stop it, Father,' she said. 'We had words before, you and I, about that sort of talk. I'm not frightened. I want you to help me get ready.'

I went to the Arranview Hospice that afternoon. 'We should have grown vegetables,' said Mrs Poole. 'That's more like it. We could have grown our own lettuce and rhubarb.'

'And radishes.'

'Yes,' she said. 'Easy things.'

The nurses came and went from the room with paper trays and small jokes, smoothing the bedclothes and positioning the morphine button more firmly in her hand. Mrs Poole wasn't much older than several of them, and she smiled as they did. She was determined to die in her own way. She feared displays of regret or recriminations and wanted in the end to sink, as it were, into that hallowed version of herself that had keened and searched for improvement. It was her higher self, and she tried to arrange for the days of her dying to meet with her rage for quality. She ordered some beautiful stationery and wrote letters to her sister and her son, saying goodbye and asking them not to judge her too harshly. 'I don't expect they will,' she said. 'They are good people. All the better for having each other.'

'You don't want them to come?' I said.

'No,' she said. 'They're near enough to me. I don't want to upset people. We've always tried to be sensible.'

'Are you sure?' I said.

'Yes,' said Mrs Poole. 'We didn't always do things the normal way. But the letters were nice. Family letters, you know? I don't want them seeing me like this when there's other good things to think about. I want them to be busy, Father. I want him to enjoy his life.'

'He will, Mrs Poole.'

'That's all I ever wanted,' she said.

I came back the next day with some elderflower cordial. 'Let me just sniff the nice smell,' she said. 'My stomach can't take it.' I also brought the Bach CD she had asked me to bring, or I thought I had. I put it on and she rolled her eyes in a dark delight.

'Wrong cantata,' she said, smiling through the morphine.

'Really?' I said. 'I could have sworn . . .'

'Never mind,' she said. 'I can learn this one. Keep it playing.'

I saw her hand go to her chest. She smiled at the ceiling and said a few words I could barely hear, and then I stroked her legs on top of the blanket. 'Take your time,' I said. Her mouth was dry. I took a stick of pink sponge that was sitting in a cup of water and ran it over her lips.

'Don't go away,' she said.

There were no last speeches from Mrs Poole. The following afternoon she made a stab at the sign of the cross. I took out my oil and slowly began giving her the last rites. Her lips opened for a second as I put the crucifix to them and she sighed into its glinting brass. Mr Poole was there and he spread the fingers of her hand over the bedsheets and kissed each one in turn, holding her wedding ring against his cheek as her breathing grew thinner still and the candle burned.

'Goodbye, Anne,' I said.

Her husband got onto the bed and put his head next to hers on the pillow and closed her eyes with his fingers. Then he took her hand. I looked at them for a moment from the foot of the bed, then went out of the room. The nurses led me through the patio doors to the cold garden and one of them brought a cup of tea out to where I stood on the grass. Through the trees one could see the River Garnock, the water flowing out of sight towards Irvine harbour and the Irish Sea. Fifteen hundred years had passed since the saint had changed the direction of the river, and there it was that day in December, sparkling between its banks, a crowd of seagulls floating slowly down on a cracked sheet of ice, moving past the trees and the town and the Arranview Hospice towards the salt water and the waves. I imagined the ice melting before it got to the sea and the birds being sent high and far into the air.

She got the burial she had wanted. Her husband asked me if I knew what to do and I said yes, the papers were to be found in their kitchen cupboard above the kettle. It was a red biscuit tin – 'She always liked a box of good biscuits at Christmas,' he said – and in it I found the papers from a company called Native Woodland. They were held together with a blue paper clip, and fastened to the top, torn from a greetings card, was a cartoon of a happy penguin with the words: 'Get Well Soon.' Mr Poole rang people to tell them about his wife's death, giving them the plans for the funeral and spelling out the address. 'Let's no' go off the deep end,' he said. 'Anne liked things quiet.'

The forms showed that Mrs Poole, some years before, had purchased not one plot but three, for a price of £2,025. In her tidy handwriting she specified 'burial, not ashes'. She had filled in the column for the second plot with all her husband's details; the third was blank. I said nothing when I saw this but simply pointed it out to Mr Poole. 'That was just like her,' he said, his hand hesitating over the page. 'She liked to be ready.'

'For an emergency?'

'That kinna thing,' he said.

The tin contained other documents: advice about her garden and a brochure for a green papier mâché pod. The brochure had a Post-It note stuck to the front saying 'this one' in faint pencil. I returned to the Native Woodland contract and paused over the small print. 'Except for approved trees and shrubs, all memorials, headstones, kerbs, wreaths, flower vases and any other forms of memorial shall not be permitted on the grave or within the site.' Beside this warning Mrs Poole had drawn with the same pencil a small smiling face.

Hundy Mundy Wood is in the Scottish Borders, not far from the old towns of Kelso and Melrose. On the way down, Mr Poole drank whisky from a paper cup and stretched his thin neck away from his tie to see the further removes of the Lammermuir Hills. Father Michael had let us bury her out of St Mary's in Irvine. He said the Bishop had nodded to the request that I be allowed to stand at the altar and said no more about the matter. The cars behind us were filled with people I had never met, relatives of the Pooles on both sides, including Irene, Mrs Poole's sister, who came down from Glasgow with the four boys. One of them undoubtedly had Mrs Poole's small features, the same timid nose, and I guessed he was Toby, the son. When we arrived there, he stood to one side of the cars and stared at the ground and the scattered leaves, as if seeking for a moment to know what the ground knew.

'She was too young for this,' said Irene. She wiped her eyes. 'Forty-three. Far too young for the like of this.'

'Yes,' I said. 'Though she never admitted to being young.'

'That's right,' she said. 'She was like that. She always wanted to be older than she was. Always that way. She wanted to be more.'

'Well,' I said, 'I suppose she was more.'

Irene just pursed her lips, a show of restraint, before sniffing and pressing a tissue up the sleeve of her coat. She took a breath and exhaled most of it in a long, wavering sigh.

The grass crackled under our feet and the pines were frozen as the boys and two gardeners carried Mrs Poole. 'This area is managed for the benefit of the plants and wildlife,' said the man from Native Woodland. 'There are notable vascular plants here: Musk Mallow, Maiden Pink. You should see it here in the summer months. Just colour.'

'And good for birds?' I said.

'Tree sparrows, yes,' he said. 'Barn owls. Yellowhammers.'

We got to a place where an eighteenth-century folly stood at the edge of the wood, the motionless, grey sky appearing through its windows. The man from the company kicked the soil off his boots and smiled into the daylight. 'It's a Gothic folly,' he said. 'Built by the great William Adam. Lines up directly with Mellerstain, the home of the 13th Earl of Haddington.'

'I want to say a few prayers,' I said.

'Here we are,' he said. 'This is the excavation.' He clasped his hands and lowered his head in a nice, agnostic way.

'Goodbye, Anne,' said Mr Poole. He said it to the small group of people around the place where she was laid, as if he were saying goodbye to the notion of others altogether, and then he looked at the opened space between the dead leaves and blew a kiss into that soft ground where his wife lay silent in her paper pod and where all their hours and all their secrets lay down among the soil. The boy came over and shook Mr Poole's hand. A fresh wind blew from the west and poured through the windows of the folly at Hundy Mundy, and a feeling most hopeful, the echo of something real, came with the good, clean air as we made our way back through the trees to our cars.

The night my father died the house was flooded. It was a burst pipe, a gusher, the man said, and the water froze all over the ground floor at Heysham. The pipe was above the sink in my father's office, so the worst of the water poured onto his private papers and medical books. My mother and I almost dared ourselves not to live once we knew that nothing good was ever guaranteed, my poor father caught short of breath in the middle of the night with so much before him. But in time his death awakened us.

Can a song be a ghost, and, if so, can it be 'Blow the Wind Southerly', which brought my father's service to a close and wanders yet in my memory through the darkened rooms of that house? The winter freeze lasted for weeks and we went there, my mother and I, to the house, to survey the damage and weigh our future prosperity. I recall the damp smell and the bitter cold at the ends of my fingers. I opened a drawer and saw his vests and shirts, an array of knitted ties, frozen in pipe water. Each drawer was a perfect block of ice. His trousers now trapped in amber. The lamp in his study was stiff with ice and the carpet crunched as I walked about the room. His medical certificates were unreadable behind mottled glass, his typewriter had locked with the cold and a slither of ice had jammed the roller, as if to silence for ever his remarks and reports about progress in the field of the human heart. His desk must have contained gallons of frozen water. And down at the bottom of the deepest drawer, I could make out, and can still make out, the submerged, magnified face of the pianist Dinu Lipatti, smiling from the cover of a Chopin album.

St John Ogilvie was bright with candles. It was Christmas Eve. People came to Midnight Mass who never came to Mass all year, and there they stood in the pews and along the back wall under the stations of the cross, the Catholic people of Dalgarnock, their cheeks pink from the cold. I entered the church and passed the nativity scene – life-size, the sheep's devoted eyes turned to the doll in the dusty manger – and immediately I detected frankincense floating through the smell of damp coats. There was a space in the corner and I stood with my back to the wall, watching the altar and the gestures of the crowd as they mumbled and lifted up their hearts. It occurred to me that the earth may be everything of heaven we shall ever know.

Some of the people had come from the pub. I could see them standing in their own shadows and shielding their cans of lager, the faces of men and women I had known. I have to say, there was something lovely in their smiles. Each of them wanted a world of cheer, and for that night only the altar gave them that very thing, its golden chalices glinting like their home tinsel as the Bishop kissed the Book of Psalms. I saw Lisa and a pale young man with blond hair holding hands. I watched them smile, and the notes of Joseph Mohr's old Christmas carol fell softly down from the choir to bless the occasion:

> Sleep in heavenly peace.
> Sleep in heavenly peace.
>
> Silent night, holy night.
> Son of God,
> Love's pure light.

Radiant beams from Thy holy face.
With the dawn of redeeming grace.

I could smell the wool and the frankincense and see hope among the faces, even the drunken ones, the hope that masked a thousand uncertainties, a hundred measures of panic and bitterness, all belonging to the day after tomorrow. I could feel their eyes as I joined the line for Communion. They followed me as I studied the trail of wet boots to the altar, the voices of the choir still gracious under the roof beams. From behind me, from the line of men standing against the back wall, there was a single shout. 'Oi,' he said. A skirl of whispers spread under the song. The line moved forward and eventually the whispering died away. I could feel my hands shaking as I clasped them in front of me and stepped before Bishop Gerard. I saw him wetting his lips as I approached; not to speak but so as not to speak. But then he said the words we'd been trained to say, and the expression on his face showed that he feared I might cause trouble.

'Body of Christ,' he said.

'Amen.'

I saw a moment's confusion darken his face. It contained an old appeal for calm and for silence. 'David,' he said. I put out my hands and received the communion wafer into them and simply nodded. The sound froze between us, and I lifted the wafer and put it in my coat pocket.

'David. You mustn't.'

I turned without looking again at the Bishop. I walked past the pews and the turning heads of the faithful and stopped for a second at the doors of the chapel, out of habit, crossing myself with water.

The Marcellists knew more than the Bombastics. In their youth they knew about the fading quality of everything: the radicals believed only in idealism and the glorious emancipations of the future, until the struggle for those too became a romantic thing of the past. The Church gave me every reason to expect a bridge between the two, it gave me hope. Our journey will sustain many falsehoods to avoid that one truth: we wanted love, and without it only the broad universe would do, with its solid, perfumed dark.

Snow came floating in from the sea as I drove for the last time up the coastal road from Ayr. It wouldn't lie, the snow, but it jigged in the atmosphere and turned cartwheels out there before landing and vanishing on the windscreen. I knew the children of Ayrshire would be glad to see the flakes and the whiteness that morning and find themselves indoors, peering out to a painted dream of Christmas Day. I left my bags in the boot of the car and parked at the edge of the housing estate, walking over the bridge and down past the primary school. The gate to the school was padlocked, and beyond the gate the classroom windows were covered in drawings of snowflakes and reindeers and jagged trees. Perhaps there's nothing so empty as an empty playground; on the grey gravel of the yard, the slushy water, like thoughts, collected in pools, and by the entrance doors a heap of crisp packets and dead leaves stood beside a brush propped against the wall. Standing there, reaching into my coat pocket, I found two silver buttons like the ones you get on jeans, the remnants of nights gone by, those nights at the Blue Bell factory with Mark and Lisa.

Mr Poole took a while to answer the door. He came with a burning cigarette in his hand. Only when I had stepped through the door did I notice how well turned-out he looked: a crisp white shirt beneath his crimson face; a scent of toothpaste and Old Spice. He took my coat and looked at me as if social rituals were a kind of embarrassment.

'You're a good timekeeper.'

'Oh, yes,' I said. 'I set off early to enjoy the weather.'

'It would put years on you, so it would,' he said.

The sitting room was a small tribute to Mrs Poole. It was filled with lamps and Aztec-style cushions, framed prints of bulbs and plants. On top of the television there were framed photographs of people I had seen only once, at Mrs Poole's funeral, and the coffee table, which took up most of the floor-space, was a neat little archive of wooden boxes, knitting needles and remote controls. On a ledge under the table I saw a couple of books: an Italian dictionary and *French Provincial Cooking*. Next to the window, a small Christmas tree was hung with baubles covered in glitter. It had lights too, and they flashed in sequence, as if each light was passing its happy message to the next, a community of celebration. The television was on when I came in: a news programme about American troops celebrating Christmas in Iraq.

'Anne used to say,' said Mr Poole, 'that the half of them don't have a clue why they're over there.'

I mused for a second and watched the pictures.

'It's all religion, isn't it?' he said. 'Not that I'm against religion. But those young fellas could be out there for years.'

'I hope not,' I said, handing him a bottle.

'You shouldn't have bothered,' he said. 'This'll be the good stuff, eh?'

'It's not bad,' I said. 'It's just right for today.'

It was actually the best I had mustered that year, the favourite tipple of my old friend Edward Hippisley-Cox, the famous 'nectar' much coveted by all those fellows, a bottle of Château d'Yquem 1986. 'I don't usually drink white,' said Mr Poole. 'But I'm drinking this one. Let's push the boat out. That's a good bottle of wine, so it is.'

It felt strange being there, in Mrs Poole's domain. I had wondered what it would be like. She had spoken about it as if the place represented a world beyond any world that I could know. Mr Poole had his Christmas cards on a string across the wall, just, I imagined, as his wife would have done, and the house felt permeated with a commitment to her ideas, a feeling that came from Mr Poole himself that day, as if he was determined to do better by Mrs Poole now that she was gone. He handed me a glass. I clinked with him and noted that the wine tasted unimaginably good.

'You're quite right,' I said. 'Maybe those boys should be home with their families.'

'It's all just fear, intit?' he said. 'We're frightened of them and they're frightened of us and it's all just a mess.'

'This is tremendously good, isn't it?' I said, looking at the liquid in the glass, the deep allure of a foreign sun.

'Magic,' said Mr Poole. He turned off the television. 'Now that's what you call a glass of wine.'

After that, he set up the kitchen table at the back of the sitting room and we ate a chicken with boiled potatoes. He poured himself a pint of Guinness and topped it up thereafter, telling me about the work he did and the early days of his life with Anne and the fact that they never got round to having children. He paused only for a second when he spoke this untruth and I straightened up, ready to speak. But something passed away in his eyes and he licked his Guinness moustache and there seemed no point in bringing him round to sadness.

He brought out a bottle of whisky and said, quite suddenly, that he wished he could have some of the years back, just to give their life together another try, with another chance to make everything good.

'We all want that, Mr Poole,' I said. 'I believe we want it from the moment we know how to want things.'

'Maybe so, Father. Maybe so.'

'Just give it time.'

'My mother died of cancer,' he said.

'I know that. Mrs Poole mentioned it once.'

The room twinkled not only with fairy lights but with unsaid things. 'It's back to the single life,' said Mr Poole. He stopped to look at the silent television as if it was a person. 'Or maybe I've always been living the single life. Maybe everybody does. You have.'

I was about to say something else as a way of saying nothing, but then I thought better of it and placed my knife and fork on the plate. 'I thought I was supposed to be the king of the double life.'

'That's only the newspapers talking,' he said, seeming to draw all the oxygen out of his glass as he drank from it. He looked around. 'It will just be me here now, and that's the hardest part.'

'It will just take time,' I said.

'That's right,' he said, but his eyes were vacant. He smiled at me and his smile rose for a second above the troubles of the past year, above the yearnings and deposits of life. The house was quiet. I saw his lip tremble and his eyes fill up as he lifted his glass again.

'Merry Christmas,' he said.

'And to you.'

Later on, he shook an old newspaper and read out an item about a mountain of fridges rusting in a part of Ireland. 'Anne thought we were using up the world,' he said.

'That would be a shame.'

'You mean shameful?'

'That too.'

'You like reading the newspaper?' I said.

'Once you get past the rubbish,' he said, 'you can find interesting things. The sport's good. I like to see how the teams are doing.'

'My father was fond of the paper,' I said. 'He read the *Morecambe and Lancaster Citizen*.' By that time he had moved onto the sofa and the drink was beginning to gnaw a little at his words and his gestures.

'Everybody has their own thing,' he said. 'I always liked this settee.'

One's life is full of rooms, and that one will always remain to me as a cell of passing warmth, the dust already settling, the memory of the man's wife now an animating feature in the continuing life of the house and the feelings of the man who still made his home there.

'Where will you go now?' said Mr Poole.

'Oh,' I said, 'there are places where I've been happy. It might be time to go and find them again.'

'That's good.'

'It's time to move on. I'm sorry to say I've been a very mediocre caretaker of my own faith.'

He looked up and the rims of his eyes were pink, and I could see from his talk that he was keen to move on himself. 'Yes, well,' he said, 'this hasn't been a bad wee meal at all.'

'Perfect,' I said.

Parfait.

When I was ready to leave, Mr Poole was looking through a tattered address book for people to call. I took the plates through to the kitchen and washed them and put them on the drying rack. As I cleared the table he would tell me things about the people in the book, who they were, how they lived, what they had meant to him and Anne. After a while, when the bin bags were all tied and the kitchen was sparkling clean, I could hear him talking to a person in what I understood to be Australia. 'Never mind,' he said. 'It's not every day, is it? It's not every day.'

He just swayed a little on the sofa and gave me a military salute when I went in to say goodbye. His glass was full and the address book was open beside him, the pages a mass of names and numbers. As I walked away I imagined he would have a long, happy night ahead of him, speaking with the near and distant people who mobbed the book. I put on my coat and heard his animated talk in the next room.

'Goodbye, Jack,' I said.

I stood on the doorstep and instantly felt the bite of the cold on my cheeks and was glad of my coat and scarf. The evening was clear and I could see from the doorstep the lamps of the bowling green and the old abbey tower floodlit against the darkness. For a moment, a flutter of nerves took hold of me as I went to step into the road, and I looked down at the bushes and saw a fieldmouse, its small eyes very still and its nose twitching at the scent of me. The mouse didn't move and I thought of the fields that were here before the houses came, before the abbey came. Bending down, I thought I saw the spires of Oxford at the centre of its beady eyes, but too quickly it darted into the bushes and was gone.

I walked up the hill and past the playground. It was difficult to think of the small feet that tramped and jumped there, the children one day walking out of the school gate for the last time into a world where adult cares would engulf them, while the school continued behind them under the same weather. There would always be something of myself left behind in those yards, in the cold high windows and the puddles of winter rain. I once knew a boy who ran at the edge of Lancashire fields. I knew him walking through graveyards with his handsome father. That comical child thought of dragonflies and the noble dead; he climbed on an elephant and waved to a crowd of wonderful strangers. I knew him very well. His hands grew to rub ice from the windows of college rooms. He kissed there, dreamed there, and knew the luck of living and the long sad terror of saying goodbye.

I knew this man who walked to the town's railway bridge and looked down to where the people lived in their houses. He was different from many people but never so different from himself. On reaching the top of the bridge he was happy to observe he was nothing much, just another person looking for faith in the cold night air. A goods train came and he watched its iron trucks go by, until there was only the cloud of his breath and the small red lights at the back of the train, the lights getting smaller and then flaring just once as it vanished into the trees.